LAST OF DAYLIGHT

Burning Cinder Book I

Nicole Hayes

IONA PRINT

ISBN 978-1-7351145-0-7 (Hardcover Edition)
ISBN 978-1-7351145-1-4 (Softcover Edition)
ISBN 978-1-7351145-2-1 (Ebook Edition)

Front cover image by Casey Gerber

Printed in the USA

Iona Print, LLC
6501 W Markham St
Little Rock, AR 72205

To my younger self who had just as many dreams about daggers and blood as she did about fairies and butterflies.

Contents

Acknowledgements

I wouldn't be here without my magnanimous husband. My relentless torture on your patience backed me through drafts of each book, but you took the brunt of it with LOD. Sharing in my pride and love for these projects really get me through them. Thank you for helping me find my confidence. Batman, you rock!

Jasmine Clark, you are an inspiration. Thanks for awarding me the best of Tameka, one of the most-loved characters. I appreciate your rousing writer pep talks during COVID. Your openness in conversations on diversity in a fictional apocalypse encouraged me to write kick-ass characters who happen to be minorities. You're a gem in a world of ash.

Ivana Radic, my Croatian bestie and critique partner, thank you. I don't know if the book would be published if I hadn't met you on the eve of quarantine. Your feedback ultimately brought my characters to life and helped transform this book from the musings of a sixteen-year-old girl into a mature discussion on so many topics. I can't wait for the world to read Project Pomegranate.

Thanks to Casey Gerber for the beautiful cover!

ONE

The Irrevocable Consequences
Of Biting Off More Than You Can Chew

{2002}

"THEY'RE REAL, YOU KNOW."

Those four words changed her life. Changed all their lives forever.

Rayne looked up from a brand-new copy of Bram Stoker's classic begging, her to purchase it. Not that she didn't already own three copies. A man stood across the display from her. No, not a man. A god. With a little "G," but still a god. Nine inches taller than her and gorgeous with black and blue hair spiked Linkin Park Hybrid Theory era music video style. He wore all black, and it contrasted against his ashen complexion. And did he just speak to her?

He chose that exact moment to smirk.

The book slipped from her hands into a pile of its orphaned brethren. When several other books tumbled over the display, she hurried to recover them. As she menaced the books, she asked, "Did you say something to me?" Pride and relief washed over her as she managed to speak without a stutter.

"Yes, I did. They're real." He pointed at *Dracula*. "Well, in a sense they are. Vampires are aliens."

The stuttering loomed. She sensed it. Her widened blue eyes blinked in quick succession. "Deer in the headlights" sprung to mind. She tried to ignore it, but a weird pain needled her temples. Like an ice cream headache.

"Uh, uhm. I-I-I'm sorry. What?!" Fourteen and doused in hormones, she struggled to handle the situation. A hot, mysterious dude declared in her parents' bookstore her favorite sub-genre of horror existed in reality set in science-fiction. Or science non-fiction, as it were.

"Would it make you more comfortable if we sat down over there?" He pointed a slender finger to a reading circle with chairs and a table. One of her contributions to the store's interior design.

As her brain struggled to catch up, she heard herself answer, "Yea, that's a good idea." Maybe if he sat his towering figure down, it might clear her head. They sat down. As it turned out, sitting with him at eye level made everything worse. His eyes shone so dark they appeared pitch black, but she saw a dark blue ring circled the outside of his iris. It almost looked inhuman. More like a doll or a shark. "So, you were saying—"

"Vampires are real. They're aliens," he restated. His tone matter-of-fact, as if he gave this lecture often.

"Aliens." She tried the idea on for size. "So, if they're aliens and we've written fiction about them, does that mean they invaded?" Look at her go. She gave herself a mental pat on the back. She not only managed to get a sentence out, but one that altogether made sense. She wondered if her hormones switched off once guys mentioned bizarro worlds. She continued to ignore the bounce of her knee a little longer. The twinge in her skull resisted her dismissals.

"Yes, a very long time ago." He sank into the armchair, one foot rested across the other knee. Comfortable. Perfectly at ease. But every twitch, wince, or frown she made, he watched. Regarded her. Across from him, she sat, rubbed her temple, and bounced one knee on the edge of her seat. He stared at her the whole time. At first, he scanned her, puzzled. Seconds, then minutes passed. His eyes tightened with a look of concern. His soft lips frowned.

"Why—" she started.

He said at the same time, "Would you like to hear the story of Icarus and Cinder?"

As soon as he said those words, the pain in her temples flared. Something. Something lingered right at the edge of her memory. She couldn't quite grasp it, but she knew it was there. The harder she reached for it, tried to recall it, the worse the pain became until she cried out. "Let go, Celindria. Stop fighting it." The tenor of his voice soothed her. It sounded so kind. So familiar. His face and his voice. Shared something with that memory she couldn't access. When she opened her eyes, she laid on the rough, industrial carpet of the bookstore. Her thick, black hair fanned around her like wings. He leaned over her, and every angle carved in his face drawn with worry. No one milled around or gawked. Close to closing time. Did he wait until the shoppers left? Did he know something might happen?

Her face scrunched in scrutiny, she finally got to ask what she wanted to ask all night, "Who are you?"

"Rayne, time to go," her mom called from the back of the store.

Her stare hardened when he didn't answer. She pushed, "I recognize you. Tell me your name." She started to sit up. He helped by stepping out of her way.

"All closed up, where are you?" her mom asked from a section closer.

The stranger spared a glance in the direction of her mom's voice. Now, Rayne stiffened in panic at the thought of her mom finding her sitting on the floor of their store with a strange man locked inside with them. She startled him when she took his hand. His skin made her fair complexion tan in comparison. While she ignored another weird familiar tug at her memory, she pulled him away from the circle. "C'mon I'll take you through the side door." He followed without hesitation. Did he not feel it? Was she not as familiar to him as he was to her?

She fished out the correct key for the side door to her parent's bookstore on the key ring she kept on her belt loop. Taking stock of the situation, she stopped herself from unlocking it. Instead, she looked into his eyes. She decided. Hardball it was. "I'm not letting you out until you tell me your name, at the very least."

3

He implored her with his striking, midnight-blue eyes. He said, "I'm afraid if I told you right now it will cause you more pain."

"In that case, you can tell me tomorrow at the Arkansas Skatium on Bowman. Have you heard of it?"

He confirmed with a nod and searched the store for her mother. "I think now is a good time to let me out," he said.

"Good, then I'll see you there sometime between 6 and 10?" She unlocked the door as something else occurred to her. "Who is Celindria?" she asked. The door opened, and he stepped out into the night. She took a sweeping glance of the parking lot behind him and noticed the single car in the parking lot belonged to her mom.

"Tomorrow, I'll tell you everything, tomorrow," the mysterious stranger promised.

For the first time since she contemplated the *Dracula* cover, Rayne smiled in front of the stranger. "Okay, I'll see you then."

"Rayne?" Her mom called, super close now.

"I'm just wrapping up," she turned to shout and wave through the stacks.

When she looked back, he'd disappeared. An eerie chill lingered.

6:01 PM and Rayne swept the crowded venue for Mr. Gorgeous Mystery Man. She convinced herself while he wasn't a god, per se, he might possess mysterious powers more equivalent to a Loki type. Full to capacity, she idly wondered how many people bumped around. She appreciated the low lighting and positioned herself under a black light to stand out in the dark surroundings.

"When is he going to show up?" Tameka stood right next to Rayne as she scanned the first comers of the night like sentinels in a prison. Of course, she told her closest friends about her encounter. As a teenager, how could she keep such a monumental secret to herself?

"Something tells me he's not showing until after dark," sighed Sagan. All three of them spent the afternoon contemplating the origins and intentions of the man Rayne came to consider *her* stranger.

"He's too old for us, of course," Rayne stated.

"Definitely." Sagan nodded, staring across the rink.

"Speak for yourselves," Tameka countered.

"Hey what are you three doing? They're about to play our song," Andrew shouted from the floor as he roller-bladed up to the wall.

The girls hesitated to admit it, but they never learned to skate. She suspected several frequent customers lacked the skill as most everyone walked laps around the different rinks and gossiped or fought or did other nefarious, teenage things. The lights dimmed lower, and the music grew louder. This place catered to teenagers and young adults as the solitary venue for stress relief after a long school week. The food tasted kinda meh and cost too much. She spent a whole dollar every Friday night. $.75 on a pickle and $.25 on a bag of ice for whoever broke their knuckles punching a wall or someone's face. But the DJ took requests. Everyone got to do the *Cha-Cha Slide,* and during all-night skates she played games on the ice-rink in her sneakers.

"We're looking for someone," Sagan explained.

Andrew asked, "Anyone that looks nearly as hot as the three of you and happens to be single?"

Tameka winced a little. She liked-liked Andrew, but neither one of them stayed single long enough to line up with when the other one was single. "It's a dude," she said.

Andrew's grin lit up the dark space. All of his teeth shined nice and white under the ultraviolet rays. He asked, "Would you like me to repeat the question?"

"There he is!" Rayne shouted and, rudely, pointed across the crowd to a dark corner near the entrance.

"Where?!" The other three shouted and strained to look where she pointed.

She ducked away without making a sound and sneaked along the wall into a well-hidden corner. Telling her friends about her stranger seemed like a good idea at the time, but she regretted it.

"I never thought you'd get away from them," came a voice from behind.

She jumped high enough to touch the exposed ceiling and almost squealed.

"I mean don't get me wrong. They seem like nice people, but I don't want to give all of you a headache on your Friday night." Mr. Mystery, too-old-for-her guy, grinned at her. She noticed his skin glowed a little less bright than his teeth.

"You came," she said. Her voice filled with awe after her heart rate returned to normal.

"I promised. So, come this way. I want to talk to you outside, so they don't see us," he said, gesturing toward the side door.

She stopped cold and leveled her gaze at him. No more fun and games. "Being with you could be dangerous. I don't know you. And now you want me to go outside. Alone. With you?" Her voice so devoid of levity and childish intentions it surprised her.

It seemed to surprise him, too. He searched her face, and when he spoke next, he kept his tone calm and even. "I'm not here to hurt you in any way. I'm worried our conversation may draw unwanted attention. Then I won't be able to answer the many questions you'll no doubt have."

"How do I know I can trust you?" she asked.

She didn't blink. She knew she didn't blink. But one second he stood a few yards away from her by the door, and the next he stood so close to her she saw his eyes transformed. The pupils of his incredible, dark eyes contracted to small slits. The midnight-blue ring on the outside swallowed his entire eye. His hand seared through her shirt where it gently cradled her elbow. She craned her neck to examine his gaze. He towered over her with the impression darkness followed in his wake. And he asked her to let him lead her away from everything she ever knew into that darkness. His voice echoed in the deep chamber of his chest as he said, "Because if I wanted to hurt you, I would have in the bookstore."

Convinced, she allowed him to lead her outside. As she grew older, she often looked back at this moment. When she followed him outside, she let go of her childhood, let go of the false sense of security that the night remained as safe as the day after sunset, and let go of any chance for a normal future.

That night Xelan told her much more than his name. He told her about herself, the world he came from, and what that meant for the human race. "So, the planet is called Cinder?" she asked.

Xelan's brows shot up, "All that and you're asking about my planet's name?" When she confirmed with a nod, he explained, "The star in our solar system super nova-ed into a red giant. Sometime before my people—the Icarus—had a name for themselves. The planet is scorched, and the atmosphere is full of volcanic ash and gases. We call it Cinder."

"Wait a minute, Icarus was that Greek story. The winged-man who flew too close to the sun? That's what you call yourselves?" she asked.

"Where do you think the story came from? Many of your stories and much of your language, it came from us," he said. "Your species was in its infancy when we invaded. You were just learning the meaning of history. Like children, it was easy to manipulate you into believing we were gods, so much so the Pharaohs that came long after continued the farce."

"What about spreading your vampiric nature with your bite?" she asked and animated spooky fangs. Her nose crinkled as she made a hissing face.

He chuckled. "No. None of that. It's not a virus that can spread through our saliva. And I've seen firsthand what drinking Icarean blood does to humans. It's not pretty. We can reproduce with you, but the offspring rarely survive. Altogether, we're not terribly compatible without the nacre."

As a fourteen-year-old living in Little Rock, Arkansas, Rayne struggled to imagine aliens invaded human civilizations of 8000 BCE without the world maintaining some recorded knowledge of it. But there was something about the pain she felt in her temples whenever he came around. It told her she understood. She knew. Deep in her bones, she knew. In the pulse at her wrists. In that moment, the fire ignited in her blood. The pain in her temples turned into white, searing agony. With her palms pressed to the side of her head, Rayne watched the world shift as she fell to her knees. She screamed. Xelan leaned her into him and cradled her against him while her world split apart like a filmstrip, leaving a vast emptiness behind.

Sights, sounds, and even smells—not all of them good—assaulted her senses. Images of slaves with boulders on their backs at great monuments flashed. The stench of blood and sweat in the hot sun as starved men, women, and even children roasted day in and day out in their work. Chains clanked, whips cracked, and voices screamed all around her. Her voice. She screamed. A woman who posed a striking resemblance to her shouted at the slave drivers—all tall men with pale skin and clean, unmarred clothes. They made for a stark contrast to the dark-skinned slaves in dirty rags. Before her eyes, the nearest warden plucked a child from his duties, lifted his neck up to his mouth, and bit into him. He drained the boy of his blood right there in front of her. The woman fell to her knees as Rayne did. She gripped a fist full of the sand with her head hung in resolution. When she opened her fist, the sand sifted through, and the Icarus in front her burst into tiny particles of light. The slaves screamed. Others shouted and rushed toward the woman. One by one they burst into light. The surrounding air wavered, and another woman stepped out of thin air. She made a perfect likeness of Sagan. Then a man who looked like Andrew appeared beside them. A Tameka look-a-alike dove from the sky and landed among them. More and more familiar faces appeared on the hill, and the last arrival, Xelan.

The image in Rayne's mind changed, and she saw a shadow of a man who stood in front of a swirling portal. She couldn't make out any of his features, but she sensed a wave of hatred and malice tested her resilience. Her fist closed and broke an unknown, yet familiar, glass object in her hand. Warm liquid spilled down from her fingertips. A high-pitched, keening sound pierced her ears, and a roar of wind shuddered through the vast chamber. The portal swallowed the shadow with little resistance. The pressure in the room increased, and the doors flew open. Thousands upon thousands of wing-ed beings drew into the conduit like air vacating a depressurized plane. At first, terror overwhelmed her. The portal might take her too, but it didn't draw her in at all. She stood there, unharmed, until all the Icari sealed behind the conduit. Once done, the torn fabric of space shimmered into nothing. Beyond stood a mirror. The mirror reflected Rayne as the mysterious and familiar woman earlier in her vision. She and the woman were the same.

When she returned to her reality, Xelan performed chest compression over her body in the back lot of the skating rink. She inhaled hard, wheezing and gasping for breath like a drowning victim. Her eyes watered as she blinked back tears. She clutched at his jacket for sanity's sake. Was this real? Was she back in her world? Or was the other place her real life, and this was a dream?

"You're here. You're here. I got you," he said in as soothing a voice he could manage with an edge of panic creeping in. When tears slid down her cheeks, he gazed up to the heavens and closed his eyes. "I'm sorry." She almost didn't make out what he said as she struggled to breathe even lungfuls of air. But then she remembered his significance to her—the past her—and she wanted to be strong for both their sakes.

"Xelan," she croaked. When he glanced down at her face, she saw tears swam in his eyes. "How long do we have?" Her voice so steady it surprised her. She regained something in that moment. Sitting up hurt, and her chest felt bruised from the whole kind of dying thing. She reached out to him and cupped his cheek. "How long, old friend?"

{2005}

"When will they come?" Rayne asked for the fortieth time. She walked away from a tree Xelan leaned against. Although the training session went well, she clung to the enduring frustration that set in the day she met the man.

He shook his head. "I told you it could happen at any moment." His tone, as always, held a wealth of patience. Tonight, it irritated her.

"But you've been saying that for three years!" she shouted, exasperated. She started unwinding the boxing wrap from her knuckles in violent, rough jerks. "How much longer do we have to wait?! How long before we just say they called the whole thing off, and we can let everything go back to normal?"

Xelan rushed over to her and took her fists in his hands, trying to stem her angry fretting. He shook them once. A familiar signal for her to meet his concerned eyes. The seventeen-year-old girl with all those muscles and all that disciplined training gazed into his eyes. He recoiled and almost dropped her hands at the callowness on her face. "Why? Why do you want this so badly? Wherever you are, whatever you're doing, he'll find you and slaughter everyone and everything around you. Why are you asking for this?"

"Because I want it over with," she answered. He gently opened her hands and took them in his own. She continued, "I hate this constant preparedness. I hate waking up every morning from terrible dreams just to live the day wondering if they'll come true this time or tomorrow. Or are we safe, now? Did it blow over?"

He squeezed and said, "Rayne, sometimes I forget how young you are and for that I'm sorry. But as long as you have those dreams, you know it isn't over."

Into the dark of the surrounding night, she spoke one breathy word that carried on the wind, "When?"

TWO

Be Careful What You Wish For Unless You're Prepared To Pay The Price

{APRIL 2006}

SWEAT DRIPPED IN RAYNE'S EYES. Deep inhale through the nose. Count to eight. Deep exhale through the mouth. Her skin burned. Not even the early spring morning air cooled her. The fire prevailed. It stoked over the last year, and when she woke this morning it blazed.

Every fiber in her quads and calves screamed, begged her to stop. Her heart rate mounted to the 180s, 185, then 190BPM. She ignored the protests from her lungs. Ignored the fatigue onset over an hour ago. Every stride won, every mile gained, every obstacle cleared, she escaped from an imminence which continued to chase her. On her heels, it soared close behind her. Breath on her neck. Flown ever closer. If she lost traction, if she slipped, or worse, if she dared stop, wings would fold around her, swallow her, and—

Halted. Turned. She howled wordlessly until her throat went raw. She faced down the trail. Her fierce gaze roved the trees, the forest floor, and the canopy for her pursuer. The pre-dawn hours offered little light. No wings. No response. But an unfamiliar surge beckoned her.

Her unit trained and exercised together in pairs. The buddy system. Restlessness and even a little recklessness petitioned her to find an additional outlet. Incapable of more than four hours of sleep, she ran the course every morning. Several times. Alone. Danger pressed into these woods, and she welcomed it. She invited anyone or anything to take her on. Attempt to, anyway. The fire inside roared, insatiable and unforgiving. The last few days it scorched worse than ever. She slept no more than an hour each night.

No unusual movement in the trees. Not a trace of life. Aside from the awful sense of foreboding. The gust in the darkness carried an ominous chill. A light whisper disguised in the breeze. A message. The words faint. Difficult to make out, but there. A male voice asked in hushed tones, "Is this enough for you?" A whisper. It echoed in the trees.

No fucking way. Alone and armed only with her anger, she turned back and bolted down the route once more. Before, the breeze went unnoticed. It offered no relief during her run. Now, it bit at her exposed legs and shoulders. Slowed her down. Eight hundred and eighty yards until home. She picked up the pace into a proper run.

Fate always chased her on these runs. She wanted to face it more with each passing day, no more extraordinary than the next. Yet, she escaped. It would catch up with her this time. Shit! The wind howled through the woods. The underbrush swirled at her legs. Unnatural. She called on the last reserves of her strength and sprinted the final six hundred yards as hard as her legs allowed. Her heart rate skyrocketed well over 200BPM. After the first hundred yards, the wind fell back. She spared a glance behind her, and it followed right at her heels. She outran the gusts. Still on they came. Definitely, unnatural.

With a grunt, absolutely not a whimper, she vaulted the seven-foot privacy fence into her backyard, squeezing her shoulders and climbing up the center. Lost maybe three seconds of her advantage. She glanced back to see the wind strong in its pursuit maybe ten yards away at this point. She crossed the half-acre lot in sixty-two seconds. She made it to the front door. Checked the door knob. No. Of course it's locked. In her scramble for the key, she fumbled it out of her hands. "Shit!" she shouted. Leaves rustled behind her. She turned, slow. Run! Why can't she run?! She decided then to face whatever it brought. Even an ugly truth she didn't want to hear.

The front door opened, and Rayne recalled some trials frightened her more than others. "Rayne. Echo. Callahan. What are you doing out at this time of night?"

If her heart pounded any harder in her chest, it might bust through her sternum. Quick, she checked outside the door to see if the tempest continued. The early AM hours returned to its usual calm stillness. She leaned an arm across the door frame, rested her forehead on it, and let out a long exhale.

"What's the matter with you, girl?" Michelle Callahan demanded from her daughter the decency to respond.

"Momma, nothing," she lied.

"How long have you been out of this house?" her mom asked.

Uncertain, she checked her watch. 5:12AM. She left the house to run the course at 3:00AM, but her mom didn't need to know that. "About thirty minutes. I couldn't sleep," she answered with a touch of honesty.

"You don't sleep. You don't eat. You don't even do your homework anymore. Then you run up on the front porch, scrambling for your keys like you're terrified of the dark. It doesn't make any sense." Her mom listed her keen observations. It occurred to Rayne that she sucked at appearing normal. "Why are you dressed half naked? It's freezing out there."

She wanted to groan so much. She dragged her dying legs into the house and across the living room. Every step heavy. She glanced at her feet to check for cinder blocks. Nope. After the stress sprints, she experienced the unfortunate side effect of noodle legs. By some miracle, she was still standing. She said, "Mom, I went for a run—"

"In Southwest Little Rock?! In the dark? I know I raised you to be smarter than that. Just last week two girls were abducted from Wal-Mart by that Night cult or whatever they call themselves. Dragging them out to Pulaski County. All their bodies turn up on Granite Mountain." Her mom shook her head and pointed up the stairs. "Go to your room. I need to think about what I'm going to do with you."

Eighteen years old. Almost nineteen, and her mom treated her like a child.

"And before you go thinking you're grown, you better remember this is my house. As long as you live under my roof you will go to school, make good grades, get into college, and make it to eighty years old. And you're gonna stop that running around Southwest Little Rock after dark or before dawn or however you want to word it." At last, she tossed her hands in the air. "I've half a mind to make you close the store every night for two weeks. No breaks."

Rayne trudged up the steps. She clung to the banister for dear life. By the time she reached the second floor, she considered crawling on her hands and knees the last step. Upstairs, she collected her clothes for her shower. Black and white. Her walls white. Her furniture black. The carpet black. Her whole life through a monochromatic lens of what was and what could be. Although her hot shower rinsed away the workout, she shivered. She needed to contact Xelan, but no one heard from him in the last four months. What happened on her run felt significant. Monumental. On the wind, something followed. She decided to search for him in the afternoon if her mom didn't force her to close.

As she prepared for the day, she passed her backpack on her desk. A short stack of homework mounting evidence of her apathy. She brushed a history essay prompt with her fingertip. She loved history and writing. With a certain future ahead of her, what was the point? Her eyes closed, and the fire returned. "When?" she asked the empty room. No answer. Frustrated, she swept the stack off her desk. She considered throwing the lamp and busting the bookcase, but contained herself. Her mom might lock her in a padded room.

Downstairs, Michelle waited with breakfast. Unusual. Her mom slept later than 7:30AM most days. Rayne's bus arrived at 7:00AM. She left before her parents woke up for the day to open the store. Her brother slept over at a friend's place.

Her mom spoke one word in a stern voice, "Eat."

Homemade pancakes with real maple syrup, scrambled eggs, and sausage. Rayne begged her tongue to water. Instead, her stomach turned. She frowned. Why didn't she want to eat? Not that long ago, after a brutal workout, she'd shovel this feast in her face faster than her mom could pile on seconds. Thirds. Where did her appetite go?

"You're stressed, baby," Michelle said. Her tone softened. The hard lines of her face followed suit.

The fire abated. "Momma?" she pleaded in a tiny voice. Why couldn't she be a little kid again?

"C'mere," her mom said.

Rayne rushed from the table to her mother's embrace. She ignored her initial urge to stop her mother from smoothing her hair. "Shh … It's okay. Listen." Her mom withdrew enough to meet Rayne's gaze. Her soft brown eyes shined with tears, "This is normal. You're in a tough place. Adult, but not enough to go out and live on your own. Your senior year. Going to college next year. It's a very stressful time." Her face grew contemplative. "Although, not as bad as when you were thirteen."

Rayne's grin broke in natural response to her mother's ribbing. She even giggled. The thought of college made her frown again. Not for her.

"I'm worried about you. Will you promise me something?" she asked.

"Anything," Rayne answered, meaning it.

"Let's you and I have a chat tonight. Tell me everything. All of what's bothering you. Even the stuff you think I won't understand. We can get some milkshakes." She held up a hand before Rayne managed a grimace, "Or whatever it is you have an appetite for these days. I'll even go on a run with you if it gets you talking to me. Deal?"

Rayne waited for mortification and paranoia to set in. The unit took an oath never to tell anyone—especially family—about their sacred duty to protect the planet. How would her mom take it? Would Xelan be mad at her if she did? Well, screw him! He deserted them. "Yea. I'd like that," she said.

"Good. Now sit down and eat half your breakfast, and then I'll let you finish getting ready for the day," Michelle said.

Rayne looked down at the heaping plate. And this time, she did groan.

The first bell rang. Rayne's eye twitched. She stood from the long lunch table, and collected her bag concealing her CD player. Twenty-eight students. Every face somewhat familiar. Four exits. Six people between her and the closest one. She counted the number of bodies between her and the rest of the exits as Kyle continued his story, "I thought, 'Surely he wasn't about to get in my face.' And then he did. He got right in my fucking face." He checked his pocket for his pen and tiny notebook.

"What did you expect? You ate his breakfast burrito." Sagan challenged as she slung her messenger bag over her shoulder.

He turned to face Sagan as he walked backward in their shuffle to funnel out of the cafeteria. His loose black cargo pants and black t-shirt, the same clothes he wore each day. "I'll have you know, Sagan, that he owed me two breakfasts at this point. I cashed in on my investment."

Rayne struggled to contain her disappointment as it mounted higher. Another ordinary day. What she wouldn't give to punch something in the face right now. The familiar fire seared beneath the surface of her tolerance. "Kyle, you told me this plan, yesterday. And yesterday, I said it was a bad idea," she reminded him without a backward glance.

They breached the cafeteria and made it to the entrance of North Hall. The North and South Halls of J. A. Fair High School sprouted from a central hub containing the entrance lobby, the main office, and the cafeteria in their respective directions. North Hall housed the most classes, and the senior lockers lined its walls. One hundred and thirteen upperclassmen crowded the steel riot gate blocking the entry. Four exits in order of proximity: cafeteria, auxiliary gym, main entrance, and South Hall. About two dozen bodies between her and each one. Not ideal. The front of the school sunk into the ground. Limited windows, also not ideal. The back opened to the bus drop-off and football field. More windows, but limited to ceiling level.

"Get back!" José shouted.

"We'll let you in as soon as you get back!" Bone Crusher reiterated.

"Not this again." Both security guards delayed lifting the gates every morning. "It's such a power move," Rayne muttered as she skipped to the next song. Her thick, black hair disguised the earphone. Disturbed's *Remember* blared in one ear. Their "Believe" album soothed the burning rage like an ointment.

"C'mon man! You're wasting locker time!" Kyle shouted back.

Incredulity stained her voice, "Do you even remember which locker is yours this year?" The devious snicker beside her brightened her dark mood. Sagan often affected her that way. Unlike Kyle, who wore his usual outfit, Sagan went for a throwback to freshman year: red corset top, black skirt, and stiletto knee-high boots. It improved Rayne's mood to see her dress the same as when they dated. The whole overworked, athletic reach girl thing didn't suit her. Rayne mourned Sagan's long brown hair before she cut and bleached it. But Sagan liked it, and nothing else mattered.

With some irritation, Kyle brushed his brown mop of curly hair out of his deep green eyes. "No," he answered in a flippant tone.

"Well, I do, and I'd really like to get to it before my A&P exam," Sagan said as she rifled through her bag. "Apparently, I left my cheat sheet in there."

Kyle's eyes widened as he gasped in exaggerated alarm. "Oh, no! You might get an 'A' minus!"

She stuck her tongue out. "Not everyone can roll with intentionally failing except for the classes where you negotiate with your teachers to sit with Rayne"

Kyle scowled. Rayne refused to acknowledge it. Sagan's tone softened, "Besides, some of us want to get into good universities."

Snapping back to Sagan almost gave Rayne whiplash. And there it was. The big bomb. Sensing the impending conflict, Kyle blew out his breath in a whistle. "Are you serious?" Rayne asked.

Sagan flinched, and her light skin blanched alabaster. Her response tempered Rayne's initial shock. She opened her mouth to soothe her, but stopped. Something alien streaked across her peripheral vision. White hair. Unable to stop herself, she spun and scanned the crowd. Her frantic blue eyes connected on each head before moving onto the next. Ninety-seven out of one hundred and thirteen. Ninety-eight . . .

"What's wrong?" Kyle asked. As rare an occurrence as winning the lottery, his voice dropped all humor and pronounced each word in a grim, flat tone. Rayne continued counting rather than answer. He'd figure it out.

This alerted Sagan, and they all searched the crowd like paranoid secret service agents. Where was it? Where did it go? More to the point, who was it? No one in the school dyed their hair white. And none of the older teachers allowed it to grow. Was it—

CLANG! The trio jumped out of their skin. "Let's go! Let's go!" The riot gate shuttered and crashed as José finished rolling it to the ceiling. Chests rising and falling a little belabored, they surveyed one another. Rayne concentrated on her breathing. Slow, deep, steady. In and out. Her body stilled. She frowned as she contemplated her sour mood. Alert. Ready to go at a moment's notice. They knew the stakes. If only they didn't. Then maybe they wouldn't be jumping at shadows.

"You all right?" Kyle asked.

"I thought I saw—" Rayne started.

Bone Crusher pressed in on their huddle, "Move it along people. Two minutes before tardy."

Kyle's face shifted as he considered cussing the security guard out. He opened his mouth, and Rayne cut in, "Move out, soldier."

"You heard her," Bone Crusher poked the bear.

Sagan's blond bob bounced when she hooked her arm through Kyle's elbow. "Escort me to my locker, good sir!"

Rayne smiled, short-lived. They moved on down the hall, Sagan distracting Kyle from his growing rage. Each of them itching for a fight. One might assume hormones. To their misfortune, teen angst occupied but a minuscule fragment of their torment. With the weight of the world on her shoulders for the last four years, she faltered on the edge of losing it. Every day the same beige-coated, cinder block walls. The same dirty white linoleum. The same off-white drop-ceiling. The same aroma of budget rubbery meat and off-brand canned vegetables lingered morning and afternoon. The same nine hundred and one faces give or take a transfer. The days blended into one another. Call it a case of Senior-itis, but if something big didn't happen soon, she might need a straight jacket. She needed it to accessorize her white button up blouse and black, ripped jeans. No glamour required for combat boots. If the others shared her disposition, they kept it to themselves. She'd bring it up at the next meeting.

"Move expeditiously through the hall, please! Expeditiously," Mrs. Mendax, their principal, shouted from all of her four-foot, nine-inches of height. Her voice carried her 'word of the week' through the halls lined with old-fashioned wooden lockers.

Passing the library, two students shouted in shrill, unified voices, "Expeditiously, everyone! Expeditiously!" Thirteen students broke into a chorus of laughter.

"Mr. Cody Noble. Mr. Quincy Green. Straighten up before I write you up," she said. Real clever and all, but every student knew she bullshitted about write-ups and detention because she never wanted to do the paperwork. More students mocked her further down the hall. For the first time in Rayne's entire tenure at J. A. Fair, the woman stomped her foot and stormed off in the direction of the office.

"Something finally got into her?" Sagan asked.

Happy to hear the casual tone returned to his voice, Kyle said, "She's on her way to smoke a blunt in her office. Helps her unwind."

Rayne's eyebrows shot up. "And how do you know that?"

Sagan chimed in, "Yea?"

"Because I smoked one with her last week," he said.

"No fucking way," Sagan scoffed.

Rayne believed him. "You can't be doing that."

He scowled. "And why not? I'm eighteen. I can do what I want."

If Rayne rolled her eyes any harder, they might fall out of her head. "It's illegal."

"You could go to jail," Sagan added.

Rayne said, "And Xelan's not around to bail you out, again."

Under his breath, he muttered, "Better than what I normally do with my 'free time.'"

Sagan either ignored him or didn't hear him. She broke off to her locker with a warning, "Stay out of trouble. See you guys at lunch!" The sound of her stilettos tapped as she walked away.

They approached the end of North Hall. Rayne's locker caught the morning sunlight as it poured in from the glass exit. She soaked in one of the few access points to the outside world. This constant alertness wore on her. Kyle watched her as he leaned against the lockers. He appeared casual, but she knew better. They all learned the same covert methods of relaxed posture and unassuming stance. Couldn't let the world know they trained to be murderers. Was it murder if it was an alien? She jerked out of her thoughts and opened her lock. She peered inside. Why bother anymore?

She replayed the conversation with her mom, "As long as you live under my roof you will go to school, make good grades, get into college, and make it to eighty years old."

"Whatever," she said to her locker.

"What was that?" Kyle asked. Again, his eyes held too much concern.

She retrieved two dusty books from her locker and stuffed them into her bag with little more than apathy. Her notebook, on the other hand. The purple cover slipped from the flattened spiral coils. She filled it to the brim with secrets, stories, and plans. She kept it in her locker after her mom "cleaned" her room one day and damn near found it.

"Everything's fine," she said. She clutched her notebook to her chest.

"Rayne, I think—" Kyle started.

"Don't you have somewhere to be?" The sass, the salt, the scorn. Tameka knew which buttons to push. And she loved to push them. Often.

Kyle scowled at her.

They dated once. Complicated and short-lived, they broke up in 10TH grade. Ever since the two of them in the same room went from fireworks to TNT. Friends with both, Rayne cautiously juggled the relationships. Tameka's eyes narrowed like emerald shards. "Why are you always following her like a puppy?"

Classmates passed through the crowd. Some paused and took notice of the scene. "You insist on sitting next to her in every class. Everyone knows about it. It's pathetic!" Tameka liked to go for the throat.

Rayne dared not interrupt. She liked her head right where it was, thanks very much. Kyle, on the other hand. Known for a short temper and melting down like a nuclear reactor whenever anyone questioned his friendship with her, Tameka threw down the gauntlet for another glorious fight.

Kyle surprised her. He ignored the bait. Instead, he smirked and said, "Everyone's gotta have a hobby." To Rayne he said, "I'll see you in Spanish. Don't forget there's a test this morning." He shook his head, the great mass of messy brown curls shaking with it. He disappeared into the history classroom beside her locker. Rayne spared a moment to recall if he ever attended the class before. After a second, she decided it didn't matter.

"I think his discipline training is paying off," Rayne said into her locker.

She grabbed her pencil case, and from behind heard Tameka go one step too far. "You know he's in love with you," she said.

While Rayne loved them both, her morning already kinda sucked, and her fuse snuffed shorter and shorter as the day went on. She hesitated to turn from her locker and confront Tameka. All this for a boy she friend-zoned. "Yes, Tameka. It's a well-known fact."

"Well, why don't you do something about it?" Tameka asked. She brushed a red tendril away from her striking black freckles against her tawny complexion.

Rayne slammed her locker and rested her head on the wooden surface. One. Two. Three. All the way to ten. Tameka was her friend. Don't go hurting friends because the morning was rough. Tameka got up in her feelings about Kyle a lot. This time was no different.

She turned as slow and as non-threatening as possible. She asked, "Why does it bother you that it doesn't bother me?"

Tameka clenched and unclenched her jaw as she mulled over her answer. She turned her denim-clad back on Rayne and shuffled through her own locker. She said, "I guess sometimes I worry you're leading him on. That's all."

Rayne cocked her head and stopped the grimace before it started. The hard edge forged in her esoteric flames crept into her voice as she asked, "You don't still blame me for your breakup, do you?" She walked halfway across the hall without thinking. She noticed halfway to Tameka. Why did she want to attack one of her best friends? She took a deep breath and planted her feet to the tile. Maintain calm.

Tameka's tresses bounced as she shook her head. Some of Rayne's anger dissipated. Tameka met Rayne's gaze and explained, "No. I really don't. I know you went out like twice, and it didn't work out for you. I also know he's asked you several times since, and you've turned him down."

Rayne began, "That's because—"

Tameka raised a hand the shade of amber. Rayne stopped. Tameka continued, "But ... it's crazy the way he follows you around this school. You lead all of us, not just him. At no point did Xelan say you needed a guardian. So, what's his motive?"

At last, something she could speak to. Rayne brushed up beside one of her oldest friends. "Tameka, I've honestly given up on getting rid of him. He's either going to follow me into college or into hell," she said in a forlorn tone.

The delicate features of Tameka's face softened. She started to say something, then Rayne cut her off. "C'mon. We're gonna be late for English."

On the way to the room, Rayne wanted to add one more quip. "Besides, I thought you had a thing for Xelan, anyway."

Tameka stopped short outside the classroom, and Rayne hurried inside.

Silence filled the halls as teachers commanded their classrooms. Tameka and Rayne entered room 124 on the English branch of North Hall. They both sat in their usual seats beside one another in the back. Rayne seized the opportunity to vent to her notebook about the argument in the hall. She poured all her thoughts not worth the fight with Tameka onto the 8.5x11 page. Why did

Tameka blame her for Kyle's behavior and actions? Couldn't she see he's the one with the problem? Tameka reached her hand out between them. Rayne gave into the urge to smile. She handed Tameka her second earphone, and they both listened to the "Queen of the Damned" soundtrack. The best medicine for Ms. Saul's lectures.

Around her bags unzipped, papers rustled, and a hushed whisper suffused the room. The final bell rang, and students rushed to catch up on their homework. Another worksheet. No wonder she blew off her homework. Ms. Saul sank below Rayne's standard for an English teacher. She struggled to control the class; she chose reading material outside the AP English curriculum; and she assigned little to no papers. Rayne's classmates no-doubt appreciated the last, but senior high school students from the Little Rock School District often failed to compete with national standards on reading and writing. Impoverished students deserved the same expectations as middle-class districts. Rayne decided when she became a college writing instructor, she wanted to teach in impoverished schools. There she might use her experience to guide students like her into jobs above the poverty line. A future.

She placed her pencil down and read the page. When she became a writing instructor? She didn't have a future. Why did she keep putting herself through this? How much more—

"Rayne?" Ms. Saul's voice cut through Rayne's melancholy.

"Ma'am?" Rayne asked.

"Weren't you paying attention? Can you answer my question about themes in the Canterbury—" An awful sound interrupted her.

Another fucking day. When she heard her office door connect with the jamb, Rebecca Mendax wrenched her three-inch pumps off her aching feet. Checking the clock, she groaned. 8:30AM. "Seven more hours to go," she sighed. But she signed up for this. Fifteen years ago when she agreed to promote out of teaching into principal duties, she understood long hours came with the territory. She failed to anticipate how hard the work would be.

Fair upheld a reputation as a different class of school then. It always scored beneath public school standards, but never as bad as the last five years. These days guidance counselors forewent teaching students how to sign up for scholarships or select the right school for them to apply for admission. These kids lucked out if they got a Burger King application at graduation. At the end of the day, all that mattered remained in the reason she got into education and accepted the principal position at this school in the first place. She couldn't forget that.

She tsked and walked over to her desk. She also underestimated how much footwork there was. She patrolled the hallways on a near hourly basis to catch kids skipping or running through the halls. Then, her least favorite time of day, class change. She shuddered as she straightened a stack of papers. At four foot nine, she impressed no one shouting at the kids to move faster through the halls. Their herd times were so slow, classes started an average of five minutes late. She failed to push them any faster. And her feet killed her. With that in mind, she swept a hand over the cushion of her seat and lowered herself onto it. Before the backside of her skirt even touched the leather surface, a knock sounded from her door.

"Yes?" she groaned.

Muffled behind the door, a voice wavered as it announced, "Mrs. Mendax, we need you at the front of the office, urgently."

Ms. Fuller, the vice principal, stood on the other side of the oak paneling. She sounded upset or bothered. Something was wrong. "I'll be right there." Sighing as she lamented the loss of her sitting time, Mrs. Mendax re-shoed her feet and hurried to the door. She opened it and narrowed her eyes.

"Ms. Fuller? How can I help you?" she asked.

The woman's eyes brimmed with tears. "Please. The front of the office. Please." Her voice shook and carried an edge of panic.

Alert and irritated, Mrs. Mendax pushed past her simpering subordinate and stomped to the front office. School violence, namely mass shootings, remained a constant concern of school staff. She hesitated to jump to the conclusion in an instant, but she felt hard pressed to think of another reason one of her VP knocked on her door on the verge of pissing herself. Prepared to talk some sense into a depressed teenager, Mrs. Mendax barged into the front office, and realized she could not prepare for this.

A man with pale blond hair an inch longer than his ass examined their intercom system and muttered, "Yes, this will do nicely." He flipped a switch with leather fingerless gloves. When he stood, his leather coat creaked, and it swayed around him. His smile brilliant at the sight of Mrs. Mendax, he said, "Hello. I'll bet this works great as a sound system." He tossed a thumb at the intercom speaker. Two men entered both front doors to the office and shielded the front of them.

Mrs. Mendax resisted the urge to recoil and asked, "I beg your pardon?"

"Oh, that's not all you'll beg for," the blond-haired man said. And then Mrs. Mendax gave in and recoiled this time. Did he have any idea who she was? As if in answer, a remote, disturbed smile crept onto his lips. "Rebecca. May I call you Rebecca?" he asked with an air of consideration as he paced away from the intercom system. He rested an arm across one of the secretaries' cubes. The secretary tried to shrivel further into her work space.

Mrs. Mendax straightened herself and shuddered as she shook off the nagging sensation of impending doom. "You may," she said, with the same firm tone she used on some of her toughest repeat delinquent students.

"Thanks." The smile actually dialed down into something that could be mistaken for charming. "I'm having girl troubles." She blinked once, slow. This threw her for a bit of a loop. She stopped herself from laughing. The situation grew more ridiculous with each moment. She stopped herself from fidgeting in her discomfort again as she listed which mental illnesses a doctor might diagnose him with. He continued, "There's this girl I really like, see? And I'm trying to ask her out. But I need a good atmosphere, a backdrop, if you will."

Mrs. Mendax nodded to show she followed along. He shined her another winning smile. "I'm glad you understand. This school," he circled his index finger around, "is the perfect place. But it's missing something."

She rose to the bait, "What's that?"

"It's not doused in blood and filled with screaming teenagers. Boys!"

All hell broke loose. The two men by the door lunged for the two smaller men behind the main counter. The secretaries and counselors burst from their desks and tried to bolt for the doors. The blond man grabbed the woman nearest him, and in an act of mercy, snapped her neck. He ran, jumped onto a desk, and leapt onto a retreating counselor. Mrs. Mendax heard the woman scream, then she heard a snarl, and then she heard nothing. The two men at the front lay sprawled dead across the counter. From behind her, where two people escaped, she heard muffled cries, and guessed more men waited back there. In a few short minutes, they disposed of the entire office staff.

"So this is it, then? The Master informed me it was happening so soon. I thought I was to be notified so I could make preparations," Mrs. Mendax explained.

The blond man stood and wiped the blood from his mouth. "He's been most impressed with you and the other followers."

She nodded. "I make good on my promises." Four fucking years of housing Icari across the world. Feeding them scraps from the socio-economical table. The Cult of Night even earned themselves a reputation when the FBI investigated them for cultist ideology. They understood so little. She straightened her jacket as she took in the blood all around the room and on the office doors. Clearing her throat, she asked, "What does the Master wish for me to do next? I can assist in finding the girls."

"Oh, there'll be no need for that. He said it was time for you to receive payment," the man assured.

She flushed with excitement. Finally, her time had come. But best play it up to the second in charge. "Payment? I am but a servant to the Pretiosum Cruor. I only wish to assist the Master," she prostrated. The second in command chuckled, and his genuine smile shriveled into a cruel smirk. When she felt strong arms grab her from behind, she cried out. "What is the meaning of this! I did everything I was told. I brought them together! I serve the Master! We all serve the Master!"

"To put it simply, he suspected you wanted a meet and greet. Picture. Autograph. You know. And this being the culmination of thousands of years of work, he doesn't to waste any time on fans. You understand," he humored. "Now, hold still. This won't hurt a bit."

The blond man crept toward her, and Mrs. Mendax screamed. She screamed as the tissue ripped. She screamed when the blood poured. And she screamed when things she knew she needed to live strung out of her and passed around. Joining the chorus of her screams, the very loud sound of metal scraping along tile down North Hall. That remained the very last sound she ever heard. The blood-smeared face of her Master's second-in-command, the very last sight she ever saw. And her aching feet, the very last sensation she ever felt.

THREE

Always Be Prepared Isn't Just A Motto
For The Scouts

SHE WOULD KNOW HE WAS HERE. She'd know before he step foot in the bland, beige hallway. She'd sense him and his kind the moment they enter the school. This was good. Nox wanted her to feel him nearby. He wanted her quaking and terrified. She would soon surrender her whole race to him, and she didn't even know it. Though he assumed she suspected: this was always meant to be.

The cloth across his back itched and pressed into him. He resented the heavy cloak, and his need to cover himself on this planet. He ruled Cinder as the most supreme King in history. His broad chest and honed backside bared for all to see the might of the King. But no matter. It served for dramatic effect. The moment he could rid himself of it, he shall. This moment, eight thousand years in the making, called for a little theatrics along the way.

Standing at the mouth of this "North Hall," he flexed his fist around his ring, and reached out for that thread that lashed him and her together. Through the connection she never realized existed, he heard music. Something sensual, something foreboding.

His exceptional canines flashed as he grinned. Perfect. He raised one laced, heavy boot, and took his first step down the hallway. The heavy masonry instrument dragged along with him. Loud. It was so loud. It resonated to the opposite end of the school, where Colita cut the sprinkler lines and prepared the explosives. At present, Korac took care of a most inconvenient errand for him. Each of them prepared for their own moment. Each of them juiced and electrified with anticipation.

Nox chuckled. She knew. He had her. He sensed the connection between them spread wide open. His hold on her grew intoxicating. And he held onto it for as long as she allowed. The journey down the hall intensified as the scent of amped-up human adrenaline enticed his predatory senses. The fear. He licked his lips, lifted the sledgehammer, and slammed it into a set of wooden lockers. Smashed. Splintered. The busted bank of lockers exposed student possessions smelling of hormones and deodorant. Weak humans pressed their faces to the glass of a nearby classroom. He snarled into the window and swung the hammer at the wall beside one door. Cement blocks crumbled away. The people stayed inside.

He wanted the buildup before the climax to last as long as possible. For the grind and scrape of the hammer to announce his presence. Her heart pounded in his hand as sure as if he'd ripped it out, himself. Through their connection, he watched the tears breach her lashes. Overcome, overwrought, and oh just a tad bit . . . excited. He flexed his fist again, nails biting his palms. He sent the image of his ring down the pipeline to her. He predicted how this might affect her. Sure enough, she bolted up from her seat. Merit tended her friend. The moment Rayne released the breath she held, he broke the connection. Time enough for that in a few hours. An eternity waited for them after today.

He approached the first off-shoot hallway, and Colita's men deployed on cue. They walked in time with him from the exits up to North Hall access. Nox continued his slow sojourn past the second off-shoot. And then he stopped at the third. He sensed her right there. Around the corner. Utterly frightened. Her lovely fair skin, almost as pale as the most beautiful women on Cinder, drained with dread. Her wide bright-blue eyes shed tears caused by the delicious adrenaline spike. Her delicate mouth parted, allowing short, quivering breaths. He desired to taste her lips, splashed with salty tears, for the first time outside one of her dreams. He wanted her to look exactly as she did now, underneath him on their pallet beside his fire. His fingers tangled in that beautiful midnight hair.

There would be time enough for that in the end. Here and now ... as the security guard approached, he flexed his fist one last time, and the invasion began.

The whole class drew up from their studies, alarmed. A grating, metallic screech reverberated through the halls. The teeth grinding, scraping sound started near the cafeteria, but grew closer. The sound amplified by the empty hall and the quiet academic atmosphere. Rayne glanced at Tameka. Tameka palmed her hidden cell phone. She stopped mid-text message. "What the fuck is that?" she mouthed.

"What the actual fuck?" one classmate shouted.

Another asked, "What is that, Ms. Saul?"

A call beckoned her. No defense to protect herself, her mind gave in without resistance. Confused at first. She sat fixed in her seat. Her eyes widened in horror as she came to understand. Tears brimmed her eyes. She opened her mouth to say his name. To warn Tameka. To warn them all. But a strangled whimper puffed out. A loud crash carried down the hall. The source grew ever closer.

"Rayne?" a voice called.

A tear fell. Her heart pounded against the wall of her chest. Every vein and artery pulsed heavy against the barrier of her skin as her heart rate excelled. Nearby, rock shattered. Tameka resorted to gripping Rayne by the shoulders. She shook hard and whispered, "Celindria."

No response. Rayne struggled to break from his grasp. She fought against the allure of his madness. The connection with him too intimate for her to bear. Bright white light filled her vision. In its place, she gleaned the impression of a large man's hand in a flowing sleeve. He flexed his fist, tightened around a heavy, engraved ring.

Voices. They swirled in her head. Xelan's voice asked, "Why? Why do you want this so badly? Wherever you are, whatever you're doing, he'll find you and slaughter everyone and everything around you. Why are you asking for this?"

She asked in a frustrated tone, "When?"

The final voice frightened her. Strong, sure. A voice she heard in her most private dreams. He asked, "Is this enough for you?"

"Nox." Rayne bolted out of her seat.

Tameka withdrew her hands from Rayne as if burned. "Are you fucking kidding me?"

Marilyn Manson sang through her earphones: *Redeemer*. She swatted them off her ears and struggled to remove her bag. She flung it and the CD player against the wall. When she faced the class, mascara spilled off her lashes into her eyes, stinging.

Tameka reached for her. "Rayne, we have—"

A chorus of stomping feet erupted, barely audible for the terrible screech right outside their branch of North Hall. *BANG!* Another explosive crash. Wood splintered and splattered across the tile. Their classmates strained in their desks to see out the door, but seemed too afraid to get up. Better not to draw the attention of the predators. When the situation couldn't get worse, the motion sensor lights shut off. The hall pitched in total darkness.

Panic mounted. One classmate asked, "Ms. Saul, is this a drill or something?"

Another, "Is there something outside?"

Ms. Saul placated her charges, "It's all right. I'm sure it's just a security training exercise."

Rayne rushed to the door, her combat boots echoing the footsteps in the English hall. She ignored Ms. Saul's questions. "Rayne, what do you think you're doing, young lady?" and "Where do you think you're going?" Her hand no sooner touched the door handle than a figure in a dark cloak walked past the door. The effect slow and purposeful. He paused at the window. The light in the classroom illuminated his face. She studied the high cheekbones and sharp jawline. Thick brows shaded the most unusual bright, yellow eyes. Designs drawn in black across his face. Pictographs. She recalled studying a face like his in a history museum featuring an exhibit on Mayan and Aztec culture.

Mesoamerican? She startled when she noticed he studied her with just as much intensity. He opened his mouth and snarled at her. Fangs. Scary, long fangs. A little over five centimeters long.

"Yip!" She bounced back from the door and collided with another student. Tameka helped her off the floor. Rayne pushed her hand through her hair as she started to pace. The class stood staring at the being beyond the door as if to convince themselves the shadowed figure didn't exist. Until he receded into the darkness.

"I'm going," Rayne told Tameka.

"Going where? Rayne, get back here!" Ms. Saul shouted.

Too late. Rayne barged out the door. Her eyes adjusted to the lower lighting quickly thanks to their training. The motion sensor lights ignored her. Nothing down toward the emergency exit that led to the football field. Good. But to North Hall? No go. The cloaked, Mesoamerican man waited, standing about eight inches taller than her. His back almost as broad as the entrance. Against her better judgment, she gave into an urge to peer beyond him.

Tameka waited for her at the door to the class. Rayne pressed a finger to her lips and tip-toed away. Close. So close to the man in front of her. He either didn't notice or didn't care. The latter disturbed her more than the former. If he didn't give a shit she crept up right behind him, then she presented no threat to him whatsoever. A bit insulting, but her pride would recover.

Beyond him, another being stood on the edge of sunlight pouring from North Hall exit. A massive one at that. At least two or three inches taller than her boy here, he took up two-thirds of the massive corridor with his breadth. Beside him laid a large, heavy sledge hammer. The cloak shifted. She drew her eyes up to the cloak's hood. Shadow. Only shadow even in the shine of all that daylight. Like the dark inside sucked it all into a void. Two, surely more beyond. One between her and the nearest exit. Nothing between her and at her six. Nine hundred and one students to evacuate. Time to go.

She backed away, terrified to unlock her gaze from the mountain in the school. As she stepped back on the linoleum, she resisted shrieking for the sake of her sanity. When out of her sight, she feared he might start swinging that thing around and come after her.

Something bumped her elbow. She jumped and bit her tongue. Tameka grabbed her; scared the shit out of her. She allowed Tameka to pull her into the classroom, and secured the door shut, herself. Every muscle stiffened and drove up her adrenaline. Her classmates and Ms. Saul stared at her. Each wearing a similar expression: eyes wide, cheeks streaked in tears, mouths grim, thin lines, and a stiffness to their limbs. Paralyzed with fear. Racked with it herself, she rallied. This was it. She refused to let them suffer undo injuries. Fear, a luxury she could no longer afford. A deep breath. In through the nose. Out through the mouth. Like running. Her heart calmed, her muscles loosened, and her shoulders went back. The fire inside her peaked.

With her chin high she said, "Tameka, can you hand me your cell phone?"

"Of course," she answered. Her voice wavered. The device exchanged hands.

Rayne paced around the room, breaking up the cluster of students. She touched one on the shoulder, patted another on the forearm, and smiled at a few. As she reassured the room, she dialed 911. Her gaze flicked to Tameka, who raised an eyebrow. Rayne shook her head. Her eyes and mouth tightened, grim.

"What's that mean?" someone asked.

She opened her mouth to volley them with more false reassurance. *SMASH!* Real close. The sound of shattering glass and clanging metal carried down the empty halls. Screams sliced through the terrifying stillness. Some of the class started asking questions, but Rayne charged for the door.

"Don't!" Tameka started. But Rayne already crept into the hall. She slunk along the wall to avoid the Mesoamerican's attention. Beyond the sweep of his cloak, right in front of her locker, laid a body. Chunks of glass and scraps of twisted metal littered the corpse. Tan, athletic, and dressed in a school security uniform, José's toes pointed to the ground, but his head gazed at the ceiling with empty, lifeless eyes. The cloak shifted, and she glanced up to the Aztec warrior. He hissed. She backed away. Her eyes never left him. She expected Tameka's reach this time and followed her back into the classroom. She slammed the door and put her back to it.

"What was—" Tameka asked.

She stopped when the lights flickered. The class held a collective breath. Bright. Dim. Bright. Dim. Super bright. Off. Screams exploded throughout the campus as each classroom plunged into utter darkness. The narrow windows at the top of the classroom provided their sole source of meager light.

She looked around and took in the faces of her classmates. None older than seventeen or eighteen. All frightened. Four years in the making. She trained, planned, and prepped for this exact moment, and it finally came. Six classrooms on this hall. Averaging thirty-three students per class. One unguarded exit. Difficult, but not impossible. As for the rest of the school, well … one thing at a time.

A classmate asked, "What's going? What was that?"

She tried her leader voice on for size. "All right, everyone. Listen up!" The students snapped to attention. The teacher, not so much.

"Rayne, everyone, please sit down. Security will handle whatever's going on—" Ms. Saul began.

"Security was eliminated, Ms. Saul. José is dead." Rayne announced. Her mouth tightened in a grim line.

Well, that sure closed Ms. Saul's mouth.

"The school is under attack," Tameka jumped in. Her voice carried a weight of concern to it. It proved more convincing than Rayne's approach. The color drained from the class, collectively. Ms. Saul, too. Tameka continued, "We can get you to safety. As safe as it can get, anyway, right?" Tameka deferred to Rayne.

Rayne took the signal and picked up the torch from there. "No time to arm you. There will be some kind of signal. Some kind of alarm to trigger the full invasion." Eyes locked with hers. Desperate. Terrified. She made certain to return eye contact with each student. "Listen to me and follow my every instruction. You got it?" Nods or either frozen stares in return. "Tameka?"

"Yes?" Tameka answered. They practiced using their ancestors' names as triggers, but never designated call signs or code names. She made a mental note to work on that.

"The back exit is unguarded. Lead them to it. I'll get into the hall and distract the intruders. Make sure to tell anyone along the way to head to the football field." Rayne's voice grew in volume. "Do you hear that everybody? Get to the football field! Don't go any further than that until we know the perimeter is safe. They may be guarding the campus, somehow. Do you understand?"

Every head bounced this time. The class's demeanor shifted from paralyzed with fear to antsy, yet determined. Some milled around and collected a few belongings: jackets, cell phones, and . . . sun glasses of all things. She took a few steps to the door, and called out behind her, "Okay. Remember, to the—"

Glass shattered. Not outside, but inside the classroom this time. The narrow windows, nine feet from the floor, crumbled into the room. Beastly limbs and paws scattered. Huge. "What the fuck?" Rayne shouted. Her classmates screeched. Off in the distance, more glass broke. Further away. Next door. Across the hall. Down the hall. Every class with windows chinked and cracked. An ensemble of screams followed suit.

"That'd be the signal," Tameka shouted over the din.

Rayne blocked the door a bit as she addressed the adrenaline-induced students and teacher. "Stop. Calm. I know it's hard. But you can't just run into the hall and go where you like. To the football field. No matter what. Get whoever you can out to the football field. Tameka will guide you to the end of the hall. Please tell me you understand?" There. Finally. An edge of concern she'd yet to manage blossomed. Through the window, two of the classrooms opened up. Chaos poured into the hall. Waves of aimless bodies foamed forth, divided down both ends of the hall. As the distant screams took shape into shrills and more guttural sounds, compassion choked the fire in her. People were dying.

Ms. Saul clutched the hand of the student next to her. "We understand. Grab her hand." He grabbed the girl behind him. And she grabbed a girl beside her. And so they went until they formed a human chain. "We won't let go until we're on the football field."

"Where will you go?" Tameka asked Rayne.

"My locker. I have a stash there," Rayne confessed.

Tameka smiled. "So do I. I'll be back."

Rayne pulled Tameka into a tight hug. Tameka trembled. Rayne understood then she was the only member of their unit who asked for this in some way. "You'd better." Rayne stepped back and smiled. Then she popped out the door. She held every confidence Tameka would keep the class safe. What she doubted was how the fuck she was supposed to get to her locker through this mess?

Bodies surged in waves around her. Pressed her against the wall. Students ran from the next classroom on her left. They all but trampled their teachers to escape. Shrieks ricocheted from North Hall. The main artery of the school pumped adrenaline and blood into the mouths of the invaders. Whether or not the school realized it, the intruders craved this pandemonium. They lusted for the aphrodisiac of fear, the temptation of helplessness, and the enticement of adrenaline. They drove the student body from the classrooms on purpose. She grimaced. "Fucking assholes."

Desperate, she shouted, "Go to the exit! The football field! It's safe outside! Don't leave the campus!" Some people in the crowd pivoted to her instruction. The rest ... Screams, gurgles, and strangled sounds followed.

Inch by inch, she made her way to North Hall access, driven by the crowd to stampede along. Aware of Tameka and the class as they skirted the opposite direction for the exit, she prayed to whoever was up there for their safety. Most of the traffic herded along in her direction. She broached the main hallway. Underfoot the vibration from the swelling masses amplified. A thunderous roar preluded horrific shrills. Structural debris—glass, beams, ceiling panels, duct work, cinder blocks—spattered and echoed throughout the school. An acrid smell filled the air. They set off a fucking explosion in South Hall.

"Oh my God." So much smoke.

"Oh my God." Everyone is screaming.

"Oh my God." The ground was shaking.

Lucy struggled to right herself. A ringing carried in her ears, and the ground shook. Squeezing her hands over her ears, she stood still in the dust, smoke, and debris. The fire alarms remained silent. Shouldn't they go off? Never mind, the screaming was enough noise. Realizing she was close to the last one in the room, she started staggering her numb limbs toward the door. Out in the hall, students squealed and funneled out of classrooms to escape the fire erupting in the Technology hallway. Knowing South Hall lay just ahead and seeing it meant two different things. So many bodies stood between her and it. She joined the crowd at the back of the group and pushed her way through. She wanted to see the sunlight from the doors just at the end there.

A rumble elicited more cries from the terrified teenagers. Lucy gazed up at the ceiling just in time to watch a huge beam collapse and crush in a classmate's face. With fresh panic and screams, any semblance of order flew out the window. Chaos reigned here, now. A wave of movement surged through the crowd as rushing forward and pushing out became the top two priorities. Lucy squished into her neighbors in front and beside her. She felt hands on her back, elbows in her ribs and face, and someone's ankle entangled hers. She thought for sure she might fall down, but the other girl lost her footing and fell under the heaving heap of stampeding students. How in the world in this onslaught of cries had she triangulated on that one girl's screams? No way to know, but it happened. She heard her screams as one foot mushed into her, another bashed her head, and then another foot stomped her, until the screams gurgled into nothing. She knew if she ever slept again, she would hear that sound in her nightmares for a very long time.

The herd of people started thinning as the one hall spilled into another. But why was everyone turning right? The exit was to the left. She emerged from the Technology hall and stopped so abruptly the people pushing behind her sprawled her onto the floor. She slid just shy of a man's combat boots. He stood in front of the exit. He blocked it with his enormous form. She looked up at him from the floor. He snarled back down at her with huge teeth and brandished a sword at her. No fight left in her, she scurried up onto her feet to rejoin the herd in their escape. She spared one glance behind her, and the man remained stationed at the door.

She ran outside of the flood now, and it refused to let her back in. Where the elbows annoyed her before, they pained her now. The aggressive jabs forced her out of the way. In one last ditch effort to keep her place, she dove into the mess of them. Someone placed the flat of her palm up against the side of Lucy's head and pushed her cheek into the lockers. The girl flattened Lucy there and ran off. Bodies brushed against her, feet rushed across her, her head smacked against a combination lock, and without a doubt, at any given moment, she might fall under the churning battery of shoes. Her screams would die after a time, like the trampled girl.

While the screaming never ceased, it took on a sort of desensitizing rhythm. As the herd approached the cafeteria, that rhythm changed into an orchestra of sounds. More than screams: cries, grunts, groans, guttural sounds, wet sounds, crunching sounds. All of it awful. Some blood-drenched students ran screaming back into South Hall. They didn't get very far before arms reached out from the cafeteria and pulled them back inside. At last swept into a break in the lockers, Lucy opened the door next to her and popped inside. She knew it by the smell of new industrial carpet and paint: the recently established band room. Cast in darkness, she focused on the shiny new room smell and tried to ignore the smell of smoke and something else she failed to recognize. The stench made her pull her wrist to her mouth to stifle the urge to gag. Fumbling around in the location of her B-Day, 4TH period class, she stumbled upon the rows of desks. Just beyond them was the podium, just beyond that was the stage, and just beyond that was the door. The way out.

She strained, listening for outside noises. Sound proof. She no longer heard the sounds of her classmates dying violent deaths. No idea what was going on. No idea how this could be happening. Or why. No answers. Well, it certainly wouldn't happen to her. She planned to get the fuck out of here. She hopped around the podium to claim the stage, when something grabbed her arm. She yelped and jumped back, knocking over a sheet music stand with a terrible clang. Sound proof. In the dark, she heard a moan.

"Who's there?" she asked the dark classroom.

A cough in response.

Nothing yet lunged at her or tried to hurt her. Was someone in the dark? Maybe hurt? She found the courage to walk back over to the podium. No grabby hands. She reached forward in the dark. There, denim. Wet denim. A moan answered her.

"Who are you? Are you hurt?" she asked.

Lucy cursed the darkness as she just recalled her cellphone. One thing at a time. Check to see if this person was hurt. Then call the cops. As soon as she hit a button, her Nokia screen illuminated a patch of denim. She raised it slowly from a pants leg, up to the hip, and then along the waist. She stopped, the light bounced as her hands shook. So much blood. The material on the abdomen appeared drenched in black. Or ... was that even blood? What was it?

Another moan made her jerk her hand up higher. Mr. Kent's face was not just awful to behold, but missing the skin entirely. She dropped her phone and recoiled. She screamed as stands fell like dominoes around her. She tripped and landed with the lot of them and tried desperately to unhinge her foot from the base of one. All the while, Mr. Kent returned her screams to the best of his abilities. Frightened and in pain, he needed help, but how could she possibly help him?

Pulling herself out of the frenzy, she lifted her phone from the ground by his feet, slow and careful. This time the phone rattled in her hand, bouncing light around the room. She took a deep, calming breath and tried her best to be a decent fucking human. She refused to be like all those students that tried to peel her against the lockers.

"Mr. Kent?" she asked.

A groan and a gargle.

"Mr. Kent, can you move?" she continued.

THUMP! She swallowed as much fear as she could, a huge gulp that echoed throughout the very nice acoustics of the vacant room. She examined him again, careful not to shine the light on his face. Whatever empathetic bone she possessed in her body told her discretion mattered here if she could help it. He might not know he looked like a monster, and screeching in his face was not the kindest way to tell him.

" ...me" Did he just say a word?

"What was that? Did you just say something?" she asked.

"Mmm...me..." he moaned.

She moved closer. "I'm sorry. I can't hear you. Can you try again?" She matched the smell she couldn't place when she barged into the room. It came from him.

"Ki-kill...me..." The words sounded so faint, she believed he couldn't say it again. His words almost struck her to the core, but it's odd how seeing perforated intestines and a face ripped off numbed her. Somewhere in her subconscious she reached the same conclusion as he while she clashed about with the music stands.

"Mr. Kent, I don't think I can do that," she lied. Physically, it might prove harder than she expected, but she worked at her parents' vet office on the weekends. She helped with euthanizations before. She understood the concept of ending another being's suffering, and right now Mr. Kent suffered a threshold of pain that warranted euthanasia. But letting other people know that you took a cold, clinical approach to creatures on the verge of death made them treat you like a sociopath. So she lied.

He groaned again. He gripped a shard of wood in his hands. What was he doing with it? He filed it against the podium as he stood there. She winced. How long did that take? It looked like a few hours. The bomb went off like forty-five minutes ago. What the fuck? She asked, "Mr. Kent, can you move?"

"Kill. Me." He muttered again.

He tried to hand her the shiv. "No, Mr. Kent. That won't work, anyway." She promptly shut up. She used the phone to scan him one more time—except for his face—no need to see that again aside from her nightmares. Those beseeching blue eyes against all that red gore. She shuddered. There, she noticed something. His bleeding abdomen presented a whole other problem. Viscera hung from him. She turned her head and tried to breathe in shallow breaths. No vomiting. She refused to vomit. Damn it, she was going to kill him, though.

"Okay," she gave in. He tried to hand her the shiv again. Once more, she pushed it away, "No, that won't work." Deep in contemplative thought, she scanned the room as best she managed in the dim orb of the Nokia's light. When the realization struck her, she muttered, "Of course." Walking over to the music stand, she picked up the bigger, sturdier of the bunch—the teacher's. She tried not to dwell too much on how bizarre the day progressed that she resorted to using the band teacher's stand to kill him, at his request. She unscrewed the two halves of the pole, dividing them. She poked at the top of the stand to see if that might be sharp enough. She wanted to put him down as painlessly as possible. Oh, who was she kidding?! This was going to hurt like hell.

"Mr. Kent, are you sure?" she asked, walking back over to him.

She made out the back of his head nod stiff and slow: up and down. "You were one of my favorite teachers," she offered as some cold comfort here at the end. He coughed and groaned louder than he had so far. Something like a sob caught on the end. With his head already resting on the podium, he managed the optimum position for what she planned to do. Before she allowed herself to think too hard or too long about it, she lifted the stand over her hand with both hands, and thrust it into the back of his neck. A horrific gurgling sound erupted from him, and she yelped back, almost screaming again. Mr. Kent's entire body convulsed against the podium. It wasn't terribly violent, just more like a really long shiver. Desperate, she tried to look anywhere else, and for a second thought about retrieving the stand and going again. But then all went still. No sounds.

Lucy stepped as close to him as she ought to and held her breath. She listened as keenly as her pounding heart allowed for any signs that he might still breathe, still in pain. Nothing. He was dead, and she killed him. That wasn't anything like the animals. Something burned her face. She pressed a hand to her cheek and felt the tears through the shock. "Thank you, Mr Kent." With that, she rushed out the back door.

Seventy-six students in the hall. Three teachers. Where did the Mesoamerican dude go? With the vampire fangs? Rayne clung to the wall as others spilled around her. She couldn't hide much in a locker that would help against explosives.

She grabbed the nearest charging student. "Run outside! Run to the football field! Tell others!" He pulled and tugged away from her. Her fuse reignited, and she jerked his tall, lanky frame hard until his face met hers.

She searched his eyes for reason and logic. "Try to be calm." He stared, but he stopped trying to get away from her. "Go to the football field. Grab others. People are there, waiting. You'll be safer outside. Don't let anyone, if you can help it, run into North Hall. Don't leave the campus, either. Stay at the football field. Do you understand?"

He hesitated and glanced at the herd. "What's happening?" The softness in his voice surprised her. She needed the reminder that not everyone was like her and her friends.

"Awful people are attacking. If you go to the football field, you stand a chance," she said.

He looked her over once more before he turned back to the crowd. "HEY! HEY!" His deep voice, more arresting than her own, stopped a pocket of the swarm. "THIS WAY!" He pointed long arms to the opposite end of the hall where Rayne made Tameka out as she sidled her way back.

"Thank you," she said to the young man.

"YO, THIS WAY!" He continued shouting. More than half the rushing student body stopped for him and turned at his instruction. He followed suit.

"Tameka?!" she called.

"I got 'em all out. Good call on the junior basketball player," Tameka said. "That's what? Fifty students headed outside?"

Forty-eight. The anger flared in Rayne. She clenched her jaw and muttered, "Not nearly enough."

The surge thinned by the time they spilled into North Hall. The ground slipped beneath her. "Fuck!" she cried. Her momentum and the debris beneath her combat boots sent her tumbling. She slid through the metallic remnants of the outer door. She caught herself with her hands and stopped against her locker. Right next to José's body.

"Are you okay?" Tameka asked as she popped out of the fear parade. She pressed herself into a door frame for protection against the churning of bodies that dwindled as they reached this pocket of North Hall. Nobody wanted to linger near the body. She scanned the pitch-black hall. Still no Mesoamerican-cloak-guy.

"I'll be fine," Rayne answered. No point in telling Tameka about her hands. The broken glass bit into her skin like sharp gravel. She stood, careful not to press into her palms. "You get your stash. I'll grab mine."

Tameka lingered near her with a little hesitation before she hopped out of her cover. "Got it."

Rayne's hands bordered on hamburger meat. The tiny chips coalesced into the tissue of her palms. No use trying to pick those out. She ripped the sleeves from her white blouse and exposed the almost masculine wealth of muscle that corded her arms. Other teens hid their arms for more nefarious reasons. She hid her obsession with toning. The Linda Hamilton look didn't really appeal to high school boys in the mid-2000s. Or girls, for that matter.

Her teeth ground as she wrapped the wounds, glass and all. She worried Tameka would watch her, but dammit, this was a war. She couldn't let this hold her back, especially not right at the start. With that in mind, the flames fueling her determination raged on.

The crowd diminished from a trickle into nothing. The hall appeared empty as far as the light reached. As she dusted bits of glass from her side, Tameka cursed behind her, "What the fuck is that?"

Rayne spun and examined her locker with a frown. A small, folded, white sheet of paper pinned to her locker by a knife. Her knife. The six-inch knife from her stash. "Shit!" she growled with feeling.

"What is it, Rayne?" Tameka asked, again.

She yanked on the knife. After more effort than she expected, it gave. "It's from my stash," she muttered. The paper slipped into her free hand. She unfolded it with her back to Tameka. This probably won't be pretty. A note written in blood. Rayne wanted to roll her eyes at how predictable it was, but as she read, a weight in her gut sank like lead.

IT STILL WON'T BE ENOUGH.

Icy-cold dread tried to chill her boiling blood. Behind her, Tameka hissed. No sense in telling her now that she read it herself. Rayne squeezed her bleeding hand into a fist and punched through her locker door. Her hand met the other side with little more than a sting in her toughened knuckles. She glanced behind her, and Tameka spun back to her own locker. Rayne couldn't afford for her troops to see any weakness in her.

"We'll get through this," she said. Her voice carried down the empty, dark hallway.

Inside, she rummaged through the splintered wood, binders, and books for the leather bag stowed in the back. A small, tactical backpack concealed, originally, four knives, a Zippo lighter, two flares, and a bundle of twine. The knives varied in size: two two-inch, one three-inch, and one six-inch. She'd love a machete right now, but the six-inch was the max she could fit in the bag. She returned it to its sheath on a strap and wrapped it around her thigh. Won't be enough, her ass. She retrieved one last item from her locker: a hair tie. Using the mirror in the back, it seemed absurd to worry about how she looked, but might as well look good while kicking ass.

She turned to find Tameka tying back the mass of thick, three-c curls as much away from her face as she could manage without a comb. She asked, "Do you think I'll still be able to find edge brushes when the world ends?"

Rayne embraced her friend from behind and rested her chin on her shoulder. "We're gonna find the others, and then we're gonna send those losers back to Cinder."

Tameka paused, retrieving her kit, and leaned back into Rayne. "We're gonna save everyone, right?"

Rayne refused to lie to her. "We're gonna save as many as we can."

A buzz cranked up around them. They split apart and gazed up at the wall above their lockers. Large red bulbs juiced up, slowly. The buzz increased as the light bathed the hall in red pools. They turned and looked toward the other end. Reality set in.

Twenty-two. Twenty-two bodies. A girl slumped against the next bank of lockers. A sophomore, though her name slipped

Rayne's mind. Rayne scrambled to check her pulse but found the tissue around her wrists tattered and torn. Veins and all.

Beyond the door beside the sophomore laid a freshman face down on the linoleum. Tameka knelt and rolled him over. Oh, but only if she hadn't. Made more obscene by the back-up lights, the sight of his smashed-in face curled Rayne's lips off her teeth. Bone and brain matter filled the cavity. More bodies littered the hall as far as the poor light allowed them to see. All lifeless.

"Rayne?" Tameka asked.

Rayne snapped to her without a word.

Tameka pressed on. "Do you think we trained enough for this?"

Rayne looked away, afraid Tameka might catch her own doubt in expression. Not to mention they spent the last four years preparing for this. No way they weren't about to win ... "Xelan wouldn't have wasted his time on us if he didn't know we could stop this," she offered.

Tameka stood. "You're right," she said. "Let's—"

The Mesoamerican blood sucker rounded the corner of the next branch off North Hall. The generous sort, he prepared to share his next meal with a friend. Both cloaked men towered at least eight inches over Rayne.

Tameka hissed, "Fuck."

The new intruder resembled a Roman sculpture from around the time Caesar reigned in office. Their bright yellow eyes stood in stark contrast against the waves of black hair framing their pale features. The red glow emphasized the menace in their stares.

"You're both just knock-outs." Rayne ignored the sharp glare Tameka shot her. She prodded on, "Have you thought about going into modeling?" She welcomed the comforting impression of her six-inch blade against her thigh. Finally, the fight she wanted. Forget college. Forget work. Forget pretending to give a shit about mundane, daily crap. She resisted the urge to crack a smirk.

A fucking classroom door opened right beside the monsters. Of course it was an Environmental Science class. Four students and a teacher clamored in the doorway. They took one look at the dudes-with-yellow-eyes and cloaks and shrieked.

46

"Get the fuck back in the classroom!" Tameka ordered.

Rayne took a step toward the smoldering duo. The Roman grabbed the closest student. Nothing changed in his expression when he pulled her to him. Rayne halted. Faltered, unsure. Her eyes narrowed. He watched Rayne's expression as he tore the girl's trachea from her throat. They watched her fall lifelessly to the floor. The girl's expression forever locked in horrific surprise, her dark eyes shining nothing.

Tameka let out a strangled cry. The teacher and students slammed the door shut. They wailed beyond it. Rayne stared at the murdered girl. The Roman startled her by laughing. A cruel, cold laugh. How many more would die? How many more had they already killed? Xelan warned her for four years of the beasts' invasion and now ... Was this what she wanted? What she asked for?

Rayne fumed. She unsheathed her knife and said, "You're fucking—"

The Mesoamerican blood drinker's eyes grew wide and his mouth gaped. Disturbed, she steadied herself from charging in. His hands gripped at his sides, lips moved as if speaking. Only strangled sounds escaped. A large, metal object erupted through the wall of his chest. A cerulean fountain splashed from the gaping hole.

Beside him, the Roman shrieked, exposing large carnivorous teeth. His eyes burned angry with hatred. A metal rod strained out of the left side of his chest. It opened a similar cavernous wound, but rather than devastated by the attack, the assault infuriated him.

A girl cried from behind the raging monster, "You missed the brain!"

Tameka and Rayne exchanged looks. "Sagan?!" Rayne asked.

The Mesoamerican soldier slumped to his knees before he fell face first onto the floor.

"Only by an inch!" Kyle shouted back.

Rayne knelt and unsheathed her dagger. She stood just in time for Kyle to fly screaming right into her and Tameka. All three of them fell to the ground. He clambered back onto his feet and dusted off his clothes before offering a hand.

"Kyle!" Tameka exclaimed. Her voice dripped with reprimand. "What kind of weapons do you call those?"

He replied in a tone dripping with vehemence, "Me and Sagan couldn't get to our stashes. The hall is a giant death trap if you haven't noticed. We had to improvise."

"Some job you're doing. If you had any sense—" Tameka started.

Before Rayne could stand, the Roman wrapped his hand around Sagan's throat. "Sagan!!" Rayne cried. She charged at the fucker.

Even with the metal obstruction stuck in his chest, he lifted Sagan from her feet by her throat. Eight, nine inches until he screamed a wordless cry in her face expressing his anguish with a hiss. Sagan struggled and scratched the hand at her throat in a meager attempt to hurt the angry monster. Rayne grabbed onto the metal weapon already in his rib cage. She shoved, hoping to force it through his side into his brain. The Roman soldier seemed impervious to pain. Voracious, it made him so much more deadly.

Still, he held Sagan at the throat. He spared Rayne a wordless, primal scream. He lashed out with his free hand, striking her. She went cliff diving just the one time. She caught a lot of air performing acrobatics. Swatted with enough force to send her flying into the wall of lockers behind her? That was new. She didn't like it. New least favorite thing. She fell to the ground and gasped for the air knocked from her. Kyle and Tameka ran toward the ravenous beast as Sagan's struggles grew less frequent and weak. Her eyes bulged and watered.

"The rod . . . push it in," Rayne croaked.

Tameka fought to loosen the soldier's grip on Sagan's throat. He squeezed harder. She faded out of consciousness when Kyle pushed the fragmented steel through the internal tissue and bone. The impact of the dull metal to the monster's chest caused him to drop Sagan. He made a few attempts at pulling it out, but short of breaking his ribs, that pole refused to budge.

The Roman warrior collapsed to his knees with one large obstruction in his torso. The bright yellow irises swallowed the entirety of his eyes. He made a strangled sound. It resembled the cry of a predatory bird. Blood gushed in thick waves down his clothes when he fell forward. He laid very dead after what looked like two thousand-plus years of existence.

Tameka helped Sagan to stand. Although the brush with death made her relieved Sagan survived, unease settled in Rayne's thoughts. Why didn't he crush her throat like the other student? Was she just lucky? Sagan took a moment to brush off her clothes. Rayne tried not to appreciate the outfit too much, lest she fall back into bad habits. Sagan looked over at Rayne and smiled reassuringly.

Rayne wrapped her arms around Sagan tightly. "I'm glad you two are safe," she said against Sagan's blond hair.

"We're not the only ones who were fighting them," Sagan croaked.

"Yeah. Nikki and John are down that way," Kyle added. He pointed down the Math/Language hall.

Tameka asked, "Are they okay?"

Sagan shrugged, "They seem to be." She hugged herself. "I was taking the A&P exam when we heard this awful noise." For a moment her eyes drifted off. "It's like I knew who it was before it started." Rayne knew the feeling. Shivering, Sagan shifted as if she found it uncomfortable to stand. "I came out anyway. There were so many people running. Screaming. I saw José ..."

She glanced at his body bathed in red light. She continued, "Kyle came out from across North Hall. We ran to Ms. Magi's room." She kicked the body of the Aztec soldier with her boot. "These two followed us down the hallway as we were getting her class out of there. We broke a few desks up for weapons—"

Kyle interrupted, "Which was fun, by the way."

Sagan shot him a look before continuing her explanation, "We heard a sound and the next thing we knew the ground was shaking like an earthquake. The two monsters at the door were gone. Nikki and John should be in the room still trying to make better weapons." She finished by motioning for Tameka and Rayne to follow.

"One second," Tameka said and held up her finger. She turned back to the environ science class. She put her face in the window and knocked on the door.

It opened, tentative and slow. "Are they all gone?" asked the unfamiliar teacher.

"No. There are more," Tameka answered. Her honesty shook the survivors.

Rayne cut in, "But if you want to make it through this, you need to get out to the football field."

"Yea, that way," Kyle pointed down the English hall.

The teacher peered at them through the crack in the door. He took in the sight of the bodies behind them. One more look into Rayne's best pitying expression, and he turned back to his three students. "C'mon. We'd better listen to them."

The students perked up, no doubt happy to abandon the dark classroom for the promise of sunshine outside. She envied them. Kyle pointed once more to the English hall as the small brood retreated through crimson flood lights. The teacher stopped one more time to ask, "Are you coming with us?" He glanced at the bodies, then to the knife on Rayne's thigh, and to their faces once more.

Rayne answered, "No. We've got work to do."

Nikki regretted wearing a white peasant blouse. Crimson smeared the poor thing and spilled down onto her blue jeans. Her flowing bell sleeves remained pristine, untouched. Until her wrists. She checked many a dead body for a pulse that morning, and each one stained her sleeves in blood.

She pretended to attack the upside down desk with vigor, but progressed very little. What was the point? Without Rayne, they wouldn't get very far. Ms. Magi's Spanish classroom suffered the same beige and white interior decorating job as the rest of the school. However, elements of the room resembled the tiny teacher's personality. Bright, colorful posters papered the walls. Red, white, and green paper chains dangled from the ceiling. Festive cultural books stuffed the bookshelves. The bookshelves they dismantled for shivs.

And Rayne charged through the door, followed by Sagan, Kyle, and Tameka. Oh, God. How bad was her hair? She brushed her hand through the silvery blond ends and caught herself. She winced. This was the fucking apocalypse. Not the time for vanity. What would Rayne think of her primping while bodies littered the hallway?

"Nikki, are you all right?" Rayne asked. She crossed the room. Her silky ponytail swinging, and the knife holster standing out against her thigh.

Nikki prepared herself. It always hurt like hell. Rayne's arms wrapped around Nikki's smaller frame. She glanced to the side and caught her reflection in a framed poster. Shame suffused her, but she was happy to see none of her makeup ran and her hair could be worse. Her freckles stood against her milky complexion. She admitted to adding a few extra because she knew Rayne liked them so. Rayne pulled away from the embrace first. Nikki bit into her lip to silence a whimper. Every. Fucking. Time.

"I'm all right," she managed. She smiled into her ex-girlfriend's face. The picture of all-rightness.

"I'm glad," Rayne said. Too soon, she turned away and walked over to John. He didn't warrant a hug, but she checked in on him just the same.

"No. I'm most definitely not okay," he answered before she asked. Blood soaked his green polo and khaki pants.

"Where's the wound?" Rayne asked.

"It's not mine," he answered. He stomped on the desktop, and it splintered.

Tameka asked, "Are we the only ones with a weapon stash on this hall?"

Nikki and John glanced at one another. She said, "We don't have one."

Sagan said, "Mine is like four yards into the dark." She pointed south. "That way." She glanced around the room and added, "It won't be enough to arm this whole group, though."

"Mine's in the Med Science Lab," Kyle said.

Rayne snapped to him, "You hid yours in a classroom?"

"Yea. I gambled on when I thought an invasion might start, and I lost. Okay?!" He grunted.

Tameka bristled. "You bet an alien race with an aversion to sunlight inspiring our myths about vampires would attack during school hours?" Her voice dripped with venom like the fangs of an asp.

Nikki winced at her tone. The two of them never stopped. John broke in, "Yea, well. When does it look like they attacked, Tameka?"

Kyle gloated and opened his mouth to fuel the flames, but Rayne cut them off. "Okay, guys. Seriously. Enough." She met each of them in the eye. "I know Xelan warned us so many times this would happen. But I never thought it would happen during school. No, not because of the time of day. But because—"

"Of the body count," Tameka interrupted. Her voice quiet.

Rayne glanced at her and said, "Yea." She put her hands on her hips and bit her bottom lip. She continued, "I thought they would strike us directly. At most, the skating rink. But this is it. We need to work through our plans and fast. Let me just say explosives were not on my list of tactics."

"Not mine," Sagan added.

Tameka muttered, "Mine either."

"Kyle, do you have anything in place for Fair?" Rayne asked.

"Well, aside from my weapons stash, no."

"Let's roll with what we know," Rayne started. "They forced the classes into the main hallways."

"Right, like they scared them out of the rooms." Tameka nodded.

"Are we all assuming to the same end?" Rayne asked.

The room grew quiet. Nine hundred and one students in the entire student body. Flushed out and butchered.

"Jesus," John hissed.

"We've got to get the remaining people out of here. Send them to the football field. They're safe in the daylight, for now." Rayne frowned and asked, "What else do we know?"

"They have explosives," Nikki offered. She radiated with warmth when Rayne beamed at her.

"Burning us out?" Kyle asked.

Rayne nodded. "Trying to make it hard on us."

"Or maybe they're driving us somewhere into the school," Sagan offered. "A partially underground school makes a great feeding ground for these monsters."

"Nox is here," Rayne blurted.

They whirled on her. Except John. He looked mostly confused.

Sagan asked, "Are you sure?"

Rayne broke away from them. Turned her back to them as she rubbed a hand down her face. "I saw him in the hall. Not his face." Her voice quieted, "Never his face."

Nikki wanted to wrap her arms around her. Rayne looked out for them, but who looked out for her?

"Then how can you be sure?" Kyle asked. He tossed his hair back in that familiar gesture.

Rayne turned back to them, but stared at the floor. "He wanted me to know."

Sagan hissed through her teeth. Nikki scanned the lot of them. Her secrets belonged to her, but if Nox was here. Maybe ... she could fix all this. Maybe ... she can save Rayne.

"I'm sorry, but who?" John asked. "I get this whole invasion thing, but you've mentioned nobody by name."

Rayne opened her mouth to answer, but someone in the doorway replied first, "In our dreams, he's the King of Cinder."

"Andrew!" Tameka cried out. She ran over to hug him. Everyone else gaped in shock. Except John. He just sorta leaned against a wall.

Andrew stood in the doorway. His long brown hair pulled back. His concerned blue eyes examined their crew. Standing at five foot eight, he appeared solemn and suspiciously uninjured. Rayne scanned him, and he legit walked into the middle of an apocalyptic invasion unscathed. How was he even here? He went to Hall high school, which was on the other side of town from Fair. Did the assault spread so far already? That icy cold dread knocked into the walls of her veins again.

"How did you ... ?" Rayne strove to think of what to ask first. "Is Hall under attack, too?"

"I have no idea," he answered. "I was skipping class until you guys got out." He lied. She narrowed her eyes at him. When he told a lie, he always casually tugged his ear. She opened her mouth to call him out on it, but he interrupted her again.

"Never mind that," Andrew said. "We don't have much time. What do you need us to do, Rayne?"

Everyone turned. They stared at her, expectation in their eyes. She surveyed the room, "We'll need at least two large weapons and a small one each. And I mean all of us. Goal One: Get to the stashes." John stood from the wall, and started sorting through the weapons he and Nikki initially fashioned. Tameka left Andrew's side to lend a hand.

Rayne surveyed the room. Book-bags, books, purses—all left in the initial rush for safety. "Get those bags," she ordered as she walked toward the Spanish office. She rummaged through the shelves and drawers until she found two plastic baggies with cotton balls, bandages, and two travel-sized bottles of peroxide. She threw them to Tameka, "Catch."

Tameka caught it and winced. "I don't think this will be enough." She stuffed it in a bag, anyway.

Rayne nodded with approval when she found Nikki, John, and Kyle all carried two backpacks a piece. She continued her instruction as she grabbed a deserted denim jacket. "Secure this hallway. Make this room a sort of safety zone until we can get to the medical science labs. We're not just going for Kyle's stash. I want to go there for the supplies, and if we find a lot of injured people—which we will—we can patch them up there and send them out to the football field. M2 is closest to the labs' exit. That's where we're going first."

Kyle raised his hand and bounced like an eager child. Rayne pinched the bridge of her nose and said, "Yes?"

"Will there be snacks on this field trip?" he asked.

She chose to ignore the question. She continued, "If I were an evil warrior species, I would place one soldier on each hall. Maybe a dozen around the cafeteria and gym." She finished ripping the jacket into large strips of material and began a search through purses.

"So, what are we using these for?" Sagan asked as she took a bag from Kyle.

Andrew answered, "We stuff them full of weapons and medical supplies."

Rayne smiled at him as she went through a black vinyl bag. She might find the circumstance of his arrival suspicious, but he remained one of her closest friends. Having him there made a world of difference to her morale. "Exactly. That way if we come across any victims, we can treat them on our way to the medical labs." She fished out a tube of antibacterial ointment and a bottle of ibuprofen.

Tameka took a backpack. She stuffed the little zip baggies and the strips of denim inside. "I'll take the medical stuff in my bag," she said. She accepted the antibiotic ointment and pills from Rayne. Nikki found two unopened bottles of water. She handed them to Tameka. Kyle and John dispensed weapons made of wood and metal from all the broken furniture in the room.

Rayne watched everyone in the room gather supplies and fill their bags. Their faces stoic and focused. She noted scrapes, wounds, cuts, and bruises on every single one of them. A wave of guilt and shame washed over her. Just this morning she wanted anything to come of Xelan's warnings and now that it was here . . . She walked over to Andrew, "I'm gonna check the other classrooms on this hall. You explain who and what Nox really is. They deserve to know what they're dying for."

Andrew stared a little too long into Rayne's eyes. They pressed as they sought more information than she felt willing to give. He said, "I don't think any of them are planning on dying, today." She looked away then, mumbled something about "Just tell them," and started for the classroom door.

As she went to leave the room, she caught Kyle spying her exit. He opened his mouth to say something to her, and Andrew swatted his arm. Kyle promptly started to cuss him out. Andrew shook his head, and Kyle listened to him for once. Gratitude washed over Rayne. She didn't think she could handle anymore probing for now.

As Andrew's voice filled in the gaps Xelan left in the story as to why this shitty town, Rayne closed her eyes to it, turned her back on it, and walked away from it into the open hall.

FOUR

There's A Method To His Madness But That Doesn't Make Him Any Less Mad

{LATE 2002}

"C'MON, RAYNE. This move isn't happening unless you practice a little patience with yourself." Xelan cranked up the encouragement to eleven.

"That's not the problem," she muttered. She pulled the workout gloves off her hands.

He caught one, then the other, and dropped them in her duffel. "Then what is it?"

How could she tell him? She just turned fifteen this year. The move involved a little too much of ... herself ... and him. She clicked her tongue in frustration. Why was this so hard? She only needed to run up, vault his height, wrap her legs around his neck, try not to think about how close his face ... Nope. She couldn't do it.

"I think I'm just tired," she blurted. The blood rush to her head no doubt ruined her complexion.

"Yea," he said. He put his face in hers as he scrutinized it. "You look like you might be coming down with something."

His breath smelled so pleasant. Like spearmint. He stood close to her. Her brain screamed at her to kiss him. "No!" she shouted in a hoarse whisper.

He stepped back. "Okay. Maybe not." His hands stuck up in the air, a sign of surrender.

The frustration stabbed at her in the most nerve-wracking of places: her head, her heart, and lower things. Why couldn't she develop a normal crush on a boy her age? She tried to console him, "Sorry. I had a short training session with Kyle and Sagan before you stopped by. I'm worn out." She managed a weak smile.

The smile he offered in response beamed. She melted. "I love to hear you guys are working together, building a unit. Even if it's with Kyle."

The joke caught her by surprise, and genuine laughter followed. "He's not that bad."

Only a few steps later and they stood as close outside her house as she wanted to get. "What are we practicing tomorrow?" she asked.

His smile merged into a smirk, "What do you think? This move until you get it right."

Feeling childish, confused, frustrated, she let out a heavy, almost angry sigh. Without a word, she stomped to her front porch.

"What?" He called after her.

"See you tomorrow, Xelan," she groaned.

Something told her she wouldn't sleep well that night.

And she was right. Xelan insisted on a training session in her fucking dreams! She couldn't place the location. Craggy rocks and rust-brown earth filled the space. This dream smelled of earth and fire. The massive burning black-flamed pyre beside them made the training ground feel primal and archaic.

Also, a tiny bit intimate. At least they both wore clothes. A black cloak draped over his tall frame. Some tight black shorts and a strappy, black sports bra exposed her budding muscular form. Spandex existed here. No shoes on her feet. She liked the moist dirt under her toes.

"Is this enough for you?" His voice came as a hoarse whisper. She strained to catch the words.

By contrast, her voice rang harshly in the silence, "What are the rules?"

He swayed left, then right. She followed his movements. He emitted a bizarre intensity here. Everything seemed more real, more lethal without him landing a single blow. Must be a result of the atmosphere.

He whispered, "Don't die."

Well, wasn't that ominous? Maybe she was too harsh on him earlier. She opened her mouth to apologize when he broke loose and rushed her. He swung at her and struck her in the jaw. It fucking hurt. Not yet had he attacked without telling her his intentions first and how to block. They only trained for six months, now.

"Hey ..." She pressed her cool hand to her sore face.

He towered over her. She strained to see inside the hood, but he shifted away. He said, "Here, I won't go easy on you." The dream distorted his voice. It still held the familiar depth, but she read no emotion from it. Without his face to read or his voice to infer, he came across as cold and unfeeling like—"Like a killer," he finished for her.

She flinched at his words, "You're not a killer."

The hood shook left, then right. "The monsters you'll face are killers. You need a space to properly train without risk to your ..." he brushed his hand down her arm sending her heart battering against her sternum, " ...fragile body." She shivered. Right next to a raging bonfire.

"Xel—" she started in a breathy whisper.

He interrupted her, "Let's begin with the basics."

The thrall dissipated a little, and she screwed up her face in irritation. "Basics?"

"You hesitate to dodge or don't dodge at all unless told to do so. You're accustomed to sparring with your friends who let you know when to move. You won't get that from me, here." As he spoke, he returned to the swaying movements and a centered stance.

"Okay. I got this," she said. She rolled her shoulders back, loosened herself a bit, and squared her feet.

He appeared in front of her. He hadn't used that particular move since they first met. He swung on her again, but this time she blocked him. Pride suffused her until his free fist landed right in her gut.

She wanted to vomit. She clutched her stomach. Why did her dreams hurt?

"Again," he rasped.

Reminded of her earlier frustration, she gritted her teeth and went with it. She stood and waited for him to swing again. He did. She blocked and then twisted under his arm. She kicked him in the crotch. And connected.

The phantom reacted slightly, leaning forward. Did she hurt him? Should she check on him? She wanted to knee him in his face now that he doubled over. Was that over-doing it?

"Don't ignore your instincts," he said.

She clutched his shoulders and rammed her knee into his face. His head went backward. Blood sprayed. She cupped her hands over her mouth. "Oh ... Oh I'm so sorry, Xelan! I didn't mean to go that hard. Are you okay?"

He shirked her off him. "You soft creature," he spat.

His words stung. She shrunk back. "I don't—"

He grabbed her arm and pulled her to him. Tears stabbed her eyes. "No ..." She fought back as a major force tugged her to the fire. The heat licked at her until she sweat. This dream got fucked up real fast.

A matching flame ignited in her. To hell with letting a man drag her into a fire. She kicked him in his kneecap. He went down. She kicked him square in the chest. He fell back into the dirt.

Hands on her hips, she sat her bare foot on the rough cloak over his solid stomach. She staked her claim. "I kicked your ass," she announced. His body started shaking, and it felt extra weird underfoot. It took her a minute to realize he was laughing at her.

She went to move her foot away, but he clutched it in both hands. His grip like an iron vice. She cried, "Let go!"

He shoved her foot up in both his hands, and she shot up into the air. High enough the ashes and embers soared around her. As she descended, she spared some time cussing him out in her head for never teaching her how to brace for landing. No more holding back in real life training sessions. The ground took her breath away. The rough soil on her back scraped her exposed skin like asphalt as she skidded to a halt.

He stepped over her. On his middle finger shone a heavy ring. She couldn't get back her breath. Why couldn't she breathe? He leant down and crawled on his hands and knees above her. The cloak let only darkness in and nothing out. Her arms and legs wouldn't move! She opened her mouth to shriek, but without air only a whimper escaped. This is a nightmare! This is a nightmare! Xelan wouldn't do this!

Inches from her face, the monster said, "You must understand pain in order to fight in this war."

Her alarm woke her that morning. She laid in a pool of her own sweat. She thought of nothing but the dream the whole day, terrified of seeing Xelan later that night. When they met up after school for her training session, everything seemed normal.

"What's going on?" Xelan asked.

In fact, he treated her like she was the weird one. No doubt the tightness of her face and timidity to her approach tipped him off. She both wanted and loathed to ask him about the dream. It really was just a nightmare. Instead, she asked him, "Why do you always let me know before you strike?" She ignored his first question.

He recoiled a bit. But answered, "To teach you to block."

"But wouldn't it make more sense not to tell me, so I learn to block reflexively?" she pressed.

He narrowed his eyes as he examined her. Finally, he said, "Do you want to fight today without the call outs?"

She swallowed, uncertain if she wanted this. She flexed her back, drawing out every sensation, and made up her mind. "Yes. I want you to do the same with the others. A little pain from a good strike might actually teach us something."

His eyebrows shot up, but he nodded. "Okay. Okay, we'll train like that from now on."

She stared at the grass beneath her feet. "Xelan?"

"Yes?" he replied.

"Do you think I'm soft?" she asked, softly.

"What the hell is going on, Rayne?" This was the harshest she knew his voice could get. It was nowhere near the callous brutality like the voice she heard in her dreams.

"If I were to battle an Icarus, today, would it call me soft?" she pressed, again.

This time, Xelan stopped to think. He muttered, "You're only fifteen. You're human. We've only been training for six months. You aren't meant to be a badass, yet. No one's expecting that from you."

"I am," she said. Her voice rang clear on the far side of her open backyard.

He shrank back from her. "What's got this in your head?"

She gazed into his eyes one more time. Nothing. No recollection or reaction. In a careful tone, she answered, "I had a dream about you last night."

He looked off to the side in thought. He brought his fist to his mouth and bit his thumbnail. He paused and asked, "Can you describe what I did?"

She shuddered at the memory and said, "You sparred with me. But … not like here. It hurt, and you didn't warn me about your moves—"

He nodded as she spoke and then interrupted, "Were we here or somewhere else?"

"Somewhere else," she answered with some hesitation.

"Describe it to me," he said. With each question his voice grew more demanding, more earnest.

She motioned with her arms, "Big, huge rock cavern. Giant fire piled high. Dirt instead of a floor."

He shut his eyes tight. "Did I say who I was?" When she failed to answer, he opened his eyes again. "Rayne. This is important. Did I ever once say I was me?"

He did. Surely he must have. How on earth did she come to the conclusion it was Xelan when he didn't give a name? Well, because up until that point he was the only man that made her feel confused with this regular, physical contact. Speaking of, Xelan grabbed her by her forearms and squeezed gently. Oh yea, she needed to answer. He searched her eyes as she told him the truth, "No. You didn't. In fact, when I tried to use your name, you—I mean—he cut me off."

"Fuck," Xelan cursed. He never cursed. Releasing her, he stepped a few paces away. He mumbled things like, "Something must be wrong with the conduit." And "How long has he had this ability?"

Fear fluttered in her chest. "Xelan?" She called after him.

He spun and stomped back to her. His movements set her pulse in a frenzy. Too similar to the dream. She stepped back from him and saw the remorse pass over his face. She crushed him, and regretted it. He stopped short and kept a safe distance for her benefit. When he spoke next, his voice sounded thick and a little strained, "That wasn't me, Rayne. Do you recall your memory of Celindria during The Vacating? The man between her and the conduit?"

She filed around for the exact moment in the flashback. The malice, the arrogance, the rage ... "The shadow ..." she breathed.

"That was Nox, the King of Cinder," Xelan explained. "He's the king of our entire race. He's also a murderous lunatic with obsessive issues. He targeted Celindria." He took a few steps closer and knelt down so his impressive height dwarfed her less. Their gazes connected. His eyes asked something of her. They asked her to be brave. He said, "Now, I think he's targeted you."

Uncomfortable, she stepped away. "But he got sucked into that conduit. I saw that much."

He sat on the grass. The fluffy green lawn gave way to his impression. She tried not to smile at the thought of grass stains forming on his black cargo pants. He continued his explanation, "More advanced Icari can project themselves into the dreams of other Icarus." He held up his hand to stave off her protest. "Any Icarean blood is good enough. It's a resonance with the nanites. They crave the technology in his blood."

Fuck it. She sat on the grass beside him. The moon cast brilliant silver streaks across them. She planted her hands behind her and bathed in it. She peeked one eye at him. He watched her a little too close for her liking. He pushed, "I have to know what else happened in your dream. There's something else he was after."

Man, she wasn't sure if she should blush or puke. The memory of the dream had that effect on her. She squirmed under his scrutiny and gave into the grass, crushing it. "Well ..." False start.

He picked up on it. "I won't judge you."
She told him. The whole thing.
He winced more at Nox crawling on top of her than when dude-man broke her fucking back.

That night Rayne paced and paced. And paced some more. She brushed her teeth, brushed her hair, changed into her pajamas, and brushed her teeth again. Pacing in front of her bed, she battled with a bout of panic-driven insomnia. How could she sleep after all that? Her aching quads and shoulders screamed in response. Xelan gave her the most intense training session of her lifetime. No call outs. No near-miss blows. He held nothing back. And whooped her ass.

The last six months of training seemed like summer camp compared to the drills he put her through after their talk. He promised to build a training course for everyone behind her house. The kid-gloves came off, and he threatened to treat them like proper soldiers.

She sat at her desk and retrieved a notebook. She started writing in journals after her first meeting with him just months ago. She filled up three notebooks, already. Teen angst, general confusion, and misguided attempts to interpret her dreams. At 2:00AM she drooped, exhausted and so beyond ready for bed. Unable to stay awake any longer, she set her notebook on her nightstand. If she dreamt of Nox, she promised to write it down and share every detail with Xelan. No matter how uncomfortable.

As she climbed into the sheets, her legs threatened to cramp. The cool cotton soothed them, and the soreness abated a little. The moment her head hit the pillow, she went under. Record fucking timing.

Wood burned and filled the air. It crinkled her nose. It almost smelled of pine, but not quite. The bonfire crackled and popped, sending cinders into the air. No sign of cloaked-and-brutal. She wore the same get-up from last time, but more straps wove their way up her legs and down her arms. Interesting.

"Quite," the distorted, hoarse voice agreed.

She peered through the wall of flames. She caught brief glimpses of a large man almost a foot taller than her, draped in the same cloak, lounged on a massive, wooden throne. Like it was made for a giant, massive. He ought to look small in comparison, but his robust frame filled it.

"Why, thank you," he said within the dark hood. Did she say that aloud? He lazily drummed his fingers on the arm. His heavy ring bore an insignia. What was it?

Cautious, she stepped around the flames, careful to keep him in her sights.

He grunted in approval. "Now, you're treating me like a proper threat."

She continued to walk closer, taking in the sight of him sprawled on the structure. She couldn't help herself. She was curious. "I got some intel on you," she confided.

"Go on," he said.

"You're the King of Cinder. It's nice to meet you, Nox. Do I curtsy?" she scoffed. The surge of confidence and defiance shocked even her.

The silence stretched, and she stopped herself from moving any closer. Tension clawed up her shoulders. She spread her feet shoulder width apart and loosened her arms. Even with her teeth clenched, she lifted her chin. Fuck this guy.

"You're too young," he replied, his voice frank. Could he hear her thoughts because this was a dream? When he shifted, she resisted the urge to step back and away. He unfolded his big body and stood to his full height. Eleven inches taller than her, he towered above her. What had he said? She was too young to ...

"Are you ready, Rayne?" he asked.

For what? Which thing was he wanting to do? She hesitated too long. He backhanded her, and she took it. She bit her lip, hard, and tasted the metallic tang of blood. He swung again, but she dropped to the floor and attempted a leg sweep. He jumped back and stopped. She sprung up.

They faced one another. Blood trickled down her lip. Although he hid his face, she sensed him smiling at her. "What?" she asked, her voice soft. She breathed a little heavy, but not bad at all considering how much exertion she put out.

"You've already gotten better within a day," he stated.

"Yea, well. You were right." He stiffened, and she continued, "The training wheels had to come off, but you'll be the one to pay for it." She rushed him, feigned a right hook, and kicked him in his hip. On anyone else it might reach their ribs, but alas. She landed each blow. A little too well.

"Good. Your improvements are already so much more satisfactory," he said. Without warning, he moved too fast to see. He clutched her by the back of the neck. She used both hands to scratch and loosen his fingers. What a fucking grip!

"We'll continue your training." Nothing about his distorted voice showed any strain. "Free yourself of my grasp."

She growled, "I'm trying." Oh god damn, his laughter set her ablaze. Using his arm as leverage and every ounce of upper body and core strength she possessed, she drew her legs up and kicked him with both feet in the face. He snarled and flung her away. She slid in the dirt, but delighted in seeing him stagger backward.

The stun of her attack wore off too soon, and he stomped toward her.

"Shit, shit!" She hissed as she scurried in the dirt to stand. Too late. He pushed her onto her back. The dirt cool there where it pressed into her pale skin. He stood over her and he sighed ...? A silken whisper just audible over the crackle of the flames, he said, "Too young."

She startled awake. And so each night carried on this way. She put off the inevitability of sleep. They fought. Sometimes he won; sometimes she bested him. Each time it ended with some obscure reference to her youth, or a confusing encounter with his hands on her skin. Or his hips ground into hers. Or his fingers through her hair. She woke only an hour or two later, too exhilarated to sleep again.

The fire started then. Not the raging bonfire that burned when she met him in combat. No, the personal rage she always tendered, fanned by frustration and unfulfilled potential. As if surviving her teenage years required additional challenges.

When she trained with Xelan, out of the corner of her eye, she caught him evaluating her. She hated it. He surveyed her moves, but also her body language.

One day, about a month after the dreams began, she completed the take down. She ran up to him, vaulted his height, wrapped her legs around his neck, and swung them both to the ground. The night time grass contrasted against their training clothes.

Exhilarated and breathy, she beamed down at him where her legs locked around his shoulder. She expected him to put his hands on her hips and roll her onto her back. Maybe pin her there for some tension. That became typical of her dreams with Nox. But Xelan's face brokered no humor nor any sensual desires. Instead, a wealth of sadness filled those midnight voids. She released him and stepped away.

With her back to him, he asked, "Are they getting worse?"

The moon shone brightly on her face. She closed her eyes and let the silver engulf her. "Yes." Short, quiet. She shuddered at the vulnerability in that one word.

"I can't protect you there," he said. His voice grew tight with disappointment.

"No," she said. She offered him no comfort.

His hand gripped her arm and turned her to face him. She opened her eyes. He said, "You stopped sharing them with me."

She swallowed a lump of guilt forming in her throat. "They got ... too embarrassing to show you."

"I see," he said. She looked away. Without saying another word, he wrapped her in his arms. She resisted at first. Too weird. Too different. The only affection she received from tall men as of late involved a fist to the face and a caress in a scathing place. Xelan offered platonic kindness, and she shied from it.

"You're human," he spoke into her hair. "You need to do human things and spend time with your human friends outside of training." She unfolded her arms and rested them against his ribs. Not sexual, not confusing. Just a hug. He pulled back enough to cup her jaw. "Go back to the skating rink on Friday nights. Have movie nights with Tameka and Sagan."

It sounded like a worthy endeavor. "What about training?" she asked.

"We'll still train, of course, but maybe we'll skip Fridays or Saturdays. You need something normal." He smiled, and it lit her up inside. "Go on a date, you juvenile delinquent."

She barked out a laugh in his face, and he joined her. "Don't let all this confuse you, Rayne. It's not your life until it is. And until then, enjoy what you have." He pulled his hand away and stepped back. A mischievous look crossed his face. "You know?" He paused. She crooked an eyebrow. "Kyle has a crush on you."

She chortled. And he went on, "It's true. When you get to be as old as me, you know these things."

"Quit playing." She shoved him.

He made a show of rubbing his arm where she nudged him and then snatched up her wrist. He examined her biceps. "I feel sorry for anyone who tries to take you out. Look at these bad boys! Kicking my ass and throwing me around your yard. More's the pity."

Just like that, any weird lingering sexual feelings she had for him vanished. Xelan fit squarely in an older brother box. It was a nice fit, too. Like he belonged there all along, and her confusion kept her from seeing it. But this also meant she swore to herself to protect him from the damage her dreams left behind. She loved this old ass alien. He didn't need anymore guilt than he already carried for whatever crimes his bastard king committed.

Before bed that night, she muttered, "Nox, it's just you and me from now on."

{2005}

Rayne ran ten miles after dinner on the training course. Every night the group ran two, but she got an early start. She recalled Xelan's eyes when he showed up. Soft, open, concerned. The steady reminder he was available to listen any time she needed him. She growled and tossed her hairbrush back onto the dresser. Not his fault. She needed to tell someone. But how could she? It would crush him.

Wearing black shorts and a Thirty Seconds to Mars shirt, she climbed into bed at 1:00AM. She stared at the wall. When sleep refused to take her, she groaned and tossed to her other side. She winced. Earlier, she mounted their highest obstacle for the first time, and her shoulder screamed in pain. She put off R.I.C.E.-ing it until the morning.

Picking up her two hundredth notebook, she counted the words on the page: two hundred and thirteen. The lines of the page: thirty-three. How many times she wrote the letter "T:" one hundred and forty-one. She continued on until her eyelids dipped, heavy. She allowed them to flutter closed even knowing what came next.

In this dream, the steam consuming the cavern limited her sight to one foot ahead. The moisture beaded on her skin upon entry. The standard work out gear shrank to a black bikini. The number and intricacy of the straps around her legs and arms increased. They even ribboned off at her biceps and hips. The whole sordid affair left little to the imagination. Absent of the fire, the lush scent of spring flowers replaced the pine smoke aroma. Water glistened throughout her hair. It twinkled like glitter. Soft light illuminated from the distance. The walls, perhaps?

This was definitely a trick. A distraction. A test of her ability to fight with limited vision. Before she took a step, she spread her legs shoulder width apart and relaxed her arms. It made no sense to put this off any longer. "I'm here! And I know you're there."

No response.

She scanned the vapor and strained to listen for any sound, any sign he lurked nearby. When none came, she frowned. "Cool trick and all. But it's not like you to hide from me in combat. Be a good King of the Monsters and fac—"

"Come forward," he interrupted. In the distance, almost three yards away. She thought she heard water displaced in the same vicinity.

"Fuck no," she shouted.

"Rayne." For the first time since the dreams started, he dropped the distortion in his voice. A deep bass rumble with a silky edge spoke her name.

She forgot how to breathe.

"No fighting, tonight. Come forward and we can speak as equals. A parlay, if you will," he offered in that dreamy baritone.

She gulped the thick air. Could she trust him? It was just a dream. It's not like he hadn't done worse at this point. Still, she needed to keep her guard up. She eased out of her stance and stepped into the haze. The floral scent grew stronger, and the humidity clung stickier the further she tiptoed into the cavern. After walking sometime she almost gave up when, "Whoa." She stepped on a warm rock slab.

The water rushing sound started again. Close. Maybe two yards away. Through the steam, she followed the rock path until it stepped down into water.

"It's only a bath," he said. Casual, normal. Totally okay that he asked her to get into a bath with him.

Just to be sure, she asked, "Are you in it?!"

He chuckled. Without the distortion, the sound held warmth. Almost mirth. The richness of it sent a shiver up her spine until goosebumps peppered her skin. In like 100% humidity. "Yes. I'm on my end, further away. I thought you might feel more comfortable that way." Reasonable. But still questionable.

"Why are we meeting in a bath?" She almost wished he'd just resume kicking her ass.

"Because this is a dream. And I decided you've more than worked yourself out, today. Aren't you sore from all that running and clearing all those obstacles?" How could he know—"In your dreams, I know what's on your mind. Not everything. Just the immediate...stuff."

She tried to stop it. The train was derailing. Nope. This was happening. She giggled. Oh god, she broke into a fit of giggles at his use of the word, "stuff." And he was right. Like her shoulder was listening, it throbbed in agreement. She needed a break.

By the time she stopped laughing, she submerged, her knees into the water. Hot, a little more viscous than typical H2O, the water appeared black. Not like scary horror movie black, but more like water with a small drop of black ink dipped into it.

"What amuses you so?" he asked. But she knew he knew.

Rayne humored him anyway and replied, "It's just not a word befitting a king, 'stuff.'"

She took another couple of steps until the water pooled at her ribs. Despite it settling, she heard the disturbance of it further in the bath. It rippled across the black surface. One, two, three, four, five ... The rings smashed into her. He said, "Would you believe me if I said I'm more than a king? I'm an architect, an artist, a poet, and a philanthropist." The water shifted again. One, two, three, four. "And on occasion, a comedian."

She snickered again. The humidity was really messing with her. Or maybe it was the flowers. Another gentle slosh of water. One. What the—? She snapped up. The fog left him in a silhouette, but he stood close enough she craned her neck to see up all eleven inches. The cloak? Gone. The water waded around his hips ... no clothes. From his Adonis belt upward, the King of Cinder shared a bath with her, his honed body bare. At least what she saw of it. The impression of long, full hair cascaded down his back. She couldn't make out the color, nor any feature on his face. Not even his eyes. He stood maybe a foot away from her, and she saw very little.

Thank goodness because what she could see sent her pulse racing, and her chest pounded just from breathing. "You said we weren't going to fight, tonight." Why? Why, why, why, did her voice sound so breathy?! How big did her eyes get? Was it super obvious she ogled him for like three minutes?

"Shh." He actually shushed her. He reached for her.

And she jerked back like a skittish kitten. So confused. Most of the time, she assumed he just enjoyed beating the shit out of her, and she fought like hell to make it more difficult on him. But almost every night he performed little tricks to confuse her. He brushed her arm when he pinned her. He kissed her neck when he locked her in a hold. He even nipped her belly once. Right next to her belly button. And god help her, she liked it. As a teenager with limited, healthy outlets for the hormonal frustration in her life, she told herself it was just a dream. It's okay to have sexy thoughts about the evil alien king planning to dominate your planet if it's just a dream. Even if he's beating your ass in said dream. It's okay.

But this. This weird bath scenario was a flavor of intimacy outside her experience thus far, and she felt woefully unprepared for it. Light as the air in the steam, she said, "I can't—You can't have me."

He lowered his hand and sent another ripple crashing into her. She expected him to lash out. To punish her for her defiance. She did not expect him to say, "If you will turn and sit, I can relieve your shoulder."

Okay. What the fuck? Where was Nox, and who did they replace him with? This must be a different dream-scape, entirely, because there is no way in hell this motherfucker would offer to massage her injury. Maybe … just maybe … she got to have a semi-normal dream for once. Maybe this wasn't an invasion. Maybe this was how other girls dreamed.

Test it. "Okay." If he didn't hit her or grab or stab her in the next five minutes, it was just a normal dream. Like a normal girl dream. Not normal for Rayne dream. She turned and knelt in the inky water. The heat coalesced around her shoulder. She tried to stop the cheesy sigh that came out of her mouth, but resisting it proved impossible.

"There are a lot of joint injuries humans can suffer. If you're less careful, you might dislocate it or tear your rotator cuff," he explained. A lecture on human anatomical injury from the vicious son of a bitch she'd yet to meet. Fascinating.

His hot hand pressed into the meat of her shoulder. A very big hand that made a very big fist she endured over many nights in this very chamber. However, when used for good, "Ahh! Ah! That hurts!" she cried.

"Give it some time," he said. He punctuated it by applying more pressure. As she settled into the rhythm of his work, he knelt in the water behind her. Was this better or worse? On the one hand, he wasn't two feet higher than her anymore. On the other hand, she became acutely aware of his form and how it framed hers. And the massage definitely felt wonderful.

He interrupted her thoughts, "When you go to mount the wall next time, try to pull evenly with both arms. Use your core to pull up through the center, between your shoulders, rather than swinging over with your side. See, when you swing to one side, you displace the balance and put more demand on one shoulder. Tell Sagan to do the same."

She froze. Just went stiff. All her muscles rigid.

He removed his hand.

Chest deep in hot water with her worst enemy at her back—massaging her back—she grew icy cold. In a steady voice she stated, "Earlier you said you could skim just the surface of my thoughts. Since I got in this water with you, I haven't thought about Sagan."

The water remained calm. He said, "You've come a long way in your progress. I want to give you something you need."

She shut her eyes. Needs. The water sloshed around her as he waded to her front. "Look at me, Rayne," he said. Not a demand. A request.

No. Please no. He brushed a strand of her half-soaked hair. Her eyes popped open. The steam still obstructed his face.

"We can do this. Just this. Every night. We can talk as warriors do. You have your wounds, and I have mine. We can meet here ... like this ... from now on and explore those wounds, together," he said. If she thought his voice sounded seductive earlier ... He brushed his hand down to the curve of her neck and pressed his thumb against her carotid. "You have needs you won't allow yourself to experience because of the life you were born into. Needs I am more than happy to personally see met."

"But—" she started.

He placed a long finger on her full lips. He came closer, and she closed her eyes. Right into her ear, close enough his spearmint breath brushed her neck, Nox whispered, "It's just a dream."

A sound wanted to crawl its way out of her throat. She opened her mouth to let out a scream, and instead Rayne said, "Yes."

{DECEMBER 2005}

Xelan grabbed Rayne by both wrists and held her aloft. She struggled, and he remained firm but gentle. "We're done, tonight," he said, his breath puffing out. His mouth flattened in a thin line.

When he let her go, she growled. "Why?!"

He shoved the ankle weights they used earlier into his duffel. The zipper closed on a scream. "Because you're unhinged," he said.

"I'm fine. You're the one—"

He cut her off, admonishing her. "Two of my ribs are broken, and the six, consecutive blows to my head put me off the mood to train. You want a fight. And I'm not giving you one." He actually took off like he meant to leave the training grounds.

"Xelan! Xelan, come back!" she called. The slight whine at the last made him pause. With his back to her, she gave in with the apologies. "I'm really sorry. You're right. Something is bothering me. I want to talk about it, but I don't know how."

He turned on his heel then, but didn't come any closer "Go on."

Did she really break his ribs? How can her body suffuse with pride and shame all at once?! She cried in frustration and fell to her knees. She pounded the frozen earth with her fists. Seventeen, a badass, and those internal flames fanned by exasperation still overwhelmed her.

He took a few slow steps toward her. "Rayne?"

His combat boots came into her line of sight on the grass. "I'm losing!" She winced at her outburst, but she no longer wanted to contain it.

He squatted down to her level, sort of. "The dreams?" He let out a deep exhale of spearmint-y breath. "Are you ready to tell me?"

With strain, she cried, "Hell no!" She lowered her forehead to the grass-spotted earth. "But ...I don't know how much more I can take."

His warm hand brushed her shoulder, and she shrank back from him. "No, don't touch me! I'll infect you with it!" she shouted.

He sat back on the grass and kept his hands to his side. The moon shifted from behind the clouds. The pale light streaked through the trees. Xelan's face fractured her heart into pieces. No. Anything but that. He frowned with his eyes squeezed tight. A tear sparkled on his clenched jaw.

"I'm sorry," she breathed.

His eyes snapped open. They did the alien thing again: solid, deep blue with a white slit down the center. He changed them on command, but she realized now they must change when he felt strong emotions like rage and grief. "Don't." His voice layered in pitches. She flinched. He raised a hand in placation. "Don't apologize for what he's done to you. Ever." Another tear streaked down his cheek.

She shook her head. "No. You don't understand. I ... I asked for this. I ask for it every night. It's so much better than when he beats the shit out of me and so much worse because I let him ... touch me."

He turned his head away and stared into the woods. Did he find it too hard to look at her? Now that he knew her shame. Now that he knew she wanted it. Would he stop training her? Stop being her friend?

"Stop," he said.

Did she say all of that aloud?

"Stop blaming yourself," he continued. His voice thick to the point of choking. He cleared it, rubbed his face, and said, "You're turning eighteen in one month. He's older than your species. Nox has been seducing women longer than humans could write. He's a predator, and he's preying on your valid, hormone–induced confusion. Also known as a sex drive." Blood infused her cheeks, and he plopped down onto the frost-covered grass. "Do you want me to pretend you're not a human with growing needs? I can do that." He emphasized, "I'd prefer to do that. I hate watching you guys grow up. But witnessing you internalizing this has been the hardest thing I've watched one of you struggle with since I was left on Earth."

She wrenched herself off the cold ground. Her limbs encased in iron. Unzipping her hoodie, she shed it and unstrapped the ten pound weight vest from her chest. Better. She shivered and shrugged back into the thermal jacket. Xelan watched her step around him on the grass. She laid down on the ground behind him and placed her head next to his. They stared at each other up close. His eyes returned to normal at some point. Little streaks graced his cheeks from his tears. She touched them. He let her. She asked, "What can I do?"

He took her hand and held it. He said, "You can talk to me about it. Or Sagan. Or whoever you feel comfortable with. You cannot internalize this anymore. It's toxic, and it's eating away at you. Also at my ribs ..."

She winced, and he grinned. "I was proud of you for landing those shots with so much ... force," he said.

"I'm so—" she started.

"Stop," he said. "Talk or promise me you're going to talk to somebody."

She turned to the sky. The clouds passed slowly over the silver disk of the moon. Her breath left in puffs, adding to the atmosphere. The cold absorbed into her skin. She told Xelan about the first dream. He blanched twice and for realzies blushed once. And she even left some things out.

"Yea ... I think I'll talk to Sagan about this from now on," she promised.

{INVASION DAY 2006}

Not long after, Xelan disappeared. Rayne's dreams went with him. She remained unsure if the two connected somehow, but she endured the losses of both for four months. Without Xelan, she possessed no guide. No compass. She led her unit to the best of her abilities, but it never felt the same. Without her nightmares, she feared the invasion might never come. Yes, she knew how messed up that sounded. She needed the invasion to happen, to validate all the shit she already went through. Normal dreams? Those weren't meant for her. The void left her afraid she imagined it all. Was there no point in training on the course every day? Did she fuck up her GPA for nothing? Miss out on dating and losing her virginity to some sweaty teenage boy like a normal girl? Heaven knew Andrew and Kyle sure tried, but both relationships lasted no longer than six months. Neither one compared to ...

She stood in an evacuated classroom under the glow of emergency lights. The desks strewn everywhere. Glass littered the floor. These things validated her. Was it worth it? She picked up a desk and slung it at the dry erase board. *CRACK!* It busted into splinters. Losing Nikki over her own emotional distance. She kicked a filing cabinet and dented the metal like tin foil. Watching Sagan suffer at the hands of an abusive asshole while she worked through her own issues. She clasped both hands together and smashed them into a desk, shattering it. Waiting and training for four years, tormented nightly by dreams of her friends dying while she got off with some demonic, alien king, unable to talk to her parents or warn them of the coming disaster. She rocked the teacher's desk and flipped it onto its side. It continued to roll until it crashed upside down in the center of the room. The wood clamored and echoed into the hall.

Flushed and deprived of air, she sobbed. She roughly scrubbed away the tears streaming down her face. Her shame, guilt, and rage threatened to burn her alive, and she trembled with the effort to resist it.

"Whatever this was, I hope it made you feel better." The only voice she welcomed at that moment called from the doorway. She turned to face Sagan, not bothering to compose herself. Rayne shook her head. A little hiccup. Sagan crossed the room to embrace her. "It's okay. It's okay. We're gonna get through this."

"How? How are we going to do this?" Rayne croaked into Sagan's hair. "That monster is here because of me. Xelan disappeared, and we aren't prepared for this."

"That's just not true. He was always coming here, Rayne, that's why Xelan came to us in the first place. But you know what?" She pulled back and cradled Rayne's face with both hands. She looked right into her eyes and said, "He made the mistake of giving us four years to get ready for him. We can fight, we can coordinate our attacks, and we can beat them. We can trigger each other with our code names." She pressed her forehead against her best friend's and closed her eyes. The next part she whispered, "And all those bad dreams of you and Nox or me and Korac, they'll never happen. Rayne, I want you to listen because this is the most important part: if some part of you wants something to happen, forgive yourself. Don't hate yourself over something you can't control. We're impressionable, teenage girls, God dammit, and our dreams have been fucking with us for four years. Don't you dare blame yourself for that or any of this. We're being invaded by aliens. Hot, asshole aliens who want to murder us. Whatever conflicting shit you're traumatizing over right now, it was always going to happen. Now take it and stab them in the face with it. Do you understand?!"

She questioned Sagan's bravado. The girl's body trembled in her arms. She harbored as much terror as Rayne, maybe more. But Rayne couldn't let that speech go to waste. "Yes," Rayne answered with a voice heavy from crying, not out of anguish but out of appreciation. She opened her eyes and pulled back from her friend. "You're right. No time for trauma. No time for tears."

"No, you're wrong," Sagan said. "There will always be time for those things, but we have to be ready to fight with them, and everything else we've got."

"How are the others on supplies? Has Andrew finished briefing them yet?"

"They were just finishing up when I left. We could honestly use more medical supplies. Although, we both know everyone needs a blade of some kind. Or a bazooka."

FIVE

A Pound Of Flesh Loaned Is
A Pound Of Flesh To Be Repaid

WHEN IT ALL STARTED, THE SCREAMS BLENDED INTO ON ANOTHER AS IN A MASSIVE CHORUS OF PAIN AND DEATH. From the moment the windows broke, Matt knew this wasn't a school shooting. Just the number of people involved to break that much glass tipped him off. And as everyone in his biology class started stampeding out the door, he slipped unnoticed into the drop-ceiling panel over his desk. Mrs. Burless didn't even spare a glance back as she rushed after her students. He tried to use his cell phone to call for help, but no signal. He kept his cool until the explosion rattled the school from South Hall. He never imagined himself as a soldier, but this certainly felt like a war zone. Why would anyone reign an assault on J.A. Fair of all schools? He wondered not for the first time in the hour since it started. Why not Parkview or Pulaski Academy? And this was Little Rock, Arkansas for God's sake, not Washington D.C. or L.A. or New York. Something didn't add up.

Despite his concerns over the logic behind the attack, nothing changed the facts: it happened, and he needed to get out of the ceiling soon. Smoke permeated the ceiling, and he suspected the intruders disabled the fire alarm and sprinkler systems. In the last five minutes, the screams died down from a chorus to an occasional solo. He was tough. He could handle a few one-on-one altercations. Also, no gunfire. Not yet, anyway. Someone emptied the whole school, blew up a portion of it, and never fired a shot? He definitely needed to find someone who knew what was going on.

He lifted the nearest tile back from the wall and surveyed the immediate area. Notta. He stuck his head out and observed the upside down classroom. Nothing. Now was as good a time as any. He hung one leg down until it found footing on the desk underneath, and the other leg followed right after. All clear, he dropped out of the ceiling and laid flat on the ground. He crawled over to the door, careful to keep low. Careful not to scrape on the broken glass. He stood and planted his back against the door. He checked the window. Left. Right. Nothing. Well, nothing but bodies. So many school mates' bodies littered down the English/ Science hallway. He gave himself a sociopath test. Should he have convinced a few to climb in the ceiling with him? No way to guarantee he might live through this, so he certainly couldn't vouch for the safety of others. But what would his friends think if they knew he let everyone run out while he suspected the broken glass was a diversionary tactic?

He shook the doubts from his head and assessed his current situation. Alone, he needed weapons, and he knew nothing about the "enemy" except they used weapons other than guns. After twenty minutes breaking up furniture into makeshift shanks, he collected his bag of dangerous goodies, and opened the door to the hallway. He approached the closest body, a brunette he never met. He nudged the girl's leg with his foot. No response. He searched her body over for any wounds. Leaning down, he pushed her hair aside and glanced over the wound on her neck. Some kind of bite, but worried at as if by a coyote. The wound caused alarms to ring in his head. She's not covered in blood. There's no pool of blood. There's no blood anywhere other than right at the wound. Exsanguination. They removed her blood from her body. Matt checked the black-haired guy next to her, same thing. He examined one more body. They all appeared exsanguinated. Bite marks. Blood loss. Vampires? That doesn't seem right aside from the fact they didn't exist. But Matt knew all too well monsters were real.

He picked up his gear and headed for the exit. A very low and deep grumble carried from North Hall. Goosebumps pricked his skin, his hair stood on end, and his spine went ramrod straight. Was it one of them? Had he lingered too long? Next came a sigh. Not really sounds he expected from an elite fighting force attacking the school and draining the students of blood. Especially not from vampires. He spun on the spot and listened again, peering into North Hall. His instincts at odds with himself. A chuff whispered from the hall. That's it. He needed to satisfy his curiosity. Marching down the hall, he stopped just at the edge with his back pressed to the corner. Careful, he took one searching glance and immediately withdrew. Two of the biggest dudes he ever saw laid out in a heap in the hallway in front of Mr. Handler's World History classroom. The one with long black hair so still aside from the occasional whimper. A metal pole stuck out of its back.

Ignoring the morbidity of it, Matt reached down and unlaced a dead classmate's shoe. His breath came hard, and his pulse pounded as he contemplated all the years of his life leading up to this moment. He lifted the sneaker, steeled himself, and tossed it at the impaled guy.

"Umph," he groaned. His head lolled over and yellow eyes rolled around in the sockets. Matt recoiled at the sight of them. But the stranger continued to lie on his back. Matt hugged the wall and crouched like he was a practiced member of the armed forces. He crept along the hallway until he reached the pile of really weird looking dudes in cloaks. The blond one looked dead. One shiv stuck out of his chest. He wasn't going anywhere. But the guy sporting the cheekbones was alive, if a little unresponsive. Matt pulled out a chair leg and dared to poke the guy. Just a groan. With a piece of metal sticking out of his chest, he wondered how the hell he kept breathing? He knew what he wanted to do next, and he didn't want anyone to see him do it. He looked down the Foreign Language hall: nothing. He looked back the way he came: nothing. All clear. Rather than retract the metal already inside the guy's body, Matt plunged his chair leg in right next to it.

The dude's tongue rolled out, and a gasp escaped, but no more sound. Dead. Matt lifted the stranger's hand, and it fell limply to the linoleum with a splat. He knelt beside him and got to work. Blue blood. Definitely vampires. Chest punctured. He removed those implements of death. With the metal chair legs gone, he explored the wound and cavity a little better. Between the unacceptable red emergency lighting, and the blood seeping into the wound, it proved difficult, but he found what he thought might be the heart. At least, if it were human, it would be. From inside the chest, he lifted a human-like brain and brain stem. Placed in a different spot. Bizarre. Blood and very thick fluids slid down his hands, wrists, and to his elbows. He set the brain aside when something caught his eye. An extra connection just at the base of the brain stem to something inside the chest cavity.

Matt lay the brain down, gently, and dipped his hand back inside. A small chamber there, not dissimilar to the sac around the heart. He felt something hard in it. A nerve cluster, maybe? Feeling on the verge of something important, he pressed into the mucus lining and grasped the hard object inside. He retrieved a tiny, shining sphere. A pearl. Embracing the inner-scientist he tended to ignore, he left his things in the hall and rushed back to Mrs. Burless' classroom. Microscopes, Bunsen burners, and vials lined the counter, but most importantly, a sink. Might as well wash his hands as well as the pearl. He placed it under a microscope to examine it. Beautiful, but absolutely indiscernible. He failed to glean a single bit of information from it. Still, he hung onto it until he understood the situation better.

After retrieving his bag, Matt froze as voices rose from the Foreign Language/Math hall. As they carried on, his body relaxed. He recognized them. He turned the corner without checking. Sagan and Rayne left a classroom halfway down the hallway. "Hey," he whispered.

They both started as if he interrupted something. He thought better of apologizing, considering there were vampires attacking the school. They seemed to come to the same conclusion because Sagan said, "You have to get out of here."

Rayne joined in, "Go to the football field."
Matt held up a hand. "First, what's going on?"

"Vampires are real my ass. Those are just dickheads on PCP or some shit. Or fucking terrorists," Sagan's ex-boyfriend shouted in Lucy's face against the backdrop of the football field. Justin's stark white skin flared red with anger. Unfortunately, that became an all too familiar sight, and everyday until six months ago he directed it at Sagan. Even the teachers cowed and looked away, dipping off to smoke with the students at the other end of the field.

Cecily tried a calm and even voice, "People are dead. We have to stay here. Rayne was the only—"

"Since when in the fuck do you listen to what Rayne tells you, huh?! Or any of those freaks she hangs out with?" He swept his arm in a gesture to indicate the entire campus. "They're probably in on this. Don't you know the freaks are the ones that shoot up schools for being bullied and shit."

"Yea man, what the fuck are we doing sitting around here for?" Michael shouted. He joined Justin on the edge of campus, just beyond the football field. "Those assholes will slaughter y'all and y'all are just gonna let 'em do it. Starting with Rayne."

"Rayne has never been one to stand for bullying. That's something you should know pretty well, Justin," Matt said. Everyone turned to see him walking onto the bleachers. Matt pulled the battery out of his Nokia and replaced it while he spoke, "You'll get in Cecily's face and Lucy's face, but you wouldn't get in Rayne's. Not after what she did to you at the end of football season. If she says she knows what's going on here and that I need to sit my ass in this football field and wait for her, then fine. That's what I'm going to do. But I will not sit here and listen to you bitch and call her shit you wouldn't say to her face while I wait." He never even spared a glance at Justin, but he knew what came next.

Justin lunged forward like he meant to haul up the bleachers and beat Matt's ass. Michael made a show of holding Justin back. Most importantly to note, Justin let him. "You don't know a fucking thing, Anderson. You wanna talk about saying shit to people's faces, you get down here and say all that to mine." And he said many more lines to that effect. Meanwhile, Matt powered on his cell phone and tried to hold it up in different directions, higher and higher.

Michael calmed Justin down while Lucy and Cecily approached Matt. "Did you get any signal?" Cecily asked.

"Naw, I don't think there's any signal to get. Did you notice the smoke plumes all around us?" He nodded in various directions. They followed his line of sight, and a new sense of dread dawned on them. "I think this is bigger than our school."

Rustling followed by Stacia screaming, "Hey, where are you going?!" grabbed their attention. Justin and Michael bolted to the student parking lot. Matt jumped up and raced the girls to the edge of the football field. Other students gathered to watch the spectacle. While Matt trusted Rayne implicitly with their safety, he wondered what would happen if someone tried to leave the school.

"Justin! Michael! Get your asses back here!" he shouted after them for good measure. Ah, fuck it. Why should he care what happened to a girlfriend abuser and his crony? He watched as the guys climbed into Justin's truck. Lifted, of course, thanks to his daddy's money. The ignition started fine, but for a brief second the fellas froze. They looked like they thought long and hard about it. They seemed too scared to move. Then Justin said something and hit the gas in reverse. They pulled out of the parking spot and drove along the pavement to the only exit on campus.

Matt, Lucy, Cecily, and the others watched them stop the truck just at the bottom of the hill leading out of the parking lot. Matt debated if he wanted them to turn back or press on. The truck started to ease up the hill toward the open gate. That's when he heard a sound he would never forget if he lived through this. A keening howl echoed through the trees and buildings making up the campus. It raised the hair on his arms and gave him goose bumps. Not to mention the near-impossible-to-ignore urge to wet himself. If that noise wasn't disturbing enough, he heard something too loud to be described as a rustle but definitely sounded like vegetation moved around by heavy force. A tree fell over close to the truck and a giant monster, for lack of a better word, thundered out of the tree line heading straight for Justin's vehicle. A massive thing and all wrong. Its skin looked charred red and black, like a lit coal. Horns on its head, and a snout like a big lizard. Teeth longer than Matt's arm, and more than he wanted to count. The wing span spread wider than Justin's extended cab with claws at the tip of each wing. It bounded up to the truck on all six of its taloned feet. Every muscle honed on its twelve foot tall mass strained as it rammed into the vehicle. The truck flipped once on its side, then stopped upside down. The girls next to Matt started screaming as if they just found the air to do so.

His lungs refused to draw air. He stood frozen to the spot and filled with a mixture of fright and anticipation. The beast stomped on the truck's undercarriage with its front four claws. The truck flattened with ease. Lucy sank to her knees beside Matt as they watched the spectacle in horror. Surely Justin and Michael were already dead. Unfortunately, as soon as he thought it, a pale hand stretched out of the driver's side window. "No," Matt muttered. While he had no love for the two trapped inside, he didn't wish this demise on his worst enemy.

"Oh, no!" Cecily shrieked. The gargoyle snatched onto the hand with his immensely large teeth and pulled. They heard Justin scream all the way across campus when the beast ripped his arm from its socket. A few people behind them started retching, and at least one or two followed from the sounds and smells. If Matt hadn't seen so much carnage this morning, he might have joined them, but now he felt desensitized to it.

A howl pierced the air, followed by another, and another. A chorus of beasts sang to each other just inside the tree line bordering the entire school. "We're all gonna die!!" Lucy shrieked and started an onset of hysterical sobbing. More tears and desperate cries filled the air. Children. All of them frightened children who worried about their families and friends. His antisocial personality disorder kicked in. Although only eighteen himself, he shared little in common with the surrounding people, emotionally. People he liked and cared about were inside and nearby, and he didn't want them to know how much fun he was having.

"I'm won't tell you we're going to be all right. But I'm gonna say that we were warned not to leave the perimeter. Now we know why. We need to stick together, wait this out, and help anyone who makes it out of that building alive." He pointed to their high school. "As crazy as it is, we've always known Rayne, Sagan, Kyle, and all them were different. They're in there trying to save us. We have to believe they're gonna make it." He looked down the hill at the student parking lot to his Chevrolet Malibu and then turned back to his captive audience of terrified teenagers. "I'm going down there to get my car." This met with many "Nos" and "You can'ts." He talked through it, "I'm just driving it back up here and seeing if I can get any kind of news on the radio. Sound like a plan?" Students glanced at each other with nervous eyes, and he understood their reservations. But Matt watched Justin and Michael closely. The monster didn't make a move on them until they attempted to drive through the gate. He made no intentions of doing that.

"I'll go with you," Cecily announced.

A thrill of panic crawled up Matt's spine. "No!" he shouted in answer. At the hurt look on her face, he raked a hand through his auburn hair. In a calm voice, he said, "No. Just in case something goes wrong, I don't want to be responsible for anyone else getting hurt." That seemed to smooth things over. He started walking in the direction of his car. "I'll be right back," he offered over his shoulder. He felt nothing as he approached the student lot. He made an educated guess the beasts meant to keep the students within school grounds. He wasn't technically violating that rule. The white interior of his little sedan shone immaculate. He kept it very clean. The machete he kept under the passenger seat the only thing dirty inside. He pulled it out for good measure. He turned the ignition and crept the car back up the hill to the football field. As he made his way up, he wondered if his kit in the trunk contained anything useful for this situation. He shook his head at the notion. Although he could explain the machete as protection, there was no way he'd be able to explain away the rest. At the top of the hill, the students gathered around his car as he put it in park. He winced, uncomfortable with them this close to his dirty secrets. But bigger issues to deal with here.

"Turn it on," ordered Stacia, who always came across as too bossy for his liking. He turned on the radio, anyway. The sound of static filled the air.

"I'll try another station," he announced while pressing the tune button. More static.

"Try AM," offered someone in the crowd.

He obeyed with a deep frown on his face. He listened to the static for a moment, and then a beeping came through the airwaves. The crowd murmured in response. "Shh, quiet," he said and leaned in closer to the speaker. The static cleared and the beeping droned into a message. The most terrifying message they ever heard:

"Earthlings, humans, homo sapiens, we have weapons capable of destruction you cannot imagine. As you can see. We demand surrender from your leaders. The sooner they deliver it, the sooner we can begin administering mercy. Not a moment before. If you resist, we have no choice but to provide another demonstration and another. If you surrender, the populace will suffer almost no casualties. We want the human race to live. Surrender."

{2005}

Fuck! God damn it! It was his turn with Xelan tonight.

Andrew groaned as he slowed the trek to his car. Motherfucker. Every Thursday. How did he keep forgetting? Every Thursday he trained with Xelan. And every Friday, Saturday, and sometimes even Sunday, his muscles ached, sore from the workout. The DOMS sucked balls. And now that they discussed his initiation into The Brethren, Xelan suggested training on Saturday nights, as well.

Fuck. That.

Although he barely got around on the weekends, they still belonged to him. He guarded his free time because if he failed in it, Rayne and Xelan planned all kinds of shit for their unit to do. He was sick of it!

He slammed the door on his car and cranked up the radio. Insane Clown Posse made everything better. He sped on the drive home in his mom's Volkswagen Passet. Nothing fancy. Just operable. He didn't care. He was one of few students at Hall High with fucking wheels. Unlike the rest of his friends, his home lacked all that convenient yard space, so he drove to the nearest park a few blocks away.

He reclined the seat and plugged a cigarette in his mouth. Lit it, took a drag, and slowed it on the exhale. They couldn't take this from him. He liked this quiet time right after school. His mom came home late. She also thought he worked part time at Rayne's bookstore in the evenings. He came by money through more nefarious means.

Knock, knock, knock! Andrew legit jumped like four inches off the seat. Xelan peered at him through the driver's side window. Andrew groaned and rolled it down. "Dude, what the fuck? It's only 6:00PM."

"It's November. We can start early." The mother–fucker smirked.

Andrew popped the door open and threw his half-smoked cigarette to the pavement. He stomped it out. His body wound tight with frustration until his neck strained from it. Deep breath. Being stiff as a board would only result in his ass getting whooped. Sooner. He cranked his neck to the left. Then to the right. The pops and cracks relieved some pressure.

He took in the trees and the expanse of mown grass around him. The twilight came early, tonight. He lamented his extra hour alone. Xelan wasn't his usual gung-ho self. He lingered off at the edge of the parking lot, staring at the pool of light under the streetlamp.

"What's up, man?" Andrew loathed to ask. He approached his frenemy's side.

Xelan brought his fist to his mouth and bit his thumbnail. A common gesture when the alien did some deep thinking. He asked, "Does something seem wrong with Rayne lately?"

This burnt his ass some. "Dude, she doesn't talk to me about what's wrong with her. She hasn't since we broke up a year ago. Find someone else to spy on her with. Maybe Sa—"

The look on Xelan's face stopped him cold. Danger lurked beyond those midnight eyes. Even during their sparring or their usual back and forth, he kept that look to himself. Under normal circumstances, Andrew noted the hint. Tonight, though. Well, tonight he rose to the challenge. "Dude, fuck you. She broke up with me because of you."

Xelan recoiled. "What are you going on about?!"

"Anytime she fell asleep on the couch—which was often, mind you—she dreamt of you. You think I didn't know what was going on?" Andrew posed the question, but he resented the answer.

"For the last time, I've no romantic interest in Rayne. I have never touched her in that manner," Xelan said this like he kept the phrase on retainer.

Andrew paced in a circle, gravel crunching underneath. He'd kill for a cigarette. Or a joint. He pressed, "You may not have ever touched her, but you know you encouraged it in other ways. The only ways that counted!"

"What makes you think she was dreaming about me?" Xelan asked. His tone evened, and his posture stiffened. Either he was about to explode or he thought of something that didn't sit right with him.

Andrew got right in his face and spat. "Because she cried out your name, moron!" Xelan closed his eyes. Andrew wasn't sure if the alien was counting to ten or getting an image out of his head. "Over and over. It took everything I had to wake her. Every single time. Then she wouldn't talk to me for like twenty minutes. And the more it happened, the more she pulled away. So yea…it was your fault. And if there's something wrong with her now, it's your fault, too. Not because I actually know that, but just because it's convenient to blame you for it."

Andrew finally backed down. No way in hell a super-powered alien with five inches on him backed down first. Just no way. He thrust fingers into his hair and bunched it up. Fuck it. He roared his frustration into the dusk. The honeysuckle bush in front of him trembled in fright.

"She wasn't calling out my name." The quiet words reached Andrew on the breeze. The sadness in them unmistakable.

Andrew spun. At the sight of Xelan's silhouette with its head hung in shame, Andrew folded his arms. "I'm listening," he begrudged.

Xelan cleared his throat, a rare sound. His words came rough and heavy, "She was asking for my help."

Andrew frowned. "Why?"

Xelan wandered from the edge of the parking lot onto the springy grass. Off in the distance, crickets sang. The backdrop offset the mood. Andrew, curious, followed. He pushed, "Why was she calling to you for help? A lot."

Xelan winced. He said, "Before you two started seeing each other, she began having bad dreams. I won't betray her confidence and go into any detail. I will say they are recurring. And I will say they have to do with the invasion."

Andrew both respected and hated Xelan for not sharing more. Their leader secretly struggled with a turbulent case of insomnia. They deserved to know as her unit. But as someone who loved Rayne ... "I won't tell anyone. Is there anything we can do to help her?"

Xelan plopped on the grass. "We can't. I mean, not directly. This is something she has to fight on her own." Andrew squatted over the grass beside him. Xelan turned to him. "You still have feelings for her, don't you?"

Cheeky motherfucker. No one said it had to get this personal. But that sting persisted. He gave a gentle smile and said, "Yea. She's one of a kind."

Xelan grunted in agreement. "You all are to me."

{INVASION DAY 2006}

After Andrew finished the speech, the group gathered as many materials as possible. Tameka found him in the adjacent Spanish department office. "Hey," she said.

Please don't ask again. Please don't ask again. Andrew hated keeping secrets from them. They wanted answers for a perfectly logical reason. Why the hell was he here? He didn't go to school here, and Hall was on the other side of Little Rock. But he couldn't answer their question. And he couldn't tell them why. Not until Xelan allowed him to do so. So he played the brooding and mysterious card.

"Hey," he said. The fewer the words, the fewer the lies. He scanned the shelves for something helpful. Like a book on how to preserve his sanity.

She touched him on the shoulder and startled him. She said, "I'm really glad you're here."

Unexpected, but welcomed, he pulled her into a hug. He exhaled in a rush against her skin. "Oh ... I'm so glad you're okay." After the mess he found when he arrived, he thought he showed up too late.

"It was awful," she said into his hair.

He pulled back and tried to swallow some of his emotions. He cupped her freckled cheek and shook his head. "It's not over, yet. You're strong. You can make it. John and Nikki need our help."

She nodded, "You're right. We'd better get in there." She tried to hide the shine in her eyes from him, and he let her. People deserved to hold back whatever they needed in privacy.

Andrew let her go and went around the corner into the classroom. Nikki and John continued on with loading materials they needed. The locked door handle shook. And everyone stopped moving to stare. Had the Icari found them? Were they ready?

Rayne popped her face in the window. The group let out a collective breath. Nikki stepped over a desk to unlock the door.

Sagan and Rayne hurried into the classroom together with bags of supplies in hand.

Kyle asked the girls, "Everything go all right?"

Andrew tried not to cringe at how fast Kyle attached himself to Rayne's hip. Dude had issues.

"Yea, we've got a few things to help with the medical stuff," Sagan started.

"But you guys have to know these weapons won't be good enough," Rayne finished. "Our first priority is the weapons' caches."

Tameka asked, "Excuse me, but shouldn't saving people be the first priority?"

Andrew winced. Tameka always went for the jugular, so direct and a little cut-throat. Not to dwell on it, but when he arrived in the school, he lost his breakfast a few times before he found them. So many dead bodies. So many died horrible deaths. The security guard, the students and teachers in the hall. Most died screaming, drained of their blood. The likelihood of finding anyone alive grew slimmer and slimmer as the minutes ticked by.

Rayne said, "You're right." She surprised Andrew by admitting fault and agreeing with Tameka. She continued, "Priority 1: Check everyone. Help anyone. Send them on to the football field. Priority 2: Look out for each other. Watch each other's backs. It's dark out there, and as the smoke rolls in, it'll only get darker. We're in dangerous territory here. Take care of each other. Priority 3: Get to the weapons' caches. The rest I'll make up as I go along."

Her smile shined. Rayne felt hope. And if she could manage some, so could he. She learned some leadership skills from Xelan after all. He said, "All right, people, you heard her! Grab your supplies and let's move out!"

Tameka and Rayne distributed their better weapons to the rest. "One for you. One for you. Here you go, Nikki."

Kyle scoffed, "That thing is bigger than her whole body. Why'd you give me a two-inch?"

Tameka rolled her eyes, and Rayne cut her off before she made a size joke. "Because you have more experience with close knife combat, and Nikki doesn't. She needs to stay back as far as possible."

Nikki flinched. "I can handle myself."

Kyle huffed.

Rayne smiled at Nikki and said, "I know you can, and with that knife you'll take them by surprise."

It broke Andrew's heart to see the impression Rayne left on Nikki. Their leader didn't have a fucking clue. He knew exactly how Nikki felt. Every smile, every compliment, every bit of attention lit them up inside. No wonder Kyle followed her around. He was an addict. Addicted to the hope of a second chance with her. They should start a support group.

At last, everyone carried a proper knife and a shiv of some kind. Tameka loaded up the medical supplies in one backpack and slipped into it. They gathered at the door. Rayne checked the window. Left down the hall. Right down the hall. Nothing. She looked back to Sagan and Andrew. "Ready?" she asked.

They nodded in unison.

"Let's go!" Rayne said and opened the door. She froze.

A faint trace of smoke traveled into the room. Mostly an acrid smell, but another scent drifted underneath the burn.

"Is that pine?" Andrew asked.

"Let's go," Rayne said and opened the door. Sagan watched Rayne hesitate, and knew she was losing her best friend to a battle she must fight alone. The weight of the guilt she carried weighed so much, Rayne's shoulders visibly slumped and the blue of her eyes dulled to gray. Sagan knew what to look for because the same happened to her. A scent rolled in on the smoky air. Rayne once told Sagan she battled Nox in a rock cavern with a giant wood fire that smelled of—

"Is that pine?" Andrew asked.

Rayne jumped, and Sagan flinched. She reached out a supporting hand when Rayne disappeared out the door. The group followed, leading up to the main hallway. "Dear, God," Rayne uttered.

John crossed himself. Andrew and Nikki hung their heads.

Kyle asked into the nightmare, "What are we supposed to do with this?"

Sagan pushed her way to the front and broke the line. At the sight, she covered her mouth with her hand. The angles and curves of her face wrenched tight with distress. Bodies, maybe a hundred or more, laid out down the length of the hall. Arranged, broken and bent into some repeating shape she failed to make out. Rayne rushed to her side, which only increased the pounding of Sagan's already thundering heart. What was she missing? Why did the sight of it turn her blood cold? It was almost as if her mind wouldn't let her make out the shape. Recognition dawned. She lowered her makeshift stake as she stared into the edge of madness. Rayne started rubbing circles into Sagan's back, but she barely felt it. She grew numb and floated away.

{NOVEMBER 2005}

"Are you disassociating again or just ignoring me?" Tameka asked.

Rayne played with the food on her lunch tray. "Leave her alone. Justin's out on his only away game, she gets to sit with us, and you're on her ass."

"Hey, it's not my fault she lets that asshole order her around like a harem girl," Tameka jabbed.

Sagan decided she wanted to stay in her sketch book rather than join the conversation. It seemed much more pleasant to work the shading on this wing or the negative space on that antenna. She anticipated going home and adding some watercolor. This was her favorite place to be: right here with her friends and her sketchbook. Even if Tameka was on her case. She admitted she never knew why she, herself, tolerated Justin's brutish control. She joined the track team because of him, and now she sat here almost unable to walk in her heels with her ankle in a brace. He told her to stop wearing makeup; she did. Stop dressing like a Goth chick; she did. Stop going to concerts; she did. And finally, to stop eating with her friends at lunch and only eat with him; she did. Basically, anything she found fun or relaxing seemed to upset him. So she gave it all up. And what did she get in return? Three bad minutes of physical "intimacy" almost daily that still failed to push away the tall, pale, devastatingly handsome invader of her dreams. She and Rayne shared their stories, together. They suffered similar curses. Only where Rayne decided guys weren't worth it, and she'd rather fight her demon away with Xelan, Sagan just found the first domineering tall, pale, moderately good-looking guy in their school to substitute her tormentor. So she was tortured by controlling pieces of shit twenty-four, seven.

"You're beating yourself up about it," Rayne once said.

"I don't know how to undo it. I can't bear the idea that I might be waiting for *him*," Sagan confessed.

"I know what you—" Rayne started, but Sagan refused to let her finish.

"No! You don't know what I mean. Or what I feel. I invite these things on myself. Justin ... Korac ... I ask for them," she shouted. After a moment where her throat failed to function for the emotion staving it, she confessed, "I want them," almost too softly to hear. Rayne surprised her by no longer offering placations. She held Sagan. And they cheated on Justin for what she calculated as the third time in the whole of their relationship. But why keep up with it? She found solace in Rayne—whether her company as a friend or something more—she just enjoyed it.

Which is why she took the risk of her boyfriend's spies snitching on her again that she hung out with her Goth buddies. Ooo spooky. If only he had a fucking clue. However she may act at school for his sake, she never became the girl he wanted her to turn into. "You might have a point," Sagan mumbled to her sketchbook in response to Tameka. She smiled and closed the notebook on her latest drawing of a butterfly. She took a second to look over Rayne's shoulder to scan Justin's usual table. There sat The Overachievers enjoying their lunches. Lucy's head popped up as if summoned. When she caught Sagan's eye, she quickly looked away and said something to Cecily and Stacia beside her. Justin would definitely hear about this.

Later that night, her training session with Xelan went sideways fast. Laid out on her ass, he pinned her, forcing a weapon to her midsection. If a car pulled up to her quarter mile long driveway and their headlights beamed on the scene, it might appear a little vulgar. She lost this contest before it started. He lived many thousands, maybe tens of thousands, of years before she existed. Thanks to his sleeveless tank, she saw his exceptionally chiseled muscles didn't even strain. And maybe for half a second she considered giving in and letting him plunge the axe into her chest. At that exact moment he rolled off her, extracting the blade.

He laid there a second beside her. His breathing even with little sign of exertion. For some reason, she stilled, afraid to move or release a breath. Then he just appeared on his feet with no movement in between. She knew now why she felt uncomfortable meeting his eyes. He was pissed. "What is wrong with you, Tameka, and Rayne?! Kyle and Andrew don't give me this melodramatic shit. I swear the three of you will be the death of me," he shouted.

She stiffened, afraid to answer. She reacted the only way she knew how to that tone of voice from a man. She sensed herself moving further away from her body, which she faintly realized was curled on its side. That was okay. It would be over soon.

"NO!" he cried and suddenly he knelt on his knees beside her. He shook her by the shoulders, gentle. "Come. Back." His voice sounded no longer harsh. He sounded terrified.

Sagan slammed back into herself almost abrupt enough to make her gasp. The compassion in his kind, midnight eyes forced something tight in her chest to loosen. "Don't go, Sagan," he pleaded. Now that she felt able to move, she uncoiled herself from the fetal position. She knelt on her knees in the dirt, matching him. "She was right. What has he done to you?" Justin, not *him*. She couldn't bear to tell Xelan about her nightly tormentor. So there's only one other "he" Xelan might ask about. He reached out and then thought better of it, lowering his hand.

Her voice came soft as it often sounded when she left herself. This was the first time it didn't involve bruising on her throat. "How can I be a soldier if I'm broken?" she asked.

Did she hear right? ... No, she must be mistaken. In all this time of knowing Xelan, the last three and a half years, he'd never even shed a tear. Now, she thought he sniffled, or even worse, wept. His form silhouetted against the moon, she failed to make out if he started crying. "I cannot protect you in the daylight. We can make you physically strong. We can even make you defend yourself against the hordes of Cinder. But this, I cannot protect you against." He paused, sighed, and stood. He walked toward the only tree in her front yard. She stayed. "This will take a toll on your human soul that I can't bring you back from. Your face during our fight? You wanted to die." He let that hang in the air.

Sagan reflected and tried to muster a decent response, "Xelan—"

"All three of you are struggling with this in ways I couldn't predict. This wait is causing suffering I wasn't expecting. You're warriors with nothing to fight. Where else would you take that fight but inside yourselves?" He came back to her. He made an effort to walk slowly with gentle movements she saw clearly. "Tell me everything. Everything that's eating away at you. It's the only way I can help you." And she did, mostly.

That night she suffered a terrible dream which became her norm in the last three years. The man's long, white hair trailed down her body as he pinned her to the bed. He leaned in—She sat upright in her bed and gripped her fingers in her blond hair. Her heart rate slowed, and her breathing became even. She laid down again under the red and black bedspread. Something crinkled when her head hit her black pillow. She sat up to examine it. A sheet of rough card stock. On it, a beautifully and expertly sketched drawing of a butterfly. Not too dissimilar to the butterfly she drew today, but this wasn't her work. It was too good. Although, this looked like a page from her sketchbook.

She bolted out of the bed. Not mine. When her bandaged foot touched the floor, she started. What the fuck? It crunched on another piece of sketch paper. She turned on her lamp. Sketches carpeted her room. Some contained butterflies in different poses of flight. But some posed pictures of her. She lifted the one underfoot. In the picture she laid on her front lawn, curled in the fetal position. She wore the exact same clothes she wore earlier that night with Xelan. Shakily, she covered her mouth with her hand. Tears poured in streams down her cheeks. Wake up! Please wake up! She lifted another sketch. The same scene, but with Xelan's outstretched arms before he helped her. She picked up another. Not the same scenery, but she laid in the same position. In bed. Asleep. Wearing the same pajamas she wore right now. She dropped all the sketches and rushed to her bed. She laid down and pulled the covers over her head. She felt her body starting to pull into its familiar safety position. She jumped out of bed and bolted to her tiny en suite. She evacuated the contents of her stomach into the toilet.

"Never. Again," she said with conviction to no one.

She padded back to the room. First, she checked the windows, and made sure they were locked. But of course they were. She locked the door to her room. She searched her desktop and drawers for any sign of her sketchbook. Not there. Not in her backpack either. Missing. Stolen. She began picking up each sketch, trying hard not to look at them: butterflies, fetal position outside, fetal position in a nightmare sleep. But only one caught her eye. The one with the message scribbled on it. No, not a message. Initials: "T.A.O." In the sketch, she sat at the lunch table with Justin. Everyone in The Overachievers group ate and appeared to carry on merrily. But Sagan sat straight up. Her eyes shaded in such a way that it carried a vacant look. Her lips drawn in a stark, thin line. She stared into nothing. This was her disassociating. She looked damned sad doing it, too.

"Never. Again."

"Butterflies," Sagan let out in a breathy whisper. "They're butterflies." He meant all the gore and grotesque show of it as a message to her.

Rayne spun Sagan to face her. "Stay with me." The familiar coping mechanism kicked in. She avoided coming this close to an episode in the last six months. Not since Rayne literally kicked Justin out of the picture.

Rayne's voice came to her steady and soothing, "You will fight him. And you will kill him, Tao."

Sagan snapped back to herself. She searched Rayne's face. "How?"

"By being a total badass," Rayne replied

Sagan's lips almost twitched into a smile. Then, she made out something through the smoke over Rayne's shoulder. Rayne noticed her focus shifted and turned. Written across the lockers, in a thick, sticky coat of blood, the Latin words, "Pretiosum Cruor." The rest of the group examined the words with her. The mantra, the chant, the symbol.

"We still have to check for a pulse on every single one of them," Tameka announced. "If there are any survivors, we have to help."

Rayne whirled to look at her, broken out of her reverie. "You're right. Check all of them."

"Oh, my nightmares can be spared that," John said.

"If you were one of them, you would want someone to check you," Nikki countered.

John shook his head. His frightened chocolate brown eyes grew wide. "The only thing I'd want if I were one of them is for someone to put me out of my misery."

Andrew said, "Enough. Check them and be quiet as you do it. We're not in friendly territory."

John and Kyle obeyed, checking vitals of the hopefully unconscious high school populace. They returned shaking their heads, concern strained in their eyes.

"I found one!" Nikki whisper-shouted. Tameka rushed over with the medical supplies bag. Sagan and Rayne followed suit. Andrew and Kyle stayed alert, searching through the smoke for signs of a trap.

A young woman laid in a pool of blood. One arm snapped at the elbow and wrenched at a horrible angle. The other cradled something close to her chest. Tameka started fashioning together a sling. "Can you hear me?" Tameka asked her.

Nikki and John looked away to join Kyle and Andrew on their watch. The rest went along with the pretense. Tameka broke the silence, "She's saying something."

Sagan knelt and leaned closer. "What?"

Tameka laid her ear against the girl's mouth. When she sat back up her face went from the color of twilight to a shade of sallow.

"What is it?" Rayne pushed. Tameka shook her head.

Sagan leaned closer. The girl said something. The same thing repeatedly. Her eyes blown wide, and her skin took on a gray cast. But she repeated the cycle.

"I will pluck your wings."

Sagan fell back and almost bumped into another body. Her heart tried to beat out of her throat. Her skin crawled and beaded with sweat. She took deep, gasping breaths, but almost vomited from the smell of the surrounding slaughter.

The horror kept coming. Rayne pulled the bound notebook from the girl's arms. She opened it with her face scrunched in a frown. As she flipped it wide open, page after page filled with sketches of Sagan in one pose or another. Sometimes she slept. In one picture she ate dinner with her parents. Another picture captured her in a moment not meant for anyone's eyes when she thought she laid alone on her bed. Then came the very last picture. She smiled, wearing a scarlet-red top and a short black skirt with knee-high boots and stiletto heels. Chin-length, blond hair styled to fluff her layers. Her messenger bag hung off one shoulder. The object of her attention, on the far side of the page, Rayne admonishing Kyle, and the riot gate even further beyond that. The expertly drawn expression on her face held peace, even serenity. The initials "T.A.O." placed in the upper right corner. Just beneath that, a "K" drawn in calligraphy.

Kyle gaped at the pad. "That was from this morning."

"No," Sagan groaned.

Rayne dropped the sketchbook and rushed to her. "We won't let him do this to you, do you hear me? Never. Again."

Sagan snapped her attention to Rayne, "Never again?"

"The only time I'll will let him near you is so you can kick his ass."

"And even then you won't be alone," Kyle added.

Tameka finished fashioning the girl's arm in a sling and bandaged the other wounds. "Ready."

They approached the girl, carefully. Andrew started, his voice gentle, "What's your name?" The girl's eyes were still open too wide, and she refused to meet his gaze. She kept repeating the line over and over. He asked, "Anyone got a jacket?"

Tameka shrugged out of hers. Crusted with Icarean blood, but it was better than nothing. Andrew wrapped it around the girl. "I think she's in shock or whatever comes after shock."

"We can't leave her here," Nikki whispered.

"You may well have to," an unfamiliar voice hissed from down the hall.

Sagan's eyes darted around, frantically as she scanned the space for the man behind the voice. Out of the classroom, a few lockers down from the message, came an Icarus with long blond hair, a long, braided beard, and dark brown eyes. He was the first Icarus they saw under six feet, but his shoulders and chest expanded much wider than the others. He carried a sturdy wooden shield in one hand, and a standard heavy mace in the other. Sagan and the rest of the crew stood and gathered their weapons. Tameka stayed with the injured girl, cradling her in her lap.

"It's rude to eavesdrop," Andrew said to the Viking.

The stout Icarus pointed the mace at Tameka's ward. "She delivered the message to the harlot. We have no further use of her."

"I don't understand. Why haven't you drank any blood?" Andrew asked. His tone intrigued, but not surprised.

Sagan diverted her attention to Andrew for a split second. What was he going on about? The bodies were drained of blood. She spared a glance at Rayne, who shared her confusion.

"Sagan! Look out!" Andrew shouted.

While distracted, the Icarus charged at her. She heard the others cry and shout in warning, but she never stood a chance. She caught the brunt of the charge, and her back slammed against the lockers behind her. All the air rushed out of her in one big swoosh. She kept her fingers around her knife. "Come now, girlie. We have places to be," said the Viking as he pulled her over his shoulder. He recovered his mace and shield.

Oh, hell no. She knew where he was taking her, and she was having none of it. Just as she heard Rayne charge him, Sagan stabbed her knife into the mountainous man's backside. He grunted, but carried on. "What the fuck!" Sagan shouted.

Rayne ran up and attempted to stab him right in the chest. He blocked with his shield and swung with his mace. All the while he sidestepped around the display of bodies. He took great pains to move further down the hall toward the cafeteria without striking her friends.

Andrew attacked next. He swung a chair leg in range. The behemoth blocked with a swing of his mace and bared his fangs. This left an opening for Kyle to hit him in the groin with a wooden shelf, hard. The beast doubled over with a groan and a hiss. Before he recovered, Sagan hopped off his shoulders. She ran into Rayne's arms, and they pulled back from mini-Thor's sweeping range. Andrew and Kyle led the front line.

"Why haven't you fed?" Andrew asked again. His voice grew more firm.

The Icarus snarled at him. He chucked his shield and reached behind him. His long arms bent and creaked as he pawed at the knife in his back. He finally gripped it and with a long, slow, wet suction removed it from him. He dropped it next to his shield. What was this guy like with less weight? She glanced at Rayne, whom she feared realized at the same time. Was he that fucking dangerous?

After all that buildup, he shrugged his massive shoulders. "Them's the orders."

"But the bodies ... ?" Andrew asked.

"For the masters only," he answered. He obliged their questions too well.

Something was wrong. Before Sagan worked that out, her brain stuttered over exactly what he said. If only the masters could eat, then all these bodies ... were the victims of two, maybe three Icari at most. All that blood to satisfy the hunger of a few.

WOOSH! Andrew flew over her head.

"Shit!" Kyle shouted.

Tameka screamed.

"Get to him!" Nikki cried. She and John ran to Andrew's side.

Tameka asked the injured girl to follow. Sagan turned back to see Rayne and Kyle facing off with deceptive mini-Thor. A blunt, iron sphere dangled by a chain from his mace. Fuck, they needed better weapons. Behind her, Andrew sputtered, so at least he was still breathing.

"Am not to hurt the blond siren or the brunette virgin, but they didn't specify about the rest of you," the bully announced.

"Fuck you, man, I'm tired—" Kyle started. He flipped off the behemoth.

"We've got this," Rayne interrupted him. Her voice stern.

Kyle's face fell sad and confused. Sagan touched his shoulder, and he lowered his arm. "Check on Andrew, Devis." She kissed his cheek for his valiant attempt at chivalry.

At the mention of his ancestral name, the hard lines of confusion softened on his face. "Aye, aye, Cap'n." He handed her the board as he walked behind her toward the wheezing sounds. She gave her attention back to the strangely accommodating troll.

"Aye, so are you ready now?" He smiled broad enough to expose his sharp teeth.

Rayne answered by rushing into chain range. Sagan followed soon after. Before he got the chance to swing the mace, Rayne slid on the congealing pools of blood beneath him. She slid right between his legs. As he prepared a defense, Sagan took advantage of the time by slapping him in the face with the slab of wood. He staggered back.

"Arrrgh!!!" he roared. The lines of his face went drawn with rage. His eyes shone feral, his teeth bared, and his beard became full of foam from his ravenous growling. Right as he wound up for another swing, his face contorted into a frightening grimace. The sound he let out came closer to an animal—sharp and coarse. He thrashed, and Sagan leapt back out of range.

"You bitches!" He snarled as his chest burst open. A feral scream rang from behind him. The knife made some progress tunneling through the immense Icarus' brain, but it slowed.

"Rayne!" she cried. She tried to dart behind the mountain. He swung out with his mace, careful not to strike her even as he fell. "HELP!" Sagan screamed.

Tameka and John stayed with Andrew. Nikki and Kyle rushed over to help push the beast. Rayne pushed with both arms into the knife and one leg onto his back. Nikki, Kyle, and Sagan ran around to help force him to topple the rest of the way over. The monster cursed the whole way. Once the Icarus fell on the ground, Nikki and Kyle climbed onto his back. They started stabbing over and over again around and through Rayne's knife. They pulverized his brain until Sagan confirmed he no longer made any noise, and his body laid still.

"He's gone," she announced.

Breathing heavily from the exertion, the four of them stood around his corpse as if waiting for him to rise again.

Tameka cried out, "You guys!" And broke their trance.

Andrew sat up. No blood on his shirt, but blood stained the corners of his mouth. "I'm all right," he assured. And he almost lasted a whole convincing second until he started a coughing fit that resulted in more crimson on the lower half of his face.

Rayne hurried over to him. "You can't go any further."

He sucked in a ragged breath and let out a moist cough before answering, "Yes." Deep guzzling breath. "I can," barely audible whisper.

Tameka beseeched Rayne with her eyes. Rayne growled and reached for his shirt. When she went to lift it, he pushed her away. "No. What are you doing?"

"I can't let you come with us until I wrap your ribs," she answered. "And you remember what happened the last time we trained with Xelan and a mace? Same thing. So we're doing this."

He stopped fighting, and Sagan turned away. Don't wanna see those bruises. Not on her friend. Judging by how quiet it got, she took a guess on how bad he looked. Instead, she locked eyes with the victimized student.

"Hi," she said. At some point during the fight, the girl stopped repeating the words. She sat up, cradling her sling. Sagan felt for her, on a battlefield with a damaged arm. "Can you talk?" The girl seemed less in shock, but not much better than any of them. No answer, but her expression came across as less empty. "Can you make it to the football field on your own?"

Now the girl looked at Sagan.

"The rest of the survivors are there. You'll be safe as long as the sun is out." No response. Sagan got closer to her, careful not to touch her. "The man who did this to you is a monster. And guess, what? We're going to kill him. I'll carve his brain out." The girl met her eyes. The others started watching once Andrew pulled his shirt over his bandaged chest. "But we can't do that until we know that you're safe."

"None of us will ever be safe again," the girl whispered.

"Maybe not while he's alive, but he's not gonna survive today," Sagan vowed.

Rayne said a small prayer to whoever was up there that nothing waited around the corner. She, Andrew, and Kyle popped their heads around. Fuck. An Icarus, almost as tall as the door, paced like a good little guard in front of the "Media Center." Not just any guard. Even in the glow of the red lights they saw he wore black leather: coat, pants, gloves with the fingers cut out, and boots. His straight, white hair flowed down to his waist looking ever-the-part of a stereotypical Anime villain. Double fuck. He screamed elevated, badass motherfucker where the prior Icarean fighters whimpered run-of-the-mill soldier in comparison.

Nikki whispered, "Think we can slip past him into the lab hall?"

Kyle shrugged. "Yeah, but we can't be sure if there's more there either."

Rayne nodded. "We'll just have to take that chance, then. That's Korac, second-in-command to Nox. We'd better avoid him. He's older than the others and a vicious son of a bitch."

They returned to the others, and she took great caution in breaking the news to Sagan. "Korac is standing right in front of the library." Sagan disguised her panic well, but not enough to hide it from Rayne. "He's armed. Two weapons, but I don't know what they are. We can't fight him with these." She shook her last two-inch knife for emphasis. "We'll have to get by him to reach the Med Lab hallway." She spared a glance at the rescued survivor with her arm in a sling. "But it can be done."

"Okay, so we'll sneak into the next hallway, take out that monster in there, and hope like hell Krack or Borak or whatever his name is doesn't catch us?" John asked. He pointed and waved emphatically as he animated the plan.

Sagan smiled as she said, "To put it simply, smart ass, yes."

He shrugged. "Just seeing if we're on the same page here. Oh, and sorry, Kyle. I didn't mean to come for your throne."

Sagan laughed, and Kyle, resident smart ass, added, "Damn straight. Try not to forget it."

Andrew muttered to the ceiling, "We're all gonna die."

Rayne took a deep breath. "Okay. When I count to three, Tameka and I will run for the next hallway. Andrew will go last with Kyle to be sure everyone gets there safely." She paused, inched a little forward. "One ... Two."

"Wait, wait," Nikki said. "Do we go on three or after three?"

Tameka rolled her eyes, and Rayne whispered, "Three." She and Tameka ran alongside the wall, slipping around the corner. Rayne glanced around the walls on either side. Korac took a drag on his cigarette as he observed a "Stamp-Out-Smoking" poster. He blew a smoke ring at it. Rayne tried to roll her eyes but she was too full of adrenaline. She signaled for John and Sagan to follow next. Andrew and Kyle last.

As Andrew slipped into the hall he muttered, "Man, I could really use one of those."

John said, "Oh, yea? Why don't you go ask him for one?" He and Andrew glared at one another. Was there tension there?

"Fuck off!" Nikki snapped. A reprimand that intimidating coming from such a tiny person caught everyone off guard. "Big picture, guys."

While they made it to the Med Lab hallway, they needed to clear one more corner before they reached the labs. The exit just beyond made this a prime spot for a guard post. Using the same method as before, Rayne, Andrew, and Kyle popped their heads around the corner expecting to find a guard. Instead, they found the decapitated body of another cloaked Icarean soldier. His head laid farther down the corridor. The group approached slowly and stepped around him with more caution than necessary. He was dead. Very, very dead.

"What do you think killed it?" John asked.

"The decapitation, prolly," Kyle condescended.

Tameka threw her hands up in the air. "Oh, my God! Can someone please get a six-inch ruler so we can get this measuring contest out of the way already?"

Kyle's response died in his throat as Andrew grabbed his shirtsleeve. "C'mon."

They headed for the door to M2. Rayne and Kyle attended fourth period, Medical Science III, in the lab.

"AHH!!!!"

The door lunged open, and someone swung at them in a blind rage, screaming. Andrew caught him and pinned him flat against the wall. "Human. We're human," Andrew repeated.

"Don't hurt him, Andrew," Nikki scolded.

He stopped struggling, and Andrew let him go slowly. He stepped back from the wall, holding the leg from one of the lab tables.

"Pablo?" Kyle asked.

"Man, I don't know what's going on, but I'm happy to see you."

Rayne asked, "Pablo, what happened?"

He answered a little breathlessly, "I don't know, man. I just know we were in class and we heard a noise like a car dragging both bumpers down the street. It was real loud. Like it was amplified, you know? Then out of nowhere someone breaks the windows in the room, and everyone ran. It was crazy, man. Some of us stayed in here. We were hiding. Lynn was in the other lab. She ran at some real freaky dude with a table leg and took his head off with it. I've never seen anything like it. His head…the mouth was still moving." He grimaced, and a fine tremor shook his hands.

Rayne could kiss Xelan right now. Without his training, she'd either end up like Pablo or like one of the students in the hall. "Where's Lynn?" she asked. She placed her hands on his shoulders to steady him.

Pablo glanced back at the door with his deep brown eyes. "We're all hiding in there."

Medical Science Lab 2 comprised the space of three regular classrooms. Regular desks lined in rows at the front, closest to the marker board. Chunky black lab tables sat in the middle of the room. The last half of the room contained stainless steel gurneys. Cabinets, uppers and lowers lined all the wall space and hugged the incinerator. It set in the room's left wall with a large glass door, resembling a massive microwave.

Several unfamiliar underclassmen huddled in the far corner of the room. They overturned the clunky lab tables to create a useless barrier around them. Pointless…but if it made them feel better…At best it provided a false sense of security. And who couldn't do with some security right now?

One student asked, "What's going on?"

Kyle said, "The apocalypse."

"Kyle!" Nikki admonished. She turned to the students. "We'll get you to safety."

"Check everyone. Make sure no one's hurt," Andrew commanded more than suggested. "Kyle, get to your stash."

Sagan nodded toward them. "They look more like they're in shock than in pain."

Rayne walked around the room, searching, shuffling debris about. Kyle barreled by her and climbed up onto one of the lab tables. She peered in the incinerator's glass front that held glaring light like a mirror. So, this was what mid-battle Rayne looked like. Her reflection should have startled her, instead it filled her with a strange sense of sorrow. No real marks yet, just a weight that made her eyes seem heavy and dark. She didn't ask for this. She adjusted her hair tie.

Sagan called from the center of the room. "Okay. You got it? You need a hand?" Kyle opened a panel in the ceiling and thumped his hand around inside. "Got it," he said. He retrieved a leather messenger bag.

Nikki called, "Everyone here is fine. Just scared."

A familiar voice said, "I'm not scared."

Rayne turned and let the relief show in her smile. "Lynn." "I killed the vampire-thing." She stated with a bit of defiance. "These idiots just screamed and ran for cover." She pointed at the terrorized group.

"Hey!" One protested.

Rayne shook her head. She couldn't think of what to say. So, Tameka said it, as always, "It's not their fault. Not everyone's been taking survival training since they were seven, Lynn."

Andrew nodded. "We need someone to take them to the football field where the rest are. Do not leave the campus." He nodded toward their charge, cradling her ruined arm to her chest. "Take her."

The bunch of huddled people stood in unison. "We can go alone," the pissed off one offered.

Lynn sighed. "Then go. It's not like all your crying is fucking helping, anyway."

Kyle hopped off the table. He pointed to the back lot, and said, "Just get out of here and go straight to the field."

They went to leave. The ballsier one walked up to Lynn. Tameka and Rayne leaned forward just in case. He stared in Lynn's eyes for one or two heartbeats and then flipped her off. The girls grabbed Lynn on either side. "Whoa ... no need for this."

The dude held it the whole way out the door.

Lynn shrugged. "C'mon! Get off! I get it. Plenty of people dead, no sense in me adding to the body count."

The girls let go, but hesitated at her side.

Rayne eyed her for another second and then announced, "We need two volunteers to stay here and take care of the people we send this way. There are plenty of supplies. Once they're all bandaged up and checked out, send them out to the back of the school. The rest will go with me to find Nox. So who wants to stay?"

Glances exchanged around the room. Lynn and Pablo spoke up. "I guess we could take care of this place," Lynn said.

"We've been here for nearly two hours anyway," Pablo added.

Tameka raised an eyebrow. "With your idea of compassion, are you sure?"

Lynn shrugged. "Kyle was right. It's not really their fault. They don't know how to fight. Especially something like vampires."

Andrew said, "We'll let's get one thing straight. They're not technically vampires."

"They're aliens," John joined in. He looked so happy to be on the knowing side.

Lynn glanced at a few of the crew before saying, "Okay. Aliens. For real?"

Pablo said, "They don't look like E.T., man."

"And why do they drink blood?" Lynn pointed out.

"Cause it tastes good," Kyle answered. His voice matter-of-fact.

Everyone in the room stopped and slowly turned to look at him.

He frowned and shrugged in defense. "What?! Like you don't like a rare steak now and then?"

Lynn turned back to the group, slow and hesitant. Her eyes narrowed and her voice strained as she said, "Okay ... I know taking their heads off kills them, but is there another way?"

Nikki said, "The heart is in their skull, and the brain in their chest. Switched from ours."

"Riiiight," Pablo said.

Andrew said, "Decapitation is your best bet. It's this whole technology thing. Some higher classed warriors might regenerate. Severing their head or puncturing their skulls stops the heart."

"Puncturing the brain has worked on two so far. So go for the very center of the chest," Sagan finished.

Pablo mouthed to himself while pointing at his skull and his chest.

Lynn patted him on the back. "Don't worry. I got it."

"We'll explain more once this is over," Rayne said. "Kyle, what have you got for us?"

"A survival manual. Three six-inch knives. I call dibs on this one." He stored one in his cargo pocket. "Two four-inch knives, duct tape, some chain . . ." Rayne and Tameka exchanged glances. " . . .super glue, and a ball-peen hammer." He laid the arsenal out on a table.

"Dude," Andrew said.

Kyle frowned. "What?!"

Rayne rolled with it. "We need to get going. Start divvying that shit up. I'm sure we can't get anyone here without the Icari noticing. You'll have to do some defending. Think you two can handle that?"

"Yeah," Lynn said.

Rayne caught Pablo staring at Lynn when she spoke or glanced away from him. His eyes kinda sparkled, and a little smile tugged at his lips.

"Pablo?" Rayne broke his focus.

He shrugged. Everyone had a pretty good idea of who would do the fighting, and they were pretty sure it wasn't Pablo.

"The taps are still working so you'll have water to clean wounds. If there have been no victims for thirty minutes, I want you to go to the football field." Rayne held up a bandaged hand to stop their protest. "After they're gone, there won't be any reason to stay. We'll be fine." Everyone knew it was a lie, but a good one.

She headed for the door, and the others followed. She turned back one last time to add, "We've had all of our A&P and medical biology classes together. I know you can do this. I'm sure if you go through the cabinets, you'll find bandages and antibacterial stuff. We'll keep what we have for on-the-go triage. Take care." She walked out without a backwards glance.

SIX

When You Check Vermin For Rabies
You Remove The Head

"**WHAT THE FUCK?**" Rayne halted outside the door to M2.

"What is it?" Tameka asked. She strained to see around Sagan, who also stopped short and stared at something on the ground.

Tameka squeezed through them. A black sign laid flat on the dirty, white linoleum tiles. "That wasn't there when we came through," she stated.

Red letters across the sign, "Stamp Out Smoking."

Sagan hissed, "He knows."

John asked, "Did that Sephiroth looking son of a bitch really just walk right up to our rebel base and leave this here for us to find it?!"

"He's messing with us," Andrew stated. "Focus on the priorities. Remember?"

"Sagan, are you good?" Rayne asked.

Tameka felt a little left out. Why was Rayne so worried about Sagan every time Korac came up? Did something happen?

Sagan gave a weak smile and said, "I'm fine. We can do this."

Rayne squeezed her hand and charged ahead. Tameka and the rest followed Rayne down the short hallway away from the medical science labs. Tameka watched Kyle claim his spot beside his master like a good dog and ask, "Do we have a plan?"

Without turning, Rayne answered, "Yes. We go to the cafeteria and we kill them."

"Good plan," John muttered to Nikki some feet behind.

Nikki asked, "You got a better one?"

Tameka noticed Rayne assumed the leadership role over the whole group. Not that she minded. Only ... Tameka knew what the others seemed to forget: Rayne was just a teen as much as the rest of them. Sure, Xelan trained some of them into more effective fighters, but a full-scale invasion? They weren't equipped to handle this. Not really.

Passing the decapitated Icarus' corpse, Tameka noticed something gleaming beneath the black robes. Rayne knelt beside him. She retrieved the large weapon from a sheath. A fucking doubleedged sword. Naw, seriously? A silver and onyx emblem decorated the pommel in the shape of a heart with a vined dagger piercing its center. The words "Pretiosum Cruor" circled around it.

John asked, "What the hell is that supposed to mean? 'Pretiosum Cruor?' It's there." He pointed to the sword. "In blood on the walls. Considering how good they are with 'body art' I'm afraid where it'll show up next."

Sagan winced at "body art."

"It's symbolic—" Andrew started.

"Hey ... I think this should be my part of the story to tell, don't you?" Kyle asked.

Tameka clucked her tongue. "Here we go."

"Ahem. My ancestor, a Progeny, forged a great device to help seal the Icari back into Cinder." He pointed to the pommel. "That's it. Stands for 'Precious Blood.'"

"How does it work?" Nikki asked.

"Well ... I don't know," Kyle answered.

Tameka prayed for the strength to resist the urge to slap him upside his head.

Andrew groaned.

She turned to Rayne when she said, "We aren't sure how the first wave used it, exactly. But Nox perverted the symbolism behind it. And now they paint it everywhere like an upside-down cross or a pentagram."

She stared hard at the sword. Was Rayne about to keep it? She held it out in front of her, assessing it. In their training, Xelan taught them to appreciate balanced weapons. Recently sharpened and in all its simplicity, it made for a magnificent weapon. Unsure why, Tameka didn't want Rayne to keep it. Not until she gave a real smile for the first time since the fight started. Well, she could have it, then. Of course it would take a sword to make Rayne happy.

The respite passed. A shadow of hopelessness or pain cast in Rayne's eyes.

Tameka's best friend angled her head, listening and glanced back at the others. "Let's go." She left without seeing if they followed. Much to Tameka's horror, Rayne took the corner without checking to see if Korac still stood in front of the Media Center.

"What the fuck, Rayne?" Tameka shouted. She stomped after her. Of all the fucking crazy ass white girl things she could do. Tameka, with the unit right behind her, turned the corner. "Oh, shit."

Half a dozen of the cloaked soldiers spanned the hallway. Someone far more threatening than her personal guard captained the intimidating blockade. Long legs, softly rounded hips, a tiny waist, and a size-challenged chest made up her tall, athletic frame. The mass of blond curls around her face and shoulders emphasized the deep blue of her eyes. Her skin the same complexion as the Icari. She smiled. Tameka wanted to back-hand her. Large, curved canines protruded. Bitch might hurt herself with those if someone pounded her face into a locker or a wall.

Colita bowed in a mock curtsy. "Celindria, Merit, and The Afflicted One." She greeted the three girls in front as she scanned the approaching victims.

"So she's real?" Kyle asked. Tameka glanced at him. His face grew flush, and his eyes found the linoleum real interesting.

Rayne scoffed, "Are you fucking kidding me?!"

"What?! It was a dream!" he cried.

Andrew and John also looked elsewhere. Rayne said, "And you two?" When their skin reddened, her jaw gaped open.

Tameka whistled. "She's been busy."

John shrugged, casually. Andrew answered in a defensive tone, "She's hot!"

Colita gasped in mock surprise. "Andrius. My, my. We were informed that you weren't to be here. I suppose we were mislead." At that, Colita glanced over her shoulder. The other soldiers took a step away from one with hair the color of mahogany and skin the deep color of rust.

"Mistress, there was no way I could know—" he uttered in apology.

She cut him off with a sharp, "SILENCE!" Her voice echoed off the walls in one harsh hiss. She treated everyone as play-things.

{NEAR 6,000 BCE}

"She lies with the serpent. You cannot trust her!" Merit shouted in vain.

"My own confidant? That's nonsense. She can help us. She can get closer to Nox than anyone," Xelan argued for the thirtieth time.

Merit struggled to see his side. In all their strategy and planning, she never accounted for Xelan's sentimental nature. She spoke in a softer voice this time, "If anyone would have an ulterior motive for betraying the human species, it would be her. She collects specimens like they were art and objectifies the male body as a possession. You confessed to me once that she planned a breeding program involving our strongest warriors for her own personal guard."

"That was before I convinced her it was wrong," Xelan countered.

Merit frowned. "She already claimed her bulls for the process."

"That was speculation—" He started again.

"You two argue like a couple well into their old age," Celindria interrupted from her perch by the window. "Always using words when you desire to use other things."

Xelan's mouth tried to drop open to the floor. Merit smiled, appreciating Celindria's insight. "There we have it. And I thought you were the genius." She jabbed Xelan in the chest.

"I-I-I do not understand," he stammered.

"Allow me to clarify it for you," Celindria began. "Merit has loved you for decades. You mistook her advances for the pawing of a youngling, all the while you entertained the terrifying affections of Colita. Which may no doubt influence her distrust of the siren, but I agree with Merit. Colita is not to be trusted." She approached Xelan and placed a hand on his shoulder. "Please, old friend. Do not divulge anymore of our plans to her. I fear the pain it will wrought." She placed her free hand on Merit's shoulder. "And if you can find the time, work this out between you and our love here. It takes a toll on the rest of us."

"She never really deserved your affections, anyway," Merit added.

{INVASION DAY 2006}

Tameka wanted to take point on this one. She called, "Colita."

Colita grinned in delight at the sound of her name. It gave her a sort of satisfaction that visibly confused John and Nikki. She stamped her foot and sighed. "I was told to deliver you a message. Korac awaits for you in the cafeteria." The bitch rolled her eyes. "Not that you'll make it there. You bleeding hearts aren't a threat to me." Her laughter tinkered like a bell.

"You should worry, Colita," Tameka countered. "You know not all our hearts bleed so easily."

Colita's laughter halted so abruptly it made the silence in its wake painful. "There are no victims, just unwilling participants." She smiled that twisted grin again. The malice in it turned her otherwise angelic face ugly.

Tameka barked out a laugh, her head thrown back, and her curls bounced. She asked, "But aren't you his victim, Colita? Don't you remain his 'unwilling participant' even now? You will always play as your Master's victim for the rest of eternity."

Colita's sky-blue eyes narrowed into vertical slits. Her hands tightened into fists. Her nails grew to a disturbing length. Her anger radiated from her like heat off a fire. Her voice came in layers, "I don't care what the Master says; I'll kill you myself for that, Merit."

"Then stop talking, bitch, and let's see you try," Tameka snarled.

Colita stiffened, her body went still, silent. Not a single movement. Nothing that indicated someone lived inside. Anybody home? The men behind her fell just as still.

"What the fuck's going on?" Kyle asked.

Sagan came up to flank Rayne and Tameka. Andrew waved for John and Nikki to complete the line. The air thickened; little sparks nibbled along the skin. Someone gasped from the effort it took to breathe. Tameka stood quiet, firm, while the others looked around for the cause, swaying with the effort to remain still. Each of their bodies strained as if fighting to step forward. Parlor tricks.

As those behind her took an involuntary step toward the barrier of Icari, Tameka held her breath. Her emerald eyes frozen, unblinking. Both women stood as still as stone while the tension mounted and thickened the air. Without taking a single step, Colita appeared in front of Tameka. She lashed out with the back of her hand. Tameka anticipated the move, much to Colita's frustration. With Tameka taking only one step back, Colita stumbled forward, allowing Tameka to use Colita's momentum against her. She wound her bronze hand in Colita's fair hair, holding her steady as she drove her knee into her stomach. Colita choked and shrieked with rage. Before Colita recovered, Tameka raised Colita's head fast enough to snap a human neck. She ran Colita over to a cement wall and then slammed her headfirst into it. Tameka heard a dull cracking sound and dropped Colita to the floor.

"Tameka?" Sagan asked. Her voice shook.

Everyone stopped pressing forward. Colita straightened and faced them. Her nose oozed a bright-blue waterfall. Her eyes, and the bridge of her nose already rocked a striking, purple bruise. That's right, bitch.

Far too soon, Colita's breathing improved. A force emanated from her, keeping the air as thick as before.

"How many fucking times do I have to ask what's going on?" Kyle asked, again.

"Apparently two," John answered.

Colita focused on her injury. Her eyes burned with rage and smoldered the blue to frosted stone. What was she about to do?

A moment of thick silence and a thread of anticipation lingered. Then came an odd sound, subtle at first until louder it became. The sound of someone chewing popcorn; crunching and cracking all at once. It came from Colita's nose. The bleeding ceased. The color of her nose faded into lighter shades of green, then yellow; the color of bad bruising. After the blow, her nose indented and swelled. Now the cartilage lifted, filled back into place with the others. Blood receded from the wound; the appearance of swelling faded with it. Had she been human, she would be dead. More's the pity.

"Instant plastic surgery ... nice. Where did you learn that?" Tameka asked, impressed.

"The regenerative upgrades Xelan warned us about." Andrew gaped.

"How the fuck are we supposed to fight that?" Kyle asked, giving Andrew his full attention.

"Let's start with not admitting aloud that you don't know how," Rayne admonished him. She never took her eyes off Colita.

When her nose corrected itself back into its perfectly, symmetrical shape, she wiped away the smear of blue on her face. Stolen blood, no doubt. She smiled with that cold rage in her narrowed eyes. "For this, I'll bury you all in a mass grave under the rubble of this school. But first, you will repay the lost blood of my soldiers." She made a gesture and the six Icari marched forward. They discarded the black cloaks, revealing similar monochrome uniforms. Each one modeled after a different time and place, one exotic warrior after the next. The uniforms shone armor over black tunics and laced slacks. From ancient Chinese to Norwegian, each Icari distinguished themselves with their heritage.

"Someone has a fetish," Tameka accused.

Rayne took a breath. Tameka could practically see her calculating the odds. "Nikki, John, and Kyle?"

"Yea?" Kyle answered.

"What?" Nikki asked.

John just gave an attentive face.

Rayne issued orders, "You take the three on the right. Sagan, Andrew, and I? The three on the left."

"What about me?" Tameka asked. Please let her kill Colita. Please let her kill Colita.

"You get Ms. Facelift," she replied with a bitter smile for Colita. She responded with a snap of her sizable teeth.

"Yes, ma'am!" Tameka's grin of anticipation made her freckles sparkle and showed her bright white teeth between her full lips.

The good guys took one collective step forward. The invading horde took a step back. Colita, took two, so she stood behind a barrier of muscle. Everyone gripped their knives and stakes tight. Rayne held her sword firm at her side, eyes scanning the blank expressions.

Tameka stared at it and broke the silence, "Do you mind if we trade for this fight?" She waved her four-inch knife.

Rayne smiled and handed her the sword, "But only if you promise to cut that bitch's head off."

"Fuck you!" Colita screamed from behind her meat wall.

A wordless scream from South Hall pierced the tension, bringing the anticipatory moment to an end. John, Nikki, and Kyle rushed their assigned set of alien soldiers. The Russian one grunted and dropped to his knees. So began the first real battle of Invasion Day.

Jessica opened the door exiting into the South Hall entrance closest to the cafeteria. She looked left. Then right. She skipped first period to practice piano in the soundproof booths in the auditorium green room. Routine thing. No big deal. Made it out in time for second period. She wouldn't miss Music Theory for the world. She wore a denim jumpsuit with a red blouse. Red stilettos and a few coordinated accessories completed the outfit. Classmates knew her throughout the school for her forward-thinking fashion.

As she took that first brave step into the hallway, her tall heels seemed louder in the bizarre silence. "Where is everybody?" she asked the empty space.

Between periods, the halls filled with students rushing to class. Prime time for skippers to slip in unnoticed. The emptiness grew more vast with each second. And what was that smell? Smoke?

She began walking toward the front entrance of the cafeteria when a metallic rattling startled her. The riot gate slammed down and missed her by a centimeter. *CLANG!* It fell with a metallic shambling sound that resonated through the empty hallway.

Through the gate, an unfamiliar, blond man stepped out of the main cafeteria's side entrance. He stood a whole foot taller than her. He stepped closer until he approached the metal barricade. All the leather he wore, which Jessica gave him kudos for such a daring look, made subtle protests with each movement. *Creak. Creak.*

Entranced, she dared not speak. Something was wrong. He took a drag on his cigarette, and it illuminated his handsome features for a brief moment. His eyes, as far as she saw, resembled a shade of gray close to white. They took on a metallic look with the flexes of darker gray in the iris. When he threw down the cigarette, the whole color looked silver.

His waist length hair swayed as he crushed the discarded butt with combat boots. The longer she stared, at him the more his hair looked silverish white, not blond. He came across as attractive in a self-endangering way, like petting a stray wolf just because it latched onto a limb or a throat.

The corners of his lips lifted in a cruel smile before he announced, "Dinner's here, boys."

From the side entrance of the cafeteria nearest Jessica, two men dressed in black robes opened the double doors on cue. She took an instinctive step backwards, her heart racing at the sight. Maybe she should have skipped school today, entirely. She felt a tear slide down her cheek, and her lips parted, releasing a whimpering sound. The two cloaked strangers took a few steps forward. Jessica hesitated only a moment longer before turning on her heels and starting on a full run. The two men stalked down the hallway, taking their time, with the blond man's laughter carrying down the hall.

"Run, run, little girl!" he shouted.

"STOP! Get away from me!!" she screamed as they continued their patient pursuit. Gotta get to the exit. It's right there. Just a few more steps. Gotta make it to the end of the hall. Gonna make it. Shit! Another imposing figure stepped out of the Technology hall. She stumbled to a halt only a few feet in front of him. Unfortunately, the force of her stopping after a full sprint strained her fragile stiletto heels under her enough that one heel broke off.

Her feet slipped beneath her, sending her falling forward. Her matching purse flew across the hall. Everything slowed down. She saw it all through a haze. The two strangers that chased her from the cafeteria stepped over her body and regarded the newcomer. A wave of despair crashed over her as she glimpsed the exit just beyond them, her only means of escape. She saw the sunlight from here. For the last time. She would die here.

Her two pursuers leapt on her back. Jessica's chest pounded like a frightened rabbit. At the slow shake of his head, she screamed one long, high-pitched shriek that echoed throughout the vacant building. She heard her voice echo back from every hallway. Couldn't anyone save her? Was everyone dead? Both men pressed against the length of her on either side.

"Please, please don't hurt me. I'll do whatever you want! Just please!" she cried through her sobs. Anything to make them stop.

The taller man from the Technology hall knelt close in front of her. He chuckled and gripped a handful of her hair, jerking her head up at a painful angle until she cried out. He wrenched her head back until she saw his face despite the pain. Their eyes locked, and she drifted.

Somewhere in the background, long fingernails tore into the tissue at her side, followed by piercing teeth. The second one on her left side reared back, fangs exposed. But all of it seemed far away. Even when he bit into the bare flesh of her neck, she only saw the stranger in front of her. Please, God, just make it stop.

As fast as the pain lanced through her, it suddenly vanished. Numb. Nothing. His dark eyes moved her. The smile on his face not cruel but majestic. Eternity passed in the presence of his greatness. His warmth pervaded, and a sense of security followed suit.

But then he laughed. A feverish wave of anguish and nausea washed over her as the bastard lifted his thrall from her while his monsters went to work. Jessica had time to blink before her mouth opened to shriek in agony. The vampire at her right tore into her side. The one on her left took his time. He came to wreak carnage from her. Humans ignored the frailty of their bodies in day-to-day life, but this day, at this school, the monsters made it paramount. He shoved his right hand into the large wound he tore with his teeth. He ignored her painful shrieking as he pushed through the tissue until he touched the bone of her left shoulder blade. Not too deep. The bone is very close to the surface. He tugged, and she clawed at the linoleum until her fingernails bled, spitting and screaming. He stretched the tendons until they snapped, and he almost tore the bone free. She reached her limit. No more. No more ...

"Please," she croaked, hoarsely. "Please ..."

They ravenously dismantled her body piece by piece. A finger on her left hand. Her right ear. She screamed through a throat scraped dry with her begging until nothing else came out. Her own blood pooled beneath her. When they began tearing at her left foot, she slipped away into unconsciousness. The last thing Jessica heard was the tall man's laughter.

Pablo closed a cabinet door as soft as possible to avoid detection. Lynn slammed one. They definitely had two different minds at this. Rayne and the rest left maybe thirty minutes ago. He and Lynn had been at it ever since. They opened every cabinet, scoured every drawer, and even busted the lock on the good stuff. Between them, they found suture kits, wound packs, and cast plaster.

"I know we promised Rayne that we'd help, but I'm kinda hoping we won't have to use this stuff," Pablo confessed.

He saw Lynn roll her eyes before she said, "First you won't fight, and now you're telling me you won't help the wounded?"

Pablo held up his hands, warding her off. "No! No. It's not that. I just hope no one shows up in bad enough shape to use it."

"They're probably all dead anyway," she said.

He blew the air out of his cheeks. "You know? I used to like you."

Lynn gave him the finger without looking away from her work. "Oh, fuck off."

"No, I mean it. You're funny in class but not like a bitch to the teacher or anything. You pretended to struggle with the material, and I'm not the only one who figured that out. But you lent me your pencil once, and that really meant something to me," he said.

Lynn busied herself with organizing the supplies on the exam tables in the back of the class. "I've lent that pencil out to plenty of people."

"Yea but that day you didn't have another one." His smile spread, assuming he made some headway. He licked his lips and made his way over to her. He went on, "You're a nice person, and I don't know why you hide it."

"Boy, everyone knows you flirt with anything in a skirt," she mused.

He approached her at the table. "But few know how observant I am." His smile softened as he leaned against her. "When you think no one's looking, you do the kindest things. You compliment and build up other girls. You help the teachers grade papers. And you'd do anything you can for anyone in choir. You're a modest saint." He brushed a braid away from her face. The softness in her brown eyes told him she finally listened. While it's true, he didn't want to die a virgin. He also really liked Lynn and wished he'd made his move before the world ended.

"Pablo," Lynn spoke his name in a husky whisper.

"Yes?"

"Lick your lips one more time," she requested.

Pablo, aware of how much the girls liked his full lips, gave her what she wanted very, very slowly. She smashed his face down to hers and pressed their lips together. Going with it, he wrapped his arms around her waist and pulled her tighter. Unexpectedly, she jumped up and wrapped her legs around his hips. Because of his undue lack of preparedness, they both tipped over and fell to the ground. She landed on top of him and didn't miss a beat.

Her nails raked along his skin as her warm hands snaked under his shirt and made their way up his abs. Thank God for his workout routine. The softness of her lips, and the sweet merciful give of them as he tested his tongue for permission to enter forced his hips to undulate under hers. Slow. Easy. Don't push.

She moaned, and all systems were go. His tongue explored the inside of her mouth; she unbuckled his pants. It all seemed to move a lot faster than he expected for his first time. Like both of them clawed desperately at each other for this fleeting moment of normalcy.

Voices from the hall made them both bolt upright. She rolled over to let him fix his shirt while she adjusted her hair. His heart pounded for so many reasons. She started to stand, but he put his hand in front of her. "I'll go check," he whispered.

He stood and tried hard not to take offense at the amused twinkle in her eyes. With caution, he approached the door. All the while the voices grew louder. Outside the pane of glass on the Med Lab door, gathered a whole crowd of people. Five of them students and two teachers. The teachers braced one limping student between them.

"Lynn, there's some hurt people out here," he called out to her.

He opened the door and stepped outside. "Hey, hey, we're human." His arms went up in the air showing empty, weaponless hands. Lynn followed his lead and raised her hands. He smiled sadly when he saw her braids remained tousled from their ministrations. If he ever got the opportunity to muss them up again, he wanted to do it right and alone with her spread out beneath—

"Hello, we have supplies in here," she offered the group. "Mr. Handler, you're all right?" she asked everyone's favorite history teacher.

"Yes, we have some hurt students here." He nodded to the girl between him and the other teacher Pablo failed to place.

"Bring them in here. We can help." Pablo waved them inside.

Pablo and Mr. Handler lifted the girl with the limp as gently as they could manage and placed her on the exam table Lynn set up. Lynn and two other students helped another onto the second table.

Mr. Handler searched around the classroom and at all the supplies they gathered. "Where's Ms. Washington?" he asked.

Pablo just shook his head. After that a sad hush fell over them. He grabbed a pair of scissors. The girl flinched and hissed. The panic stressed her injury and caused her to groan. "I won't hurt you. I just need to cut your jeans to see better."

She bit her lip and looked over to Mr. Handler for reassurance. He patted her hand. "He's going to do what he can to help."

Their high school ranked as a science magnet school divided into three categories: technological, environmental, and medical. Pablo and Lynn took the medical science route. As juniors they took Medical Science III, along with AP Biology, and Anatomy and Physiology. They weren't experts at first aid, but they got certified in most of it. They were more than qualified to handle the supplies in this room.

Well, except maybe setting a bone without an X-Ray, which this girl needed exactly that. After he pulled away the blood-soaked material of her jeans, Pablo just shook his head as if that might remove the image from his brain. Her tibia, the lower leg bone, broke the skin of her shin. He tried hard to see it for all the blood and tissue, but he thought maybe her fibula appeared broken beneath it. Monsters like these never settled for just flesh wounds. They gotta go for the bone.

He couldn't guess at what was going on outside of the school, but if Rayne and Sagan thought it was on a global scale, they were screwed. He worried that if any hospitals were still standing they'd be full and run out of supplies and doctors quick. He heard a sharp intake of breath come from Lynn. He looked across his table to her. Even though he faced her back, he saw the fine tremor of her shoulders. Everyone around her patient stared at the girl as if they wondered how she made it this far without dying. He grew determined to recover this for the victims' sakes.

He prepared the splints and readied the wraps. "I'm going to tell you the story about a girl named Rayne and how she and her friends will save the world." He set to work.

{AUGUST 2005}

"Stay down!" Xelan ordered for the third time. He walked away from Tameka and headed for the playground equipment. He left their bags by the rope tree. Her backyard opened onto an elementary school in the Meadowcliff subdivision. A great location for training, as it turned out. And making out. Though, Xelan stayed too focused to find out, much to her disappointment.

And to that end, Tameka wanted none of his orders tonight. Her biceps bunched as she threw herself into a kip up and charged at him. Her lungs burned, her head ached, and her bruises screamed. Why was she doing this again? Oh yea. Cause there was no chance she was ever staying down.

She never made a sound, but she came at him from upwind. Big fucking mistake. As soon as she came in range, he spun into a tornado crescent kick, and sent her crashing back into the dirt. She groaned and coughed out the little particles of earth.

"You are so damned stubborn! By far the most tenacious of the Progeny I've ever met." He stepped up to her and reached out his hand. "Why can't you just stay down?!" Above him, the stars winked and played in their games. It would be a shame to waste such a night.

She took his hand and twisted a foot around his ankle. She pulled, and he came tumbling down on top of her. Elbows and knees jabbed in uncomfortable parts of her body until he spread out above her in a little push up. Not well thought out, she admitted, but it got him down on the ground with her. She took his face in both her hands. "Look at the stars with me," she said. There. An innocent request.

"Of all the things for you to do, and of all the things for you to say right now ..." He broke into a grin. She smiled in return. "Fine. Ten minutes, then I'm heading to our fearless leader's house." He rolled over beside her. Not an improvement, but at least she had him for a little while.

"It's not like she sleeps anyway," she said.

He grumped, but his eyes gazed into the night. "There are better views. The city's too bright. One day I'll show you a better night sky." He turned to her with a gorgeous, genuine smile. Her breath left her. Future plans. With Xelan. The smile twisted just a little. "Breathe," he said.

Deep inhale. Let out on a sigh. He looked too pleased with himself. A thought occurred to her. "Why do you stare up at the stars so often?"

"The sun swallowed Cinder before I was born." He expanded his hands to cover the whole sky. "There are no stars. Just the fire." He stared into the black with his hands resting on his stomach. After a quiet second, he asked without even a glance, "Tameka?"

"Yes."

"What else have you noticed about me?" He kept his eyes on the cosmos.

She sputtered. "Well, uhm ... You see ..."

When he turned to her, she swallowed hard. A heaviness settled into his eyes. So sad. A little lost. She reached out to him and touched his face. He let her. She traced the angle of his cheekbone, and the strong line of his jaw. When she got to his lips, he took her hand. "Tameka, we can't."

"Why not?" Her voice sounded petulant even to her.

"Because you're too young. I was there when you were born."

She drew her hand from him and stifled a groan. The same old tale of how Tameka's birth signaled the invasion. The first born in this line of Progeny, Baptist Hospital and everything within a one-mile radius lost power. History to her. "I'm seventeen." She tried to ignore the urge to cross her arms and sulk. She turned away from him and back to the sky.

He shook his head. "I'm ancient. It would be taking advantage of you. You have a whole life to build. So many wonders to experience. It would be selfish of me to stand in the way of that even if I am extremely attracted to you."

Well, that got her attention, but when she opened her mouth to say something, anything ... nothing came out.

He dared poke her on the nose. "Besides, I'll still be devastatingly hot when you're old enough." Laughter bubbled out of her and then ... the dreaded snort. His smile broadened until all his teeth gleamed. "That's my girl. Now," he climbed up off the grass. "Let's tuck you in."

{NEAR 6,000 BCE}

"You were right!" Xelan cried from the entryway. Under normal circumstances, that phrase delighted Merit to hear.

Unfortunately, this time he followed it with a grunt as he fell to one knee.

She dropped the Icarean book and hurried to his side. "My love!"

He slumped face first to the earthen floor. She pushed him over onto his back and hissed. "Who did this?!" The wound split his abdomen from hip to breast bone. It gaped and gushed rich, blue blood. More astonishing than the wound itself, was that it did not heal. "What has happened?" she hissed.

"Colita. She revealed our plans to the King." He winced as she peeled cerulean soaked cloth from skin. "Argh! I was ambushed and taken to his chambers." A groan. "He told me to stand aside and let him deal with the vermin, himself. Told everything back to me I confided in Colita over the last two years." His voice broke into a gargle. "That snake."

"Do they know of the Pretiosum Cruor?" she asked. Her tone urgent and firm. Of all the plans they devised over the years, that one maintained 98% predicted effectiveness.

He looked down the length of his body to her hands on the wound. "No. I never told her of it. Please give me more credit than that."

She pulled her wrap off her red hair and began packing it against his wound. "Why does this not heal?" She tried to conceal a sniffle with her words.

He heard the panic in her voice and reached for her dark hand with his bloody one. "Merit. Love, look at me."

Slowly, she turned her head to face him. "It will not heal any longer," he said.

"No, no, why not?" Her voice shook, and tears filled her eyes.

"He took it. He took from me the nacre which regenerates my cells."

"What is that?" She tried to ignore the fresh cobalt blood seeping through her compress.

Achingly slow, he raised his arm, and cupped her face in his hand. She leaned into it. "Each of you differ from the other experiments because of the nacres I gave you," he said pointing to her chest just above her heart. "With mine gone, the regenerative cells will not work again."

She shook her head, still cradled in his hand. "What will we do? Tell me, what can I do?"

"Leave me. Warn Celindria and the others. None of you are safe—"

"I will not leave you!" she cried. She took his hand from her face, and laced their fingers together: his pale, hers dark, yin and yang. The salt of her tears burnt her face, and the gravity of her decision weighed heavily on her heart. "Wait here, Xelan. I will fetch you some water."

He muttered a few statements between choking coughs, "Must. Tell. Celindria." She turned the corner into his laboratory. There on the cold, metal surface of his work table, a razor-sharp instrument. Her resolve renewed when she grasped it. She jabbed a wide, cork stopper into her mouth, and shoved the instrument under her breastbone. The immediate pain brought her to her knees, and she furiously bit into the stopper to stifle a wail. Yet even as she worked, she could feel the regenerative properties of the nacre healing the fresh wound around the scalpel. Quick. She had to work quick.

After several tries and much screaming around the bit, she returned to their living chambers. He laid where she left him. He was still. So very still. "My love?" No answer nor flinch. Not a single reaction. "Xelan, I brought the water."

She set her emerald eyes on the face she loved for forty years and crashed to her knees beside him. "No! You can't go!"

Her heart hammered as she examined him. His eyes fixed open: unblinking and unseeing. His mouth left agape with a drizzle of blue down his cheek. "I will not allow you to die!" She gritted her teeth, ripped his fine cotton shirt the rest of the way up his chest, and bore down on his mortal wound.

The major anatomy of the Icari varied from humans and Progeny by extension. Their brains sat in their chests and their hearts in their skulls. Just below the brain stem she found a chamber similar to the one near her heart. She pulled the delicate pearl computer from the folds of her wrap and worked her way into his chest cavity. Sweat beaded on her brow and dripped from her lip. The salt mingling with her tears. Her vision swam with little black dots, and she found it steadily more difficult to breathe. All that aside, she smiled when she felt the chamber swallow the nacre.

"Yes! Save him!" she croaked. She rocked on her knees as she watched. Until finally she swayed all the way over, laying along the length of him. Her breath no longer came without forcing her lungs to drink air in and expel it out. She strained to keep her heavy eyelids open, and they stubbornly refused her. A hitch caught her breath, and she felt it echo in her pulse as it slowed. She was dying. But all she wanted was to live long enough to see him move his eyes. In a voice light as the air she commanded, "Breathe."

Xelan's chest heaved hard enough his back bowed. His great swallow of air punched into his lungs. She became too weak to incline, but she made out something stitching the wound closed as if the two halves no longer wanted to be apart. She knew how they felt.

"Listen, my love," she rasped. "I cannot be with you much longer for I fear your desperation." Slackened and slowed, he turned his head. His mouth still open as if his body couldn't muster enough resources to close it. But she saw that he listened; his fresh tears told her as much. "I will not risk you for the revolution needs you far greater than it need I." She coughed and copper blood filled her mouth.

"Thank you for finally seeing me. All I ask is that you not waste time with the next love. See them and know them. Be with them. Know that I am ... always ... with you." Horror filled his eyes and unable to take the sight of it any longer, Merit gripped the instrument and thrust it the rest of the way into her heart.

As Merit considered whether she believed in an afterlife, she decided she wanted her last words to make a mark. To leave the most lasting impression and summarize her personality in one final line. "Take ... the bitch's ... head."

Four out of six of Colita's guard sprawled out on the floor with gulfing wounds in their chests, eyes, and necks. The remaining two soon to join them. Sweat beaded against Tameka's topaz skin. She stood over a prone Colita as distant screams echoed through the school. Tameka held the sword's point to Colita's throat, but she watched the end dawn the alien's blue eyes. She sought mercy in Tameka's expression, and Tameka gave her the unforgiving cold of a Russian winter.

Colita's eyes flicked around, she licked her lips, and tried to reduce her assailant's determination. "Nox is here for Celindria; not you. Do you really want to go any further? Do you have any idea what he'll do to you?! He wants her blood and her soul. He'll spare you for her!"

Tameka knelt, straddling Colita's waist. She enjoyed the exaggerated show of laying the sword against Colita's throat. Still Colita attempted to sway Tameka's resolve, "I wouldn't wish that fate on even my worst enemy. Not even on you, Heaven Dawner," she screamed to Rayne. "You should try to escape this place! Do you really believe that you could defeat him? That you could kill him?!"

Over Colita, Rayne let a soldier fall behind her, the brain removed from his chest. Rayne knelt on one knee, leaned forward, put her lips to Colita's ear, and spoke a quiet, "Yes."

With a deep sense of satisfaction, Tameka's fiery curls bounced as she pushed the ends of the sword until Colita's head severed, and the blade punched linoleum. Her icy-blue eyes opened wide in a permanent expression of shock. Tameka stood with the sword drenched in fresh blood. Rayne stood next, and Tameka handed over the blue-coated weapon.

"Thanks," she smiled and patted Tameka's shoulder.

Kyle nudged Colita's head with his foot, staring as it shifted without response. "Do you think she's dead?"

Nikki's eyes widened. "Can they come back?"

Sagan shuddered with a sense of eerie revulsion. Rayne glared at Kyle as if she reprimanded a small child. He shrugged with a cavalier air.

Andrew spoke up, "It's time to go."

Tameka reached down and lifted the head by the blond tresses. Icarean blood poured onto the linoleum.

"I think I'm going to be sick," John muttered.

Rayne approached Tameka with no sudden movements. "Tameka, I know how you feel right now. It's confusing." She tilted her head and stared at the girl speaking to her as if her best friend mistook her for someone else. "What you're feeling is over. It's the past. It's Merit."

Tameka lowered the head as some of Rayne's words sunk into her.

Their leader continued, "As much as I'd like you to have that trophy, it wouldn't be manageable to take it with us and honestly that's the only good reason I have."

John raised a hand, timidly. "I can think of a few others."

Andrew shushed him, sharply.

"Can you put that down?" Rayne asked Tameka.

Something deep in her refused to put the head down. Something ancient and primal. Behind Rayne, Andrew looked sad. Tameka focused on that expression, on the way his eyes softened and his shoulders slumped. His lips fell down-turned, and he raked his hand through his hair. He appeared almost dejected.

He stood just beyond Rayne. "What's wrong?" Tameka asked. Rayne turned to look at him as well.

He jumped at the sudden change of focus. "I just hate this for us. I hate that we've been turned into killing machines by people who had plenty of chances to end the war themselves." He took a few steps forward and stretched out his hand. "Give me the head, Tameka. This isn't you. You hate getting your fingernails dirty. Why are you holding a fucking head?" Startled out of her trance, she jumped back, accidentally releasing the trophy. When it bounced on the floor with a wet thud, John started dry heaving.

Rayne touched Tameka gently on the arm. "Are you all right?" When Tameka nodded and turned into Andrew's awaiting arms, Rayne turned to the others, "Right. They should be patrolling the area outside the cafeteria. I want everyone to spread out, but not so far that you're out of hearing range. Make sure you can see at least one of us at all times." Even Tameka nodded along in agreement with no questions and a sense of anticipation.

Rayne gave a small smile, "Let's go." Tameka leaned forward, glancing at Rayne's hand holding the sword. Tiny red droplets fell from the soaked bandages. Their leader turned, stepped over the bitch's body, and all the while smiled faintly. As they walked away, Tameka spared a furtive, longing glance at Colita's head.

SEVEN

Stay Out Of The Way Of A Man With An Axe To Grind

THE JANITOR'S CLOSET CONTAINED MANY DIFFERENT THINGS: A MOP AND BUCKET, BROOMS, A PACKAGE OF SAW DUST, A FEW HAMMERS, AND A FEW THINGS MISSING FROM THE IMPRESSIONS ON THE WALLS. An underlying odor of ammonia permeated the small space. Kiñatta sat leaning against a wall. For the past hour she rocked herself into exhaustion. She continued rocking until the screams in the halls beyond silenced. The small closet in the Tech hall kept her hidden all this time. She wiped a hand over her tear-stained cheeks. They came unbidden, but came nonetheless. A fine tremor threatened her nerves. Her muscles grew sore from the tension seizing her. All that fear ate away every thought. Only her instinct to hide kept her safe in the closet. Smoke from the fire steadily crept its way through South Hall. She smelled it; knew the fire drew close. Yet, still, the threat of mutilation frightened her more than burning alive.

What time was it? Maybe the Fire Department would be there any minute.

The sound of footsteps resonated through the hall. Their proximity unnerved her. So close. Her heart pounded in her throat. Please. Please don't come this way. The sound grew louder as they grew nearer. Please ... Then they stopped right at the door. She closed her eyes, breathing short and shallow. Her heart beat like a hummingbird. She might swallow her pulse. Not a sound. Just silence. She almost heard her blood flowing through each vessel from her pounding heart.

Then, slowly, the latch on the door turned. Her eyes opened against her will to the sound of the tumblers giving. When the door opened by inches, she realized what went missing from the closet.

A man with long, white hair stood at the door holding a sledgehammer. She stared, wanting to scream, on the verge of hyperventilation. He raised the mallet. In the end, she screamed one high-pitched, ragged sound as he plunged the heavy thing into her head several times until she only saw red darkness and heard black silence. The fire continued to spread.

Rayne struggled with the war inside herself. And she was losing. When she first picked up the sword in the Med Lab hall, for a fraction of a second she thought about slipping the blade into her ribs, and ending the oncoming suffering before it ever began. She blinked back into truth and reality. The farthest thing from her mind. It wasn't her thoughts. While she stood with her back to the others, her eyes searched for something unseen, non-corporeal. Then she heard it: deep, malicious laughter echoed inside her head. He toyed with her. He would have to do better than that. Now, she charged away from their first victory, her crew—she needed a better word for them—followed suit.

"Are we just going straight in there?" John whispered.

"I am," Rayne announced loudly to anything that might overhear. Not sure if she harbored a death wish, or if Nox was fucking around in her head, but she knew one thing: she wasn't about to let her friends down. She had a world out there to protect. This ended today—here. At this school.

As they finally reached the end of North Hall, the group spilled into the school center and froze. In the open space separating the school offices and the cafeteria main entrance, someone with an artistic inclination got very busy. The emblem of the Pretiosum Cruor drawn in smeared blood: one heart in the center impaled by a dagger or a sword and surrounded by a spiraling vine. In the center of the heart sat a human head, unlit beyond the reach of the emergency lights.

Kyle said, "You'd think in the middle of a war zone they'd have better things to do than leave us all these love notes."

"They don't think they're in a war zone. They think this is a playground," Andrew commented.

Sagan walked by Rayne and stepped over the lines of blood.

"Do you really have to know?" John asked.

Nikki answered, "If your loved ones wanted a list of this battle's casualties or survivors, you'd want your name marked so they could mourn you."

Rayne glanced back to Nikki. Why was she working so hard on John's lack of good sense?

Sagan gasped. "It's Justin!" she cried from where she knelt on one knee inside the heart.

John surprised Rayne by murmuring, "Good riddance."

Even Kyle rubbed his neck and looked off elsewhere. No one wanted to comment on how little Justin's death affected them. But it affected Sagan.

She picked up an object beside Justin's head and shoved it into her skirt pocket. Rayne almost didn't catch the movement, and she supposed that Sagan wanted it that way. Ask her later in private. Right now, they needed to press forward. This battle ended today, remember? Gripped with the desire to end it all one way or the other, Rayne walked on.

Behind her, Kyle said, "I don't know about you guys, but seeing severed heads is more disturbing than they make it out to be in the movies."

Andrew grunted his agreement.

Korac loved making an entrance. He was the best at it. But this time was different. It was special. He needed to impress her.

Not officially met, yet. After waiting eight thousand plus years for her to come into existence and waiting another eighteen before he allowed himself to even approach her. At the tender age of fourteen, he started living as her shadow without her knowing. He saw every A+ paper and test. He witnessed her first attempt at human relationships. He watched it fall into a series of punishments he understood all too well. The abuse angered him. If she desired pain wrought, he could deliver it to her in spades. She need but ask. Those screams should be his screams. Those hateful glares for his eyes alone. Of course, he only visited her in her dreams. Dreams where they shared beautiful and intimate secrets though she would never admit it. In breathy tones, in piercing cries, and in little giggles she told him she loved him. He considered each confession a triumph, and drew from them her soul. He got so close to possessing it. It might take a few scratches and bruises to convince her to leave with him, but having been in her life for four years now he knew where to leave his marks. What a puzzle she was.

He gleefully popped his new CD into the disc player and connected the converter for the headphone jack. This moment he planned to relish on the long drag back to Cinder with both Sagan and Rayne in tow. He expected neither one of them to say yes. Their training with Xelan all these years gave them a false sense of confidence. He had to give them credit: they worked their asses off. Every night, they devoted at least two hours learning how to kill his kind. And that traitor showed them every method known as of ten thousand years ago. Even with him and his scientists gone, others came forward to improve their technology beyond the predictable deaths. It was unlikely Xelan possessed this information.

Over the past eight thousand years, Nox took Xelan's betrayal hard. Although he never admitted it. No, Nox lost trust in anyone. Korac remained the only member of the high court he refused to execute on regular rotations since Xelan fucked them all. Nox withheld trust of others with any plans of actions or big adjustments to the Operating System. So why would anyone volunteer to be on the court? He pulled them from the servant class. Said he wants representation from the weaker of their species. He gave them the juice, and overtime they grew more elevated and all that entails. This engendered the undying gratitude only servant born could supply. It proved as a surprisingly successful methodology. It also ultimately meant Xelan's out of the loop and the girls with him.

As he considered the song he selected, Korac recalled how he kept Sagan out of the loop the whole first year they started "seeing each other" in their dreams.

"Mmm ... that was nice. Why did we wait so long?" Sagan purred as she curled back between his legs, cozying against him, her back to his front.

Sitting against the wall, Korac threaded his pale fingers through her long, brunette tresses. They fell mussed, and he liked them that way. He liked the sound of her purring. But most especially, he liked this feeling of anticipation building within him for almost a year.

"I wanted to make your sweet sixteen special." He pecked a kiss on her fair shoulder.

She tilted her head back until he saw the freckles that graced her nose. "Well, I certainly feel special," she told him. Then twisted her whole body around and leaned in close until she faced him. "And I don't know about you, but I'm ready for round two."

A satisfied grin stretched his mouth wide until the sharper canines glinted. "Anything to keep my love happy." Intentionally, he wiped the expression from his face and replaced it with a mask of sadness. "But there's something I have to tell you, now."

She leaned back and knelt. Everything about her so glorious and beautiful. He memorized every soft curve, hard muscle, and tempting bone. He reserved these memories to motivate him as he forced two more years of waiting before he finally allowed himself to touch her. She peered hard at him now, as if she already pressed him while he fell deep in his thoughts. He wanted to crack his knuckles and stretch his neck. This required quite a nuanced performance, and he certainly felt more than up to the task.

He started by brushing a finger into her hair. She kissed his palm, sensually, and he rested his hand against her cheek for the start. Contact made the "bad news" easier to accept. He said, "Remember as I tell you this truth, that I love you and I have cherished all these moments we've shared."

Some concern tightened her eyes, but she leaned against his hand and kissed his wrist. "Go on," she pressed. No force. Just a gentle push.

Now, to throw in the theatrics. "Oh, Sagan. I don't know where to begin. I'll start from when I first came to you here in the dream. I want you to know that I had every intention of just providing additional training. I wasn't expecting any of this—us—I wasn't expecting us to happen."

She nodded, eyes growing wider. Her attention utterly captivated. He also had to give her kudos. A two-thousand-year-old Icarus didn't listen with the uninterrupted rapture of this sixteen-year-old-human on her birthday. Especially not while intoxicated on endorphins. He flushed with pride for his pet project. He filled his eyes with sorrow and said, "I...I lied to you in the beginning, last year."

The violet in her eyes hardened to stone. "What do you mean?" she asked.

"I am not a member of The Brethren. Nor am I some random Icarean citizen looking to stop the oncoming war."

He watched her breath hitch in her throat. He noticed how her bare chest heaved as she held it, waiting for the bomb to drop. He hoped it wouldn't disappoint. "Sagan, I'm Nox's right-hand man. I'm his general. His second in command."

Her mouth had such a pretty way of dropping open when she was surprised. And then the hand. Yes, his favorite gesture. She prettily covered her gaping mouth with one graceful hand. She blinked once. Then twice. Then rapidly. Tears filtered through her lashes and dropped onto soft, freckled cheeks. She was a masterpiece worth painting. Her pain an ecstasy he made damned sure he never lived without.

Stony, she sat up straight. When the cold air caressed her body, and hard not to notice when it happened, she became reminded of her nudity. Delicately, with shaky hands, she wrapped the sheet around her exquisite form. He took in every gesture, every tear, and every stage of grief she entered. He loved every second.

But the show must go on lest he push her into isolation. "I'm so sorry, my love. I can't apologize enough for misleading you. My mission was always to gauge your fighting performance and then leave."

She shook her head, and little tears sprinkled away. Finally, a soft, breathy sigh broke, and he damned near came. Onward, he pushed, "You have to believe me: I only stayed because I started to fall in love with you. From the very first conversation we had, I couldn't stop thinking about you. You're incredibly intelligent," sprinkled in some truth, "and so funny and just fun to be around." She peered up from her lamentations. He was getting to her. "There's no one like you on Cinder," he said, speaking the Elden's honest truth. "Until the day I met you, I didn't think there was anyone like you in the Vast Collective."

She heaved another sob, and he reached for her. He expected her to recoil. She stayed. When he brushed his fingers through her hair, his favorite gesture, she let him do it. He tried to control himself, but the sight of her shaking at his confession and his touch breached his performance. He leaned forward and took her full bottom lip, salty with her tears, into his mouth and kissed her, soft and gentle. She quit resisting the pain and gave into the tears and the crying. She pretty-cried like no woman he encountered before. He swallowed every sob that resulted from his engineered romantic machinations. She dropped the sheet and embraced him. He pulled back just enough to rest his forehead against hers and speak into her mouth, "I don't want to lie to you anymore." With quivering lips she kissed him, lightly.

"Then don't," she said in a voice heavy with grief.

"You won't like the truth."

"Then don't tell me," she demanded, surprising him with her brazen tone.

He allowed the genuine shock to show on his face as she pulled back from him and gazed into his eyes. Her own matured fifteen years in one sad moment. "You've told me enough that I can't pretend unless I choose to do so. It's my choice."

He nodded.

"Then I'm choosing this. I want my nights to be with you just like this." She lifted his hand and kissed his palm.

This turn of events was unexpected. He prepared for the sadness and maybe a fight. Then he figured after a few lonely nights without him, she might beg to know and fuck the real him. This? How could he prepare for her to beg him for a fantasy while she ignored the truth? A deliciously unexpected turn of events.

When she sucked one of his fingers into her mouth with newfound confidence on the matter he didn't have to exaggerate his reaction or hide the physically obvious one. He rolled his eyes back, closed them tight, and lifted his face to the sky. She sucked the next finger a little less gently, then licked the tip. That was it. That was how—without a word—he agreed to play her fantasy dream Icarus, at least for a little while.

The next day she accepted Justin's request for exclusive dating after ignoring him for a year. It was interesting to follow her development as a young woman living a double life. She needed the punishment during the day for what she enjoyed so much at night. The guilt gnawed at her. He watched her transform from a beautiful, pale brunette all strength and confidence into a frail, tan blond who found grace in pain. She stopped spending time with her friends. He noticed she looked miserable with The Overachievers Club. She stopped wearing the revealing Goth clothes that he very much liked. She stopped participating in Track & Field. He was always quite proud of her run times. Now she sat lonely wearing large over-sized hoodies and sweats at Justin's bequest surrounded by people in which she shared nothing in common.

Korac respected pain, punishment, and torture. Honestly, all of those were his favorite things. But it lacked art . . . a finesse. That adolescent puke didn't understand the subtly of superbly fucking a girl, keeping her on the brink of orgasm, and then refusing to let her finish for four years. That was pain. That was art. Brutishly bruising her or fucking up her ankle, that was just juvenile.

Korac rolled his eyes and hopped off the counter. The link between him and Sagan tugged as he walked closer to the cafeteria. He watched through the blood-washed windows as she stepped into the middle of the lobby and collected the gift he left her. Yes, that expression right there. That was ecstatic torture at its best. Take that lock of hair she told him so many times she loved. Feel him nearby. Know that he was coming for her.

All conversation stopped when they passed through the entrance. The cafeteria stood as a dismal reminder of a time long past. School's a safe place. Come have breakfast and lunch in the cafeteria. Live in your naive world. Not after this morning's events. The scene of the cafeteria made that fact more of a reality. The white walls washed with a thick coat of blood. All of it human.

The eight long tables served as a gathering place for students enjoying a midday respite and venting to friends and classmates. The sight of them in that moment would forever stain Rayne's memories with nightmare fuel. A little under two gallons of blood in the human body and it saturated those tables, she guessed around two hundred students died for that effect alone. It wasn't just the blood. No, it was so much worse. The remains of her classmates splayed across the long lunch tables. Limbs, torsos, and heads, but not a single fully assembled body. Viscera, long and squishy, lined every table. Larger lumps of squishy things were more difficult to identify in the low light, but she could take a few guesses.

A young girl made up the center of it all. Her name was Shannon, a junior Rayne never saw without a smile. The girl's body hung suspended upside-down from the drop ceiling paneling by a rope tied around her bare ankles. Unsure why she thought it a small mercy, they stripped her down to her underwear and left her somewhat unexposed. Even still, they left too much of her bare. Her eyes appeared dark in death, her mouth open in a silent scream, and her blood went everywhere. Long, deep incisions on her wrists, ankles, neck, thighs, stomach, and back. Tearing at her inner elbows like teeth. A missing thumb on one hand and her index finger on the other. The blood formed little rivulets against her dark skin. The crimson fluid cooled, turned shiny, and congealed.

Several of her people closed their eyes, but she knew they saw it no matter what. As they came closer, her face became more visible. Her eyes weren't closed. They were missing. Blood and paler, thicker fluids pooled in her empty sockets. Deeper lacerations across her face. The white color of her cheekbones stood stark in their wounds of her dark skin. To complete the horrific scene, every bit of the metallic stream dripped away into a large soda-on-ice canister the monsters so strategically placed under her. They even found the lost digits inside.

The whole while her team absorbed the horrific sight, they held a collective breath. Their lungs forced them to breathe again, reluctantly. She wasn't sure which smell hit her first: the sickly sweet scent of blood or the shit slaughter of perforated organs. Everyone pulled either their arm, hand, or shirt over their nose and mouth. Groans and gasps throughout. John took too deep a breath, fell to his knees, and retched. The sounds of another person vomiting cost Nikki her self-control. Though, unlike John, she found the nearest waste container, and lost her breakfast there. For a moment, she seemed fine before she saw the length of human intestine at the bottom of the barrel. She vomited to the side of it, instead.

"Jesus Christ," Kyle murmured against his arm.

Rayne closed her eyes tight and held the back of her hand under her nose. She whispered softly, "I'm so sorry, Shannon," to the long-dead girl. She ran to Nikki's side. "Take small gulps of air," Rayne coached.

But when Nikki looked up, her eyes filled not with disgust but with absolute panic. "Nikki, you can't afford a panic attack right now. Come back!"

Nikki's massage paled in comparison to its usual splendor. The man of her dreams, no pun intended, rubbed her shoulders a little rougher than normal. With each pull he irritated her old, broken clavicle injury that healed two years ago. This bothered her even more as he knew full well of it since he started appearing in her dreams around that time. Around the same time she took an interest in a new freshman girl with black hair and shocking blue eyes. Nikki loved Rayne's hair.

"Ow!" she whined at him. "Why are you being so rough tonight?"

"Your mind is elsewhere. It is not here with me," the shadow's deep voice answered.

Well, that was true. She became distracted by how well her relationship with that now-sophomore turned out. When Nikki gained a moment to think about anything other than schoolwork and chores her hormones drifted to her girlfriend.

At that moment her dream-partner actually growled. "Wh-What's wrong?" Before he gave an answer, he turned her over with rough, jerking hands. She no longer lounged on a massage table in an elegant spa. She found herself laying on a rough, earthen floor with a large black fire beside her. A very large fire.

"Where are we?! You haven't taken me here before!" Her voice trembled, and she tried to steady herself on her knees.

"SILENCE!"

She went stone still. He prowled around the pyre until he circled back around to her. When he stood before her, a cold chill shot down her spine. She closed her eyes. Her blond lashes laced tight. Wake up. Just wake up. It's a dream.

"It is more, and you have always known that," rumbled the shadow.

Her eyes snapped open and locked onto the face she never quite made out. His long hair brushed against his forearms and ribs. "Are you going to hurt me?" she asked, an edge of desperation in her voice. Ever since she broke her collarbone, she grew terrified of feeling pain like that again.

He knelt down in a motion so sudden it made her flinch, but his hand just brushed against her hair, cupping the side of her face. "Not I," he started. "Look into the fire. Look and see what you are afraid to know."

She trusted him. She did. He gave her advice on everything from what part-time job to get to what colleges she should apply to. She got into every one of them, and the job she worked for qualified as valuable experience on those applications. She needed to trust him.

Slowly, as if afraid to take her eyes off him, Nikki turned and looked into the blaze. The images she saw there took her breath away. Rayne sat at the lunchroom table beside Nikki. They both looked content. But when Nikki looked away, Rayne peered at a table on the far side of the white-washed space. Sagan sat there searching the room. When she caught Rayne's eyes they both exchanged a smile Nikki never quite saw from either of them until now. It glowed radiant, and their eyes shown in equal brilliance. In love. They were in love. Before Nikki or Justin turned back and caught them, they both glanced down. The moment ended as quick as it started. Heart broken, Nikki wanted to squeeze her eyes shut and turn away. But the images went on.

The next scene took place in the cavern she found herself in now. She recognized the rough dirt floor and the fire blazing away. Bare limbs peeked through the dancing of the flames. On the other side of the black flames she made out the shadow's pale, bare backside. Completely unclothed. His long hair swept aside. Some motion, like he moved. And then the sounds finally reached her. Oh, it was those kinds of movements. Why would he share this with her? Such a terribly intimate scene. Nikki wanted to ask him, when the face of a woman appeared over his shoulder. Her black hair matted damp to her forehead. Pale skin beaded with sweat from the heat and exertion. Nikki need not see her eyes to guess their color. The girl kissed him long and deep. The satisfied moans echoed from across the vast chamber. Their kiss ended. Rayne's eyes opened and looked right at Nikki. Nikki jumped as if to move away. Shutting her eyes tight, she didn't think she could take anymore.

When she opened them again, the imagery changed. The final scene choked a scream in her throat. Nikki laid face up, her mouth open in a never-ending scream, and her pale-blue eyes glazed over in death. The initial horror subsiding, she leaned in to gather any clues as to her demise. Pretty much the same age as now, so that provided little comfort. Her body streaked in bruises that started healing before she died. She leaned closer to the flames. There, just under her loose blouse, a terrible sight. She died in agony. Bones broken, organs crushed, and burnt flesh. She gagged, and the fire took the image away. A small mercy.

"I don't understand. Why did you show me all of that?" she asked, her voice devoid of hope.

"To protect you," he said.

She looked at him with her eyes narrowed. "Protect me?!"

He continued, "Every single image is avoidable. Do you want to know how?"

"Yes! Yes, of course!" she cried.

"Let Rayne go," he stated.

"What?!" No. She wasn't about to do that. She loved Rayne. Although ...

He repeated, "Let her go. She isn't and won't be faithful to you."

"But I love her," she argued, her voice drawn weak.

The shadow shrugged. "She didn't appear to reciprocate those feelings."

"You don't know. You don't know anything about how relationships work!" she shouted, sick of his disregard.

He said, "I believe relationships are in actions like that smile shared between Rayne and Sagan. Or passionate like her efficacious liaison with me."

Nikki wasn't the most secure teenage girl to begin with. Add a very realistic image of a very possible interaction between two exes and a dash of crazy naked sex scene with a strong shadow-dream dude, and some doubt might worm its way in. "I don't understand the third scene," she whispered in defeat.

"Simple. You avoid that end entirely if you avoid Rayne. You will never know pain like that," he answered.

Decision made, she hung her head in shame of her weakness. The shadow leaned forward and placed a gentle kiss on the pale crown of her head.

"I love her," she sniffled.

"We all do."

"Come on, Nikki!" Rayne continued to shout. John and Kyle gathered closer in case they might assist in any way.

Kyle asked, "A panic attack?"

Rayne nodded, unwilling to look away from Nikki.

"It's been like two years since she had one, right?" he asked.

Nikki came around. Her pupils shrank from the dilation during the attack. "Are you with us?" Rayne asked.

"I want to be with you," Nikki finally answered, her voice quiet.

Kyle and John stepped back out of Rayne's line of sight. She appreciated the privacy. She spared a sad smile and pulled Nikki into a hug. "I can't let you break down on me right now. We have to get through this together."

Nikki clung to her tighter than expected.

Sagan shouted from the kitchen area, "There's two people alive back here!"

Andrew shouted back, "I don't want to know your definition of alive right now!"

Rayne gave Nikki a reassuring smile. Nikki let her go and lied, "I'll be all right. Go to her."

She, Kyle, and John hurried to Sagan while Tameka and Andrew stayed behind to search their sanity. Nikki stayed on the floor, recovering.

Two students sat upright on the cold floor near one of the warming, food-well service stations. As far as Rayne gathered, they showed no signs of external damage.

"Are they injured?" Rayne asked.

Sagan shook her head. "They don't appear to be."

Kyle knelt, snapping his finger in their face. One of them stopped trembling long enough to focus on his eyes. "What happened?" he asked.

"What d'you mean, what happened? Look out there, you fucking idiot," Rayne snapped.

Sagan interrupted, "Be quiet both of you." She turned back to the students. "Are you able to walk?" The trembling freshman nodded. "You know M2? Try to help your friend up and head that way. Two people there will help. Okay?" No response this time. The boy put his arm around the girl and staggered away.

Sagan and Kyle walked back to the open area. Sagan asked him, "What kind of question is 'what happened' right now?"

"C'mon, I was asking for specifics, sheesh," Kyle answered. The two carried on around the corner.

Rayne glanced around the kitchens, her frown deepened with confusion. Where was the blood back here? The chatter stopped.

John's voice brought her back to the here and now. "Hey, Rayne?"

Music played over the school's intercom system. Not just any music. After the quiet electric guitar intro, the lyrics to *Sweet Dreams* started. For the second time since this all started, Marilyn Manson performed the soundtrack to her worst nightmare.

She stepped around the corner, sword in hand. She looked up, but felt lost as she contemplated just how much she wanted to lose her shit on this dude right now. She noticed the lights switched on in the cafeteria. In the periphery, the contrast of the bright blood across all the white walls, white floors, and white table tops overwhelmed her at first. And she seriously avoided making out the lumpy shapes on the tables without the cover of darkness. She counted three brains, twelve small intestines, and four livers before she stopped herself from self-inflicting anymore nightmare fuel.

"Celindria," a sinister voice hissed.

At the mention of her ancestral designation, she grew empty. She gave no movement or response. Apparently, Sagan and Kyle made it only this far from the kitchen before they, too, realized they had company. They both stood only two feet away from Rayne in the lunch line doorway.

The sinister voice belonged to none other than General Korac. His long white hair pulled tight from his face and held by an Asian hair pin, letting the ponytail cascade down his back in silver waves. His stark pale eyes, even lighter than Colita's, held absolutely nothing as he faced her down. No rage, no searing hatred. Just business.

But when he looked at Sagan, several things—passion, obsession, hunger, and a slight hint of anger—materialized through every feature of his face. It shone in his eyes and pulled his lips into a secretive smile. Whatever burned under the surface of Rayne's self-control, his eyes on Sagan, fanned the flames.

He brought his friends with him. More Icarean soldiers, without their cloaks, holding tools from the janitor's closet in their hands—broomsticks and hammers—one or two of them wielded swords like their fallen brethren. Twenty-two warriors total. Did they bring a small army to attack the school? How the fuck did they get that many Icari in here during the day? Three stood sentinel at each entrance to the cafeteria, and three flanked Korac.

Kyle muttered a soft, "Shit." Rayne checked, and Sagan's eyes darted anywhere, trying to avoid contact with Korac's gaze. The more uncomfortable she seemed, the more loose and relaxed he got. He was a very insistent stalker.

Andrew spoke gently to the very still Rayne, "Are you with us? Come on, we have to finish it."

No need to reply because she finally looked into the Icarus' face. Silver ... his eyes were silver. He realized she stared at him because he switched his focus from Sagan to her.

"What say you, Celindria? You and Sagan come with us, and we'll leave. No more of this ..." he spread his hands, indicating the entire room, " ...carnage. You and I both know this is pointless. All this fighting—Nox will take you, anyway. But if you go now, no more innocent people will have to die."

"Why did you say Sagan goes, too?" Nikki spoke up. She stepped forward with a blue-tinted, bloody piece of metal.

Korac observed Rayne's reaction as he replied, "His Majesty promised her to me. And I have waited a very long time." There was a history to them; a purpose for his infatuation.

Rayne must not have reacted the way he wanted. He frowned in disappointment at her unchanged expression. Sagan turned and inspected Rayne behind her. The lyrics droned on about submission and abuse. Rayne gripped the sword tight in one hand. So tight her knuckles mottled white. She clenched her free hand so hard she wrung drops of blood from the glass in her wounds. She didn't feel a god-damned thing. She just wanted the fucking music to stop.

The lights flickered above.

"What the fuck?" John asked.

Andrew spoke in a soft voice, "Rayne?"

Everyone in the room glanced up except Korac. No, she held his undivided attention. Likewise, she never moved her gaze from his. But that anger in her flared with every line of that song. His lips stretched into a gruesome smile. He knew.

The intercom speakers crackled, the music distorted, and eventually everything stopped. His smile never wavered. "Do you have any idea how hard it is to find good music on Cinder?"

Footsteps stopped outside the door. Shadows appeared through the glass window. The door opened, turning slow. Come on just try it. Lynn went to stand flush against the wall. She started to swing with a metal pole before she recognized the two intruders as frightened students.

"Shit! Sorry!" Lynn said. She dropped the piece of scrap and urged them inside. "Are you all right? You're not hurt, are you?"

Pablo sat the girl down in a chair. She failed to recognize her or the boy. Lynn looked over at Pablo. "I guess they made it to the cafeteria already." Relief washed over her. However, it seemed like ever since the group left, people escaped hiding places in droves and made their way here. The injuries all fearsome and almost every single one required hospital treatment. Historically, field medicine never really provided a good answer for broken limbs on the battlefield. And that's exactly what this was.

The boy nodded. His shocked eyes made large disks in his face. The girl kept herself in complete silence. Must be too frightened to speak. Pablo wrapped a blanket around her shoulders. He looked up and said, "I think she's in shock." Lynn turned her back on them, rummaging through the bag of supplies.

The boy stepped close, talking loud and clear, "It was horrible. Blood everywhere ..." He continued speaking, but Lynn concentrated on her search for the materials. She diverted her attention on the task at hand, but she thought he took a step closer. The pole when he picked it up made a metallic clang, but she heard it too late to stop him. The pole hit her at the base of her neck. Motherfucker! Darkness swirled through her vision.

The girl sprung for Pablo, speaking for the first time and now they knew why she stayed so quiet. She couldn't speak English.

Her dialect comprised an ancient, begotten version of Spanish. Her hands clasped around his throat, forcing him back against the black lab table. "Hey, wait a minute!" He pushed her hard enough that she stumbled back.

She screamed in that ancient tongue and lunged for him one more time. He tousled with her like the whole situation threw him off. He got enough time to search the ground for a weapon. He noticed something and appeared to form a plan of action. When she fell on him, he used her momentum to throw her over his head. She landed on one of the upturned plastic chairs with the metal leg impaling her. She shrieked a loud cry of pain. He grabbed the bastard attacking Lynn by the back of the neck, pulled him off her, and slammed him into the purifier. He pounded the red button and watched as the monster's head exploded inside the incinerator.

Pablo ran to check on Lynn. "Are you all right?"

She had her hand to her neck, finding a scratch there. "Yea, I think so."

Pablo grinned. "Next two are yours."

She laughed. Their eyes locked. She stared into his gaze, longing to finish what they started. This whole thing with the sneak assassins meant the time for distractions was over. They couldn't afford to spare even ten minutes together. They had work to do. She stood. Sadness filled her eyes. "I don't know if there's anyone else to save here ..."

Pablo frowned. "I think there should be more people to help. We've only seen maybe three dozen."

"I know."

His expression deepened in confusion. "So what do you mean?"

Her tone gentle, she answered, "Either they're at the football field or ... they're all gone, Pablo."

He lowered his head and sniffed.

Rayne turned her wrist, spinning the sword in her hand. Blue blood sluiced off the blade, spilling on the floor, and mingled with the human blood. Her body covered in so many things. Of the twenty-two Icarean soldiers, only thirteen plus their leader remained. Andrew tried to help John relocate his knee, Kyle bled from a sword gash on his upper left arm, and Nikki killed the Icarus that blackened her eye. Twelve left.

In taking that moment to survey her troops' progress, Rayne failed to notice the bastard behind her until he lifted her bodily from the ground, and slammed her back onto the nearest table. The drop on the table surprised her. It didn't hurt that much. Not as substantial as she always assumed.

She kicked at the monster's face, shouting, "Fuck you!" He dodged her kicking feet and pinned her to the wet, bloody surface with a meaty hand. He took the time to lean down and snarl all his many sharp teeth in her face.

She said through gritted teeth, "Your breath wreaks, wingless." Rayne knew at least she and Sagan should be delivered whole to their Icarean masters. So no matter how much he bared his teeth, he wasn't about to hurt her much. There were other ways to torment her, unfortunately.

Fuck. From where he gripped her no-longer-white blouse, he pulled her along with him as he ran down the length of the whole table. With every slippery, wet foot she felt long, squishy portions of intestine slap into her fallen hair and back. Harder, fuller organs bounced off her and splatted on the floor. Cold, sticky blood clung to her entire body, soaking her from head to foot. He lifted her from the table and slammed her against the wall with her feet dangling off the ground. Her back squelched against the blood-drenched cinder blocks.

"What's the matter? Afraid to take me out without daddy's permission?!" She stuck her tongue out at him. Her breath came hard against the press of him on her chest.

That did it. He pressed harder. But if he killed her, what would he tell the boss? It was an accident? Fortunately, this ruse came together as it allowed Sagan enough time to run up behind the Icarus and shove a makeshift stake into his chest. Brain impaled. Girl power! He screamed and let go. Rayne slid down the wall, but landed on her feet. She needed a second to recover from the sternum pressure.

"Are you all right?" Sagan asked.

Rayne answered, "I'll be—Down!"

Sagan dropped without hesitation and missed the glancing blow from the sledge hammer by a narrow margin. She executed a perfect leg sweep on the floor, and Rayne nailed him to the linoleum with her sword through his brain centered in his chest. Eleven.

A little breathless, Rayne said, "Nice leg sweep."

"Badass bitch impaling," Sagan complimented.

Oh, what the hell? Rayne threw up a hand, and Sagan gave her a high five. Both grinning despite the gore that covered them.

When the girls turned around, they stopped dead in the center of the cafeteria.

Korac awaited there in his leather-clad splendor. Who was his stylist? They needed a bonus. He switched eye contact between Sagan and Rayne. Emphasis on Sagan. His face appeared locked in that permanent, condescending grin. He spread his arms wide, and the two pale soldiers flanking him removed his leather duster. Like, seriously. Swept it off him and away. Rayne straight-up rolled her eyes, but he paid her no mind. His eyes locked on Sagan for the spectacle's sake. To Rayne's surprise, Sagan peered at him with wide eyes. Her chest heaving from her shallow breath. Her lips parted. Not good.

Underneath his coat, he wore a sleeveless black shirt that bared his corded arms and the hilts of some kind of weapon at both hips. One of the blood suckers ruined the moment by barreling into Sagan, knocking her over. Before Rayne could assist her, he landed on Sagan's stake when he fell on top of her. Impaled himself. She rolled the dead body off her, but retrieving the stake from the corpse proved impossible. So she collected his sword instead.

Back on her feet, she looked at Rayne. "Sweet," she said with a smile.

Korac seemed just a smidge disappointed by the interruption and frowned. He looked back to the soldier holding his coat. In a nonchalant tone that suited his irritatingly pleasant voice, he ordered, "Kill the rest."

One went for Andrew and John, one went for Tameka, and the other stalked toward Nikki and Kyle. Appearing satisfied,

Korac turned back to Rayne and Sagan. Oh, but no. Please, not that. His infuriating smirk returned. "Shall we continue, then?"

With a flourishing cross draw, he unsheathed both weapons in a fluid, simultaneous motion. He practiced. Probably in a mirror. He probably practiced naked in said mirror. Silver fucking battle axes. Both polished to a gleam and worked with intricate designs at the grip and pommel. It boasted the symbol of the Pretiosum Cruor in the center of each blade. Predictable. And they glinted, sharpened to perfection.

Beside her, Sagan's eyes widened into dinner plates, and she thought Sagan even gulped. Rayne's hair stood on end, and her muscles constricted with tension. Her breathing shallow, and her heart rate quickened. In her periphery, two Icarean bodies fell. Eight more to go. But looking at Korac...damn, this would be harder than she originally thought. The smell of smoke in the air gnawed at her subconscious and distracted her. Not afraid. Totally not afraid. Were her hands shaking?

Korac advanced first. He so would. With one foot he took a step forward, and Sagan took a step back. Rayne glanced at Sagan and tried to read her. She fought a losing battle inside. Hell no. Not happening on Rayne's watch. In his single-minded determination to obtain Sagan, Korac ignored Rayne altogether. He stepped right in front of her with no sign of defense. Here goes. She plunged the borrowed blade right into Korac's center.

Before she sunk anything home, she jolted when Korac's eyes locked right onto hers mid-attack. His smile no longer condescending. It molded into something determined, focused. He was here on a mission and be damned if Rayne got in the way. He reacted to her move by disappearing.

"What the fuck?!" she shouted in a pitch that went far higher than she ever meant to let out. Especially on a battlefield. He seriously, completely disappeared.

"Behind you!" Sagan cried.

Rayne's whole body went tense, and she froze to the spot. It was like when she was home alone, and she heard a loud sound somewhere else in the house. Her mind argued with itself—go investigate or rationalize it away? Her instincts begged her to do some rationalizing. But four years of training with Xelan made her refuse to weigh that option.

Stiffer than she wanted to be about it, Rayne turned around. Korac, in fact, lingered behind her. Fuck her, but he looked entirely too pleased with himself. Over the course of their training, Xelan taught them to track, and even imitate his speed moves, which to untrained eyes looked like disappearing tricks. Not only did she not track Korac's movements just now, she couldn't even sense a spatial disturbance. That wasn't speed. How was she supposed to fight an enemy that can properly disappear and reappear? Xelan never told her Icari were capable of those abilities. This wasn't going well.

When he spoke, she recoiled. "In no uncertain terms am I allowed to injure you. The King reserves that pleasure all unto himself, as is his right."

Rayne felt a smile creeping onto her face. "Is that so?" He nodded, still pleased with himself. "Then you don't mind if I—" She feinted a punch with her free hand and thrust her sword at his ribs. The sword pierced air. He fucking disappeared, again.

Sagan cried out. Rayne whirled around. He held Sagan in his arms, his front pressed to her back. The axes crossed over her chest with the points of the blades too close to her throat.

"I will fucking end you," Rayne screamed.

To her disgust, he pressed his face closer to Sagan's hair and took a deep breath. Her eyes went even wider with terror, and Rayne knew this manifested Sagan's worst nightmare. Only, she had some advantage. "Sagan," she spoke her name in a calm voice.

Sagan's eyes focused a little, and she answered, "Rayne."

"Tao."

Her head snapped up, and the demeanor of her body transformed from a frozen statue to a loose, balanced stance. Rayne watched Sagan process the message. Sagan's hand gripped the sword, tighter, her confidence returning.

Rayne charged at Korac. As always, his relaxed expression came across unconcerned. The shine of his eyes told her they amused him and little else. When she tackled into him, he let go of Sagan and disappeared. Rayne crashed to the floor, grabbing at air.

So, he didn't take her with him. More than likely couldn't in this case. No passengers aboard Icarean Airlines. From the floor, she heard a low grunt. She sat up and pulled her sticky hair from her eyes. Korac staggered a few feet away from Sagan. His neck started bleeding from a wound. Sagan held her sword at her side.

No obvious anxiety marked the lines of his face, but there a hint of disconcertion settled in the slight tightness around his eyes. "I see Xelan trained you very well."

Rayne approached Sagan's side. What was going on?

He took a step toward them to start the fun over again, but Sagan thrust out her free hand. She spared the chance, and turned to Rayne, "The smoke is growing thicker. It won't be much longer before we can't breathe. We still have to fight Nox, and this is such a mess. Tell us what to do, Rayne. What will make this stop before we all die from suffocation?"

"Fall down at my feet and beg me to take you with us?" Korac suggested, his silver eyes shining with silent laughter.

Rayne glanced around to take in the fight itself. Tameka fought two. Andrew helped John regain his footing, and they took on three. Kyle and Nikki battled three of their own. Kyle knocked off the head of one as she watched. Fifteen alien soldiers down. The one Nikki marked stopped, looked around at the fifteen Icarean bodies, and retreated to South Hall. Nikki pursued him on her own. Only six left, now.

"You kill Korac, Sagan. I'll go find Nox," Rayne ordered.

Korac chuckled. She wanted to kill him for how silky and sexy it sounded. What a crime.

Sagan shook her head. "No way. Not alone."

Rayne pulled her into a one-armed hug. "I'll come find you when I'm finished." She pulled away and gazed into Sagan's violet eyes.

Sagan's reassuring smile satisfied Rayne. Sagan nodded. "Go and be careful." Rayne wondered if Korac would let them have enough time for a kiss? The creak of leather caught her attention. She peered at him over Sagan's shoulder. He shook his head as if answering her unspoken request. The stormy darkness cast over his eyes suggested he tired of their parting gestures. Fuck him. She gripped Sagan's neck and kissed her like it was the last time.

Then Rayne turned and went for the opening where John and Andrew struggled with their three warriors. She walked up to one from behind, thrust the sword into its brain, and withdrew it from him. She smiled to Andrew.

"Rayne? Where are you going?!" Andrew called. One Icarus tackled him about the waist.

"Take care," John shouted.

Rayne nodded, going to Nox with fresh, blue blood on her sword. Her friends would be safe. They could take care of each other. Only five left. She took one last glance at the opening event.

Sagan turned to face Korac. A vague sense of apprehension occupied the scene. He stood there, smiling with all his amusement and arrogance. He spun both axes in his hands. She charged for him, and he met her halfway. Her sword fell between the two crossed axes. And there they faced one another like they'd met that way before.

EIGHT

Never Meet The Men Of Your Dreams Because Odds Are They'll Ruin It For You

ONE OF COLITA'S BROOD FLED RIGHT INTO HIS PATH. Nox flexed his fist, and the Icarus disintegrated into dust. Running from human children. How pathetic. Nikki barged around the corner in pursuit of her quarry. She stopped short. She recognized him. He grinned with satisfaction. He had a promise to fulfill.

"You really are here," she whispered, her voice hoarse with exertion.

"Yes, pet," he confirmed with a chuckle. Such a tiny thing. Measuring below his chest, she hardly weighed over eight stones. He considered her frame delicate, her facial bone structure like that of a pixie, and her beautifully fair skin and fair hair elicited instincts of possession and protection. To a human, anyway. To a being like Nox, he interpreted her weak, fragile body as a challenge. How many ways could he break it? His predatory instincts showed on his face because those lovely gray eyes of hers widened. So enticing. She surprised him by brandishing her sword. He resisted the urge to look behind him as if to patronize, "You wish to fight moi?" But he wanted to let her own this moment. Die with some dignity.

157

"It's a dangerous game you play," he offered instead.

"It's not a game. I won't let you take her," she vowed.

He nodded in approval. Her death wouldn't be quick, but he would honor her as a warrior. Well, as much as he could without bothering to draw his sword. "Then be swift in your actions, woman. I will not play pity to your stature."

She lunged at him. Pathetic. He feigned a narrow evasion of her very obvious demonstration. He trusted the Icarean traitor did a better job on Nox's girl. Otherwise, they wasted four years.

She lunged again. He exaggerated the effort to jump aside. He took cruel enjoyment watching the confidence build in her moves and the determination to slay the dragon grow on her face. Such heart. Maybe this wouldn't be such a bad appetizer to the main course after all.

It was time to get a few of his own offensive maneuvers in. While dodging another attack he asked, "What do you think will happen after you defeat me?"

Sweat beaded across her brow. This close to the fire, humans would have trouble withstanding the increased temperatures. She withheld an answer but grunted cutely as she attempted to slash him. He intentionally inflated the twirl of his cloak as he spun away. All the while she made her advances, he drew her further into the smoky corridor of South Hall.

He prodded again, "Do you think you'll be the prince rescuing the princess?" Her slashing intensified, and a fierceness cast a deadly look upon her face. Meanwhile, he maintained a cavalier air even with his flourishes to boost her confidence. He heard a huff. Her breath came heavy and in the denser smoke that might prove difficult for her. She stepped back in a defensive pose.

"I save the day," she finally deigned to answer him.

"And then what?"

No response. She need not say anything. He already knew what this girl's childish mind imagined for the outcome of this battle. He tsked. "You get the girl, and you both live happily ever after?"

She faltered. For a second, the confidence drained out of her into a hopelessness she carried since he convinced her to break up with Rayne two years earlier. Between heavy breaths, she said in a small voice, "If that's what she wants." The sliver of desperate hope in those words might almost break his heart. If he had one.

Time to end this. "Well …" he said as he straightened the gloves on his fingers and cracked his knuckles. He rolled his shoulders back and rotated his neck. All the while, she watched and her eyes grew less fierce and more aware of her surroundings. "I'm afraid that's just not how your story will end, pet."

In the empty hallway, through the building's silence, in the smallest voice he ever heard, she said, "No. No, it was never going to."

Ahh, so she understood. It was meant to end this way. Well, he gave her credit for her bravery and her devotion. Her loyalty was not unlike Korac's to himself. He respected that. "It won't be quick. And it won't be painless." He warned her.

She squared her shoulders and gripped the sword tightly. She seemed to lack the strength for anymore words. She just nodded.

He swung one fist into her face. He used the other to grab the sword she attempted to impale him with. He ripped it out of her hand and sent it flying toward the Technology hallway, where it most likely fell from her reach for the worst of the fire. With not even a sliver of effort, he grabbed her upper arms and hauled her off her feet. She never let out a scream. Just grunted and even that involuntary. She tried to kick him. He admired that. He threw her into the nearest wall.

Her eyes already swelled shut. Her lip busted. Her ear bled. She struggled to pull herself back up off the floor. There, hot tears streamed from her good eye. It was enough to send him over the edge and make him drain her dry. But he refused to drink from her. Affiliating with the Progeny was a contamination to his kind. Only Celindria reserved the honor until now. He would pass it on to Rayne.

He slammed his fist into the other side of her face. Might as well make the bruising even. That time she screamed and spat out something solid. He chuckled when the tooth bounced on the floor. He couldn't help himself. Humans were such weak things. She tried to punch him in the crotch. He grabbed her fist and wrenched her arm back.

"Now, I think you've had enough fun," he said. He lifted her by her throat and threw her into one of many heaps of flaming rubble.

She cried out. She screamed until her voice went ragged. She rolled and turned until she doused the flames.

He felt that familiar, satisfactory grin creep onto his face again. Ever since he saw the construction of this school he really, really wanted to try this. He lifted one hand into the air and pulled the riot gate down. The awareness filled her eyes, and she tried to spit out a scream. She blew a blood bubble instead. Hilarious.

The gate slammed into her midsection. Her partially cooked body writhing treated him to an aphrodisiac. Again. He had to do it again. He raised the gate high and paused. He wanted to watch the futility fill her eyes. She disappointed him, barely managing to look at him at all. Her head lolled in a pitiful sight to one side. Blood oozed out of her mouth and ears. Her swollen eyes left her unrecognizable from the delectable creature he started this little tiff with.

"Come on! Put some fight into it!" he demanded.

He got a gurgle in response. He decided this was pointless, but before he finished her off, he leaned in close and whispered, "You remember your visions I showed you?" She struggled to glance at him, but he saw the recognition in her eyes. Good. "If you think about it, the one about you dying in pain came true." He paused, waiting for her to acknowledge it. After a long time, her bloating face nodded just once. He smirked. "And you know without a doubt the one about her and Sagan was true." Again, a weak nod of the head. "Then, I promise I'll do everything in my power to make the third one happen. And when I finally do, I'll be sure to think of you while I'm enjoying my time with our girl."

The human heart. How it ached. It was so visible! Despite the painful swelling, fresh tears forced their way out of the corners of her eyes. And there . . . on the edge of his hearing . . . a sob. "Mmm," he moaned as he stood back to his full height. "Good night, little prince." And he slammed the gate for the final time.

The thick curtain of smoke hung in the air, darkening the red-lit hallways. The smell of charred wood and beneath that the smell of rot so thick it caked to her tongue and made it hard to swallow. With every inhale, her lungs screamed. Gripping her sword tight, Rayne came to the corner before the South Hall opening. A small knot of fear formed in her stomach so tight it almost convinced her to walk back to the cafeteria. Just run away. No one would blame her. Except maybe Kyle. It was a relief to be reminded she was still human.

She took a deep breath, that final step, and let her eyes sweep across the destruction. She clutched the riot gate in front of her and peered through. Flames climbed the wooden locker-lined walls and licked the drop-ceiling tiles. Charred and melted clumps of rubble and what looked like a body all a ruin in flames. The four riot gates separating sections of the hallway anchored half-raised. Everything made into props for the backdrop of her nightmares. The cries of her friends from behind contributed as a soundtrack to the mayhem.

Rayne took a step back from the gate and shoved both hands into her hair. Everyone depended on her now. Gotta get a grip and get in there. Once she crossed that threshold this ended only one way. She dropped her arms and strode back up to the gate. When she bent forward to cross under it, something cold brushed the nape of her neck. She spun, frantic to catch it. Nothing. Absolutely nothing. Chalking that one up to strained nerves she pressed on, observing the surroundings. Where was Nikki? She came this way a while ago. The burning corpse at the far end? Wrong hair color.

She scanned the area once more. Her eyes strained in the dark, caustic smoke. Her heart slammed into her chest. Near the body, she made out a dark figure just beyond a mound of fallen lockers that crumbled into nothing. The figure towered over the lockers. His body forged of heavy muscle, and the hooded-cloak he wore failed to contain the unearthly strength radiating from his alien being. As if on cue, he swept the hood back. He relieved his naked, broad shoulders of the cloak altogether. She tried to focus on anything but him.

How? How was she supposed to do this? Look at him and not think about—She refused to see his face. Her heart pounded like a stone knot against her sternum. But how could she end this here, if she blanched from his face? She surveyed his hands. He bore that heavy silver ring with the god-forsaken Pretiosum Cruor insignia. If his extreme height, and his majestically honed body, didn't scream "King of Cinder," the ring certainly did it for him. He had much to answer for.

After agonizing over it, she lifted her chin and examined the rest of him. Wearing heavy boots, loose black trousers, and bare from the waist up, he personified her worst nightmares. His black, silken mass of shoulder-length hair plaited down his scalp. A few loose strands framed the angular features of his pale, masculine face. A ruefully, handsome face with heavy, angled eyebrows, high cheekbones, and soft, full lips. Thank goodness she never saw his face in her dreams. She might not have woken up. Searching his face compelled her to meet his eyes. Nothing more calculating or sinister as the dark depths of his ravenous gaze. And those eyes smoldered with a thirst, a hunger for primal power. Almost as if he lusted for nothing else and could not be sated of it.

Staring into his eyes brought a wave of dizziness. She reached her hand out to steady herself against the grating. Those eyes blemished every one of her nights for the last four years. Haunted and enthralled by them, her body knew no difference. She remained drawn to him all the same. When the world stopped swirling around her, she gazed back to where he stood. The flames, the thick smoke, it made him so unreal aside from his eyes. Rayne shook her head and straightened. Her grip on the sword tightened. Fear clenched in her stomach. She was more determined than him. She had more to lose. And she wouldn't let that happen. She was ready.

"Nox."

Sagan's pulse threatened to strangle her as if her heart lodged in her throat. It beat so hard that her wrists ached with it, making her grip on the sword uncertain. She refused to give even an inch. The blade of her sword fell solid between Korac's axes in a demonstration of strength. No. No, she wasn't winning. And the grin on his alluring lips suggested that he knew it. Got to think of something.

"What's the matter, little butterfly? Are you struggling more than Xelan told you you would?" Korac teased and exerted more pressure against her sword. "All those up close and personal sessions with our wayward brother amounted to very little." He gained against her offensive, and with every detail of her life he divulged she lost the strength to keep him down. "And how steamy some of those sessions were. I'd wager you were more likely to orgasm wrestling in your front yard with Xelan than you ever were with letting that juvenile thug you called a boyfriend rutt at you."

A strained cry escaped her as he reached his full height over her. And he continued on with his banter, "But my favorite—oh yes—my favorite moments were when you thought no one was watching you and Rayne—"

Enraged, she screamed in his face. Red heat lit her skin on fire. Sick of his mouth and his intrusion on her life, she decided. No way. No way was she going to make this an easy or quick death for him. Fighting became all that mattered. She kicked his ankle, unsteadying his balance. That wiped the smile off his face. He stumbled back, lowering each axe to the side.

She seized the fault in his guard and swung for his midsection. Fuck! Korac regained his balance sooner than she expected and evaded her strike. He used one axe to block her sword and sliced at her with the other. She spun outward, away from him. She avoided the worst of the blow, but caught the axe in the meat of her shoulder. The wound bled immediately, and her breath came hissing out through gritted teeth.

Sagan's turn to step back and regroup. She took a second to examine the wound. Small but deep. Unlike the Icari before him, this motherfucker actually thought he had the rights to hurt her. Just because of their connection in her dreams. Well, fuck him.

When she gazed up into his face, her eyes burned with rage. He blew a kiss at her, and she lunged for him sword first.

He disappeared before her blow landed. She jumped to the side, fast and agile, and swung a punch into the air in front of her. He materialized at that exact moment her fist connected with his face. Why hadn't she used her sword and just plunged it into him? Fuck, she would regret that.

He lashed out with an axe, and she fell back onto her ass to avoid it. Rather than take advantage of her current vulnerability, he concerned himself with the mark on his jaw. He rubbed it back and forth, checking his reflection in an axe. She stood back up, slow and steady, and took a step away. His total disregard unnerved her. Come on. React. The hair on her arms stood on end, and her skin bubbled in gooseflesh. The same thickening of the air as the fight with Colita emanated from him. Focusing on his face, she watched the mark she gave him fade away to her dismay. He should have to keep his marks, too. When his striking, silver gaze returned to her, she watched him assessing everything from her height to her muscle mass.

"You don't have the nacre," he said, his voice turned contemplative.

"What the fuck are you talking about?" she asked. Her skin crawled under that stare.

He disappeared in response. She whirled around, and his face appeared right in front of her. His expression filled with bewilderment. He vanished again. She scanned the corner of the room near John and Kyle. He appeared on the table there, perched on a stool.

"Look out!" she cried to her friends. Busy with their own issues, they tried to stay further out of the periphery. No need for collateral damage here.

He paid her team even less regard. He crouched on the stool like a great bird. The bewilderment on his face left, and calculation replaced it. When he disappeared again, she spun to the side almost out of reflex now, and he reappeared before her. Every angle of his face oozed displeasure. "How are you doing that?"

"It would be stupid of me to divulge a tactical advantage," she answered, automatically. Where did that answer even come from? Honestly, she just thought about where he might go and that's where he was. But she wasn't about to share that with him. Pride suffused her, and she let it show on her face in her own grin. Her shoulders held straighter, her grip on the sword surer, and her stance steadier.

The displeasure melted from his face. His eyes shone with something that frightened Sagan: excitement. His smirk grew secretive, as if only he and she knew the inside joke. "I'm afraid I brought this on myself. No matter." He dematerialized. She gawked up at the ceiling. She wasn't sure what she thought she would do when he appeared directly above her, but getting out of the way seemed like a good idea. She darted over, but too late. The skin of her backside cleaved open. She shrieked and sprawled onto the floor. Korac landed in a three-point stance.

"That's twice now you passed on the opportunity to kill me," he assessed.

Like last time, she tried to crawl back without him noticing. But unlike last time, she held his complete and utter attention.

"Yea? Well, you're making me regret those little mercies," she quipped. He struck with one axe. She blocked and held back with her sword. The angle felt all wrong, and judging by the gleam in his eyes, he only toyed with her.

He struck the linoleum next to her head with his free axe. "Don't forget. I have two." She yelped, sure he meant to strike her in the face with it. He twisted the axe locked against her sword until it bent her arm away. The sword lay beside her head. Kneeling on one knee, straddling her waist, and an expression full of triumph, she feared Korac, but not because he planned to kill her. He wanted to take her with him. She feared herself more because a part of her wanted to go.

He leaned closer until she stared into the darker gray flecks in his otherwise colorless eyes, and she smelled the peppermint of his breath. "I will convince you to come with me."

His voice. The deep timbre, the elegant cadence, and the silken tone of it drove her crazy in her dreams. Here? Her breath hitched, her heart pounded against the linoleum beneath her, and she strained not to turn away from his proximity. "Not willingly. Never."

"By the time I am done with you here you will cry my name for every sexual encounter you allowed him to force on you. You could easily defend yourself." He brushed his fingers through her hair. "Those moments were meant to be mine."

Hot tears streamed from her eyes, down her temples, and into her blood-soaked hairline. She muttered, "I know."

He lifted his hand, a tear delicately balanced there. He brought it to his lips and tasted it. His eyes closed, and the muscles in his neck strained. The moment he let his guard down, she grabbed the sword, and slammed the pommel against the top of his spine with a cry.

He grunted and rolled away from her. She backed farther away from him and tried to ignore the searing in the flesh of her back. Where she crawled, she trailed a considerable pool of fresh blood.

He retrieved the buried axe. Sagan's eyes grew wide when it lifted a chunk of foundation with the linoleum tiles. He caught sight of the realization dawning on her face and smirked. "My name. Seven hundred and two times."

Everyone drifted away from Matt's car by now. Listening to the message repeat on the radio made no one feel any better. They needed to focus on the here and now. Surely anyone able to come outside already did so. A bustle of students that belonged in hallways lined with lockers, not a broken-up parking lot and pavilions surrounded by a haze of acrid smoke.

Lucy sat in the grass behind the school, knees hugged to her chest. Someone called, and she lifted her head.

"Lucy?" Cecily called again, approaching her friend.

"I'm here," Lucy's meager response. With a timid hand she touched the bandaged injury on her forehead.

Cecily sat beside her best friend on the grass and noticed the movement. "I never asked. What happened?" Her voice full of concern.

"I saw one of *them* in the hall. I was running when someone ran into me, and someone else slammed me against the wall. I was nearly crushed." Lucy felt her eyes hollow with the memory of it. "Do you remember when Sagan came to school with that bandage on her forehead?" Lucy asked.

Cecily sat in silence, her face stricken. Nearby, Lucy noticed Stacia eavesdropping with very little subtlety. Well, good. She needed to hear this, too.

"I remember puzzling over what happened. I remember thinking, 'Oh. I guess that happened, again.' Now that I have my own bandage, all I can think is, 'That must have hurt and what a piece of shit Justin was for doing it. I'm glad he's dead,'" Lucy said in a firm tone.

Cecily rolled her eyes. "You don't mean that. She has responsibility in it, too. She stayed with him. We don't—"

Lucy interrupted her, "No, it gets worse. Because we were pieces of shit, too. We told him everything she did when he wasn't around, and we were almost eager to tell him when it was something he wouldn't like. We just wanted him to quit bullying us for a minute, so we let that girl be the whipping boy."

Cecily's eyes widened, her brows came down in confusion, and the lines of her face drawn in hurt.

Stacia saw her moment to step into the spotlight and took it as always. "You can't talk to her like that. We weren't there. We don't know what Sagan did to Justin."

Lucy looked straight into her face filled with all that indignation and said, "And we deserve to die, too."

Stacia spat in Lucy's face and stomped away. Cecily gaped at Lucy with wide, stinging brown eyes. Lucy just gave her the full force of her self-loathing. With a sudden hop, Cecily popped off the grass and ran back to Stacia. So much for The Overachievers Club. R.I.P.

"You did the right thing."

Lucy glanced up into the brilliant, sunlit sky, and squinted under the shade of her hand to make out Matt's face. She replied, "Thanks, I guess. I don't think I deserve it."

The grass crunched under him as he sat beside her. "Well, I wasn't exactly giving you a compliment. Sometimes doing the right thing, especially if you're a little late for it, isn't something to congratulate yourself about."

His words stung, but they were the truth. Which, if she was honest with herself, she hadn't heard from another person in a long time. She thought she would go a little deeper. "When his truck flipped over an-and what happened, happened ...my first feeling was relief. I knew that was awful, so I went with my second feeling, which was mostly horror. But some of that horror was directed at myself. We'd let him push us around for four years, and I assisted in a terrible cycle of abuse. And you know, maybe sometime down the road I could make amends for that. Before today. That message on the radio ...I'll never get the chance."

Matt replied in that reasonable tone of his, "There is no making up for it. You have to own it and move on. Don't feel guilty for feeling relieved. Justin didn't have the best impact on the world. But you still could."

"Thanks, Matt." They both sat in silence for a bit.

The day seemed to stretch on in its horrific torture as if they became somehow separated from the world just beyond that barrier of smoke clouds, almost like the sun blacked out.

Lucy squinted harder into the sky, and then realization struck her. She cried out, alarming Matt. "What is it?" Matt looked around, but saw nothing.

Someone close stood, and pointed toward the sky, "Look! It's the sun!"

That's when Matt seemed to notice what Lucy saw. A fraction of the sun turned dark and this strange blackness consumed the fiery ball in a gradual filter. The surrounding daylight weakened, diminishing, seeming darker through the smoke. All around them people cried in collective terror. The monsters could come outside, now.

The atmosphere closed in around her, inducing claustrophobia. Rayne sensed Nox examining her. She tried to prevent it but a bout of self-conscious anxiety overwhelmed her. What did she look like to him? Soot and ash clung to her skin. She tried sipping the air in short breaths. This made her throat raw and her chest burn. Her eyes watered from the caustic air. She tried to focus them through the acrid fog. That predator fared better in his ideal conditions. It's not that he didn't breathe so much as he was accustomed to breathing volcanic gases with ease. His eyes saw sharper in the darkness. Did he notice the blood dripping from her fingertips? Did he see how labored her breathing became? After her fight in the cafeteria, blood splattered across her white shirt, shimmering stark vermilion against the slick skin of her throat. The sword she gripped coated in cobalt blood. The blood of their fallen kind.

"Is this enough for you?" His voice resonated like a low roll of thunder through the blanket of smoke and flame.

She closed her eyes to ward against him. He knew. He knew how she felt. How he affected her. "You're about four years too late," she responded in a hoarse voice that shook to her dissatisfaction. "Why did you keep me waiting so long?"

He noticed her reaction. She knew it as sure as she knew he enjoyed his influence over her. "It was more entertaining this way. We allowed you to learn to defend yourselves. What amusement would I gain from slaughtering five helpless fourteen-year-old pests? A great strategist permits the opposition the illusion of victory." With every harsh word he spoke, his authority over her loosened. "I see Andruis and The Afflicted One are here. How convenient they should—"

At the mention of their ancestral names, the personal triggers, the bonds snapped, and that internal flame burned through her. She interrupted him, venom dripping from her voice. "Don't you ever, EVER, call them by those names again. You are in no position to threaten them. And you know pretty much my whole life at this point. So don't patronize me about my friends." Defiance engulfed her.

The silence that followed her outburst stretched something tighter and tighter inside her until it wanted to snap. She flinched when Nox's roaring laughter filled the hall, loud enough to reach those in the cafeteria behind her. Every hair on her body stood on end. A chill shivered up her spine, and a shaky breath passed her lips. She stiffened, all her muscles gone rigid.

Every instinct screamed at her to maintain a visual on him through the smoke. The soot collected in her eyes. So dry. So heavy. In one blink of her eyes, he vanished.

"Fuck!" she shouted.

He appeared in front of her. So close, as if Nox wanted Rayne to peer into his eyes, shining like black pools. Her lips parted as if ready to beg for forgiveness. Anything to deter—His ringed fist collided with her face. Skin scored along her cheekbone as sudden blackness staggered her. The coppery taste of blood filled her mouth. Instead of showing some mercy and letting her fall, he wrenched her up by the collar of her blouse. Rayne stared down into the face of the man who proved capable of beating her to death in a hundred dreams, feeling exhausted by the moments yet to come. Her single comfort, cold as a corpse, Xelan told her they needed her alive.

"I will drench these walls with your blood, and take what's left of you back with me," he growled into her face.

In the dreams, she woke up whole. No blood. No broken bones. This was not a dream. She knew that. But if she learned anything from the last four years, she refused to go down without talking some shit. Fueled with a fresh sense of rage, a fierceness overtook her. "Only if I'm dead, shark fucker." She spat blood from her teeth into his face and kneed him in the crotch.

She expected him to drop her, so when he instead took her upper-arms in a firm grip, she groaned. "Do you even have anything down there or is it all made of iron, your highness?" she asked. She wiggled in his hold and batted her eyelashes. At a loss for ideas, she gazed into his eyes.

His fingers bruised, and his long nails bit into her skin. Something swam in those inky pools of his face. Determination. No matter the cost to her, he intended to execute his plan. Right now, that plan was kicking her ass. He slammed her into the nearest wall of lockers. The combination locks pressed into her back reverberating, through her lungs and kidneys. Her breath left her in a pained gasp. No fucking way. Least favorite thing. Ever.

Again, he gripped her shoulders hard, dragging her feet, and slammed her into the wall opposite the other. She cried out. Black blossomed in her vision again, and she lost all her strength. In an instant, every muscle in her body loosened, and the sword fell to the floor. She followed, sinking beside it, blood trailing along the way. Her breathing labored.

"This should be more of a challenge," he said. "I'm disappointed." Nox loomed over her. Not a single bead of sweat marred his pale skin, and she hated him for it. Meanwhile, sweat pooled everywhere imaginable on her body as flames licked the very walls around them. Watching him as carefully as her heavy eyelids allowed, she almost sobbed at the sight of him unsheathing a very serrated sword. A slow, agonizing reveal. A show for her.

"Naw, your majesty. I'm just getting warmed up." Rayne struggled to reach for her sword. He kicked it away from her. She let out a strangled breath. He wrenched her hand up closer to him, balling it into a fist around the wrapped wounds.

"No. No. What the hell do you think you're doing?!" She tried to jerk her hand back to her. His grip like a vice, he held steadfast. She just wanted to make some attempt to prevent him from whatever he planned to do that caused the sparkle in his eyes.

"Lover, don't stop fighting. Struggle more." He laughed at her pitiful resistance as she tried to pull away. He held her hand firm and steady. With morbid fascination, she watched as he cleaved the blade into the bony flesh of her knuckle. Even though she witnessed the lot of it, the exquisite pain still surprised her.

"Nooo!" she screamed and struggled to pull her hand back. If only she could cradle it to her, and nurse it, then the pain might dull to something tolerable.

He continued laughing at her futile attempts. "Doesn't this remind you of our third night together?" He raised the jagged blade again, high enough for her to see it above her hand, and angled just right so it framed the glean in those obsidian mirrors. Her lungs breathed ragged and haggard, but it came shallow and fast.

In a breathy voice, she begged, "No. Please." He sliced another slit down a white, clenched knuckle. He repeated this process on the following fingers, slicing down the white joints. She writhed, tugged, and screamed. It was like taking repeated blows during training, and the pain eventually rolled into itself until it wasn't felt altogether. This was profane. Every. Single. Time.

"Oh, God! Let go!" Tears streamed down her cheeks, leaving pale ruts in the soot. What could she do? Through the awful pain, she took stock of the floor solid beneath her. She steadied herself with it, risked a chance, and kicked out against his knee. With relief, she watched as his knee bent at a bad angle. This inversion brought Nox down to the floor on the uninjured knee. He let go of her arm.

Rayne spared a quick moment to cradle the bleeding hand to her chest before crawling to where her sword laid. She grabbed it, turned on her knees, and held it before her against her bleeding palm to block the blow she sensed coming. Nox recovered and gave her a devastatingly attractive smirk when his sword struck down onto hers. She held him off.

"Not so wise, my dear," he purred.

A twinge in her wrapped palm caused her to shout, "Fuck!" Only then she realized the sharp edge rather than the flat of her blade bit into her hand. It pressed through the blood-soaked bandages.

"You're not thinking quick enough, Celindria." He smiled, pushing his weight against her.

"Wipe that smirk off your fucking face." Rayne winced, fighting the urge to cry out. The skin of her hand split, welcoming the sharpness of the metal. He actually chuckled at her.

She gritted her teeth and pushed back, forcing the blade in faster. She managed enough space to stand up. Still straining against his resistance, she feigned a weakness on one side. He took the bait and fell into it. Closer, bent at an angle, she collided her knee into his stomach. The strike had enough momentum to knock some life out of him.

She raised the sword with both hands and prepared to bring the blade down on the exposed base of his neck. Shit! He recovered so fast! He clutched her wrists, and she knew by now what she was in for. He really seemed to enjoy throwing her into things. The lockers further down the hall did not provide anymore give than the others. With every slam, her lungs and kidneys vibrated, and her breath left her.

Between slams, she coughed, "What's your deal with the fucking lockers? Don't you have anything new to show me? I'm getting kind of bored."

He slammed her against a different bank of lockers and took both her wrists in one hand. He stretched her arms high above her head. Her abused, sore muscles strained. Turbulence overwhelmed her as he leaned his face into hers. So close that when he spoke their lips brushed. The same spearmint ... She regretted the little thrill of excitement it gave her. She searched his eyes for anything at all resembling the more tame creature from her later dreams. He gazed into hers, and in the black she saw nothing.

"In this, I obey," he said in a deep voice gone husky with anticipation. Her lungs burned. The heat got more intense by the second. She tried to swallow through the dryness, unsuccessfully. Her neck and back slick with sweat. Her mind swirled with apprehension. Why was she like this? How bad had the invasion gotten? Were the others safe yet?

To her left, further down to the end of South Hall, she peered through the broken doors. The light. Where did the light go?! Were they too late? Darkness inside and outside. Flames kissed the walls and ceiling as smoke hurried to escape in black plumes.

Nox brought her back to him with a caress of his hand. She expected a rough gritty texture, but like Xelan's, his hands felt like velvet to the touch. He plunged his fingers into her hair and gripped a fistful until her neck arched at a painful angle.

Did she scream? No. Did she whimper? No. Two years of wet dreams/nightmares with the king of an alien race while remaining practically abstinent in her real life. And what sound did she make at the first intimate contact? She fucking moaned. She could never tell her friends about this part of the fight.

His breath left on a satisfied sigh of spearmint against her hair. "I'm so pleased you're coming ... around, lover."

Her eyes fluttered closed. She tried to squirm, pressed firm between the lockers and his muscular build. A wall of wood and a hard place? Very hard. She let out a pathetic cry when his soft lips brushed her neck.

"I have not taken Progeny vein in eight thousand years," he confessed. The bass gravel of his voice vibrating against her throat.

Almost recovered. Just a little longer. How to keep him distracted without letting herself get distracted? She strained against the hold on her hair, against his tight grip. She brushed his ear with her lips, and whispered, "My king."

He snapped to her. Suspicion ladened his voice, "Rayne?" Why couldn't he be dumber?

"I'm prepared to negotiate terms," she stated, leaning back against his hand.

He laughed, a full, throaty sound. A genuine one. It suited him. He said, "You're not exactly in a position for negotiation." Something passed over his humorous expression. He leaned in close again, his lips over hers. "However, I will grant a few amenities to you and one other you choose in return for a willing surrender." She both wanted and really didn't want him to kiss her. Every fiber of her being yearned for both.

He trailed his free hand, light and soft, along her neck to her collarbone. Staring into her eyes, he admitted, "I am a generous king."

Ready to go.

His holding her entire weight at her wrists afforded her an advantage. She tucked her knees to her chest and kicked him in the face. He growled, "Bitch!" and tossed her closer to the flames.

She tumbled a bit in the hot debris. After one or two rolls she leveraged enough momentum to spring into a cartwheel and right herself. Before her heart took a beat, she started a flat sprint. He straightened and waited for her. She jumped and kicked one foot off the locker to gain some height. She wrapped her legs around his neck and swung them both to the ground. The take down. Straddling his neck, she boxed his ears for good measure, and hoped they rang like hell.

She wrenched back for a good right hook to his jaw, her tight knuckles screaming from the torture he wrought. Too late. He caught her fist and ground his thumb into the pulpy tissue of her palm. "Argh! No!" she shrieked.

His expression betrayed no pain or fear. In fact, his eyes sparkled in the depths of those abysmal pools. Was he toying with her? He bucked her and tossed her over to the side. "My turn?"

Lynn formed the stirrings of a plan. Pushing the mass of braids behind her shoulder, she continued searching the drawers of cabinets. "Great," she muttered to herself. Found at least one thing she wanted. Unscrewing the bottom of the flashlight took a short eternity. When it opened at last, she groaned in disgust. "It's empty."

"Yea well if they left the batteries in they would die. Check the same drawer for the batteries," Pablo offered unhelpfully, although she knew he meant well.

"Check the same drawer for the batteries," she repeated in a mocking tone. She rifled through the drawer, louder than ever to cover her complaining. How could she let herself fall for his bullshit? How could she pounce on him like a thirsty woman? She cringed anytime she relived the "lick your lips" line. Worse yet, she couldn't get a single second of their contact out of her head. Visions of his velvety, brown eyes behind low lids as he sneaked peeks at her during their kisses harassed her non-stop. If she wasn't treating a dire and devastating wound, her brain tormented her with their whole scene on perpetual replay. In slow-mo. And with an embarrassing soundtrack.

She roused a happy, "Aha!" when she found the batteries in an altogether separate drawer. She started loading it up. She wanted him to witness the moment in which he was wrong, but when she looked up, he stared out the back window. She shrugged and continued her task while her inner monologue berated her. Sure, the kissing was amazing. She'll give him that, but it's only because he had so much practice. He flirted with every girl in and above his grade. Despite all that, she always had a thing for him. He was nice and funny. It was hard to determine how smart someone was in this school. Most people seemed to hide it, aside from The Overachievers, of course. But she guessed he probably was. It didn't help he was handsome, and he hadn't even grown into his face, yet. It's a wonder the boy was single. Come to think of it, she couldn't remember him ever having at least a public relationship—

"What the fuck?" Pablo barked from the window. A small mercy as it broke the dangerous spiral of her thoughts.

Lynn diverted her attention away from the flashlight to spare him a glance. "What is—" Before she finished asking, she saw what made him swear. She stood and walked over to him. They both watched in horror with mouths wide open. The daylight outside receded. The light diminishing until only a deep shade of darkness remained. It was unnatural. Noon cast in a blanket of reddened darkness, for the sun's rays still graced the smoky clouds. Yet it was dark. If the Icari could really leave the shelter of the building, then all was lost.

"Lynn?" Pablo asked. She turned to him. "How many do you think are left?"

"Aliens or students in the building?" she asked.

He stepped forward and glanced through the doorway. "Icari."

Lynn took a hair tie from her bag and began gathering her braids away from her face. Her teeth clenched around the tie. She responded, "Well, if Nox is anything for Rayne to worry about, then we should definitely assume he came prepared for this ..." She slipped the weight of her hair through the tie and walked back into the Med Lab. She tried hard not to think of him as a piece of sensual meat while they dealt with an apocalyptic crisis.

Pablo followed, asking, "Where do you think they'll come from?"

Lynn proceeded to the large cabinets in the left corner of the room. "What do you mean?"

"These anemic posers came from somewhere, right? But they can't be out in daylight, so ..."

"So how did they get in the school to begin with?" she finished for him with provoked curiosity. Wait, did she just finish his sentence? She shook her head and started rummaging through storage. She retrieved an industrial-sized bottle of denatured alcohol and fifteen empty glass specimen jars. She relished the mixture of confusion and surprise written on his expression. "They had to come from somewhere underground, but where is there an underground entrance to this school?" She started applying labels to the bottles and filling them with alcohol. "Hand me your over-shirt, Pablo."

On the labels, she wrote, "Do Not Fuck With."

He complied and inquired, "What are you doing?"

Rather than answer him, she tugged his shirt with her teeth and ripped it into strips. She ignored how much it smelled of him.

"Hey!"

"I'm making a surprise. It'll be useful for where we're going." She soaked the strips of cloth in the alcohol and shoved them into the tops of the containers.

"That's not what I meant. Here." He handed her a pair of scissors openly displayed on Ms. Washington's desk. She tried to keep her eye roll to herself. "Where are we going?" He grabbed three, and she tossed four more his way.

This being exactly the distraction she needed. She shoved eight bottles and four stakes in a bag. She marched to the door. She almost made it out with her mini armory when she replied, "To find where the Icari are coming from."

"What?!" Pablo exclaimed as he ran to catch up with her. "Hey! Wait a minute!"

NINE

Pet The Tiger Through The Bars
But Never Uncage Him

WATER SLUICED FROM KYLE'S FACE. His hair dripped in mass. The defined muscles of his arms strained against the sides of the toilet bowl. No telling how long he had before the toilet filled back up with water after flushing it, but he certainly had to get that boot-licker the fuck off him. Where the hell was Nikki, anyway? She was supposed to back him up. He wondered if she was okay, and felt a spark of guilt he really couldn't afford to worry about right now.

The unreal strength of the irritating tyrant pressed down on the back of his head. He gathered a large gasp of lung-burning, smoky air and started reaching for the handle again as the water restored. The sight of the water filling up the toilet sent him into a panic. How many times had he done this now? Two? Three? Was he developing a phobia? The water washed up over his face, rushing around and pressed at his eyelids and nostrils as if asking for permission to enter. For the first time in two years, he wished he cut his hair. In the water, as it started looming around his face the claustrophobic sensation of its presence made his heart race and incited the urge to thrash. He and Xelan never practiced drowning torture techniques, but in all those years the one thing he recalled, "To remain calm is to remain in control." So he remained calm, and it rewarded him with an idea.

He pushed himself enough off the floor to kick the Icarean soldier's hip, and the bastard stopped drowning him. Standing in a rush, Kyle rolled his eyes in growing frustration. "Man, I was hoping that was your nuts." He sniffed blood back against his sleeve. "Unless you're a eunuch ..."

The monster's eyes flared, and rage seeped into them. He screamed words needing translation in a ragged voice and lunged at Kyle. With his hair dripping bleach-y toilet water, he squelched as he sidestepped the beast. He close-hung the dude using his own momentum. As the Icarus doubled over to choke on his breath, Kyle shoved into the soldier's chest with one hand, and slammed an elbow into the middle of his back with the other. That looked like it hurt.

Before the monster recovered, Kyle pounded his knee into that snaggle-toothed face. Blue blood sprayed the white-washed cinder block walls. "Do you understand English?" The beast stumbled back and faced him with cerulean liquid rushing from his nose and mouth. His teeth stained a weird cast of blue. No answer.

"Do. You. Un-der-stand. En-glish?"

Just a wordless snarl in response.

"Good. Cause I want you to understand me when I say, 'I'm about to fuck you up.'"

Oh, yea. He got it. The butt-biter launched at him. Kyle turned, centered his balance with ease, and side-kicked the vamp-wannabe solidly in the chest. It went flying into the bathroom stall. The cherry on top? His head fell into the toilet. Kyle jumped on the stall door. The soldier righted himself as Kyle swung the door back at him. If the school built the door out of stronger materials, the blow would decapitate him. Alas, it made for the perfect throat crushing technique. Knowing full well how fast the beast recovered, Kyle spared no hesitation in grabbing the knife and finishing him.

He swung his soppy hair back and laughed, nudging the corpse with his foot. Lucky these cloaked guys didn't have the same skills Korac used with Rayne and Sagan. Maybe not every single blood sucker on Cinder was super gifted. "Ooo ... what's this?"

He knelt beside the body, shoved aside the folds of his cloak, and snatched something from his belt. A rather familiar dagger made of solid gold. From the pommel to the blade a golden-leafed vine swirled in delicate art. Was this . . . ?

"You forged this?" Celindria asked. She stared down into the magnificent vessel.

Pride warmed Devis' chest. His smile broadened at the awe in her eyes. Grateful for the rare gift of her praise, he said, "I named it Pretiosum Cruor, which means—"

"Cherished Blood," they said in unison. She smiled at him over the surveyed artifacts.

"How does it work?" she asked.

Devis understood Celindria always focused on business. She desired nothing more than to save humanity from the Icarean horde. He respected her for it, but he also wondered if she ever got lonely. Many in their group paired off. Even Xelan and Merit stopped dancing around it and started spending time together. But Celindria went off on her own, planning every detail of their revolution. He would never stop loving her.

"Devis? Is something wrong?" Celindria pressed.

"Oh, sorry! The work taxed me greatly." He laughed away her concern. "Here." On the silk he laid the dagger and vessel. Both forged with smelted gold. A metal which beared adverse effects on the monsters. He touched the empty heart-shaped glass of a receptacle. A golden sword pierced it, and a delicate golden vine surrounded both. "This is for the blood as we talked about. I designed this to chamber it. Releasing the blood will open the conduit and set in motion the final step in our plans. Once we gather The Brethren and discuss our strategy, we can start vetting volunteers for the process. One person. One bond. Forever."

"How do we get the blood into it?" she asked.

"This dagger." He touched a four-inch golden blade surrounded by the same swirling vine. "The technology Xelan provided us will prevent oxygen from reaching the blood. Straight from the vein to the glass with no exposure."

Celindria faltered and let the podium hold her weight. "Are you all right?" Devis asked, holding her elbow.

"Yes. I apologize. Must be the heat from the forge," she answered, her voice breathy.

"I will fetch water." Devis rushed to the center of the camp and collected the ladle from the trough. The Icari granted "free" humans pitiful access to water. They kept only the cattle hydrated. Never fresh, but the desert night cooled it to mask the taste. After filling the flask, he sealed it, and rushed back to his forge. Upon entering, he knew without words something went wrong. He dropped the flask. His eyes grew wide, and his mouth fell agape. "No," his voice quiet and thin.

Celindria offered a sad smile as if afraid she disappointed him. "This is the way," she offered.

"You can never understand what you have done," he accused.

"The nanotechnology will recognize my blood for the Vacating. It will accept no other."

"Forever, Celindria. It will not accept the blood of another so long as the technology exists," he elaborated.

She touched him on the shoulder gently and relaxed a little. "It could be no other way. Never would I ask any other to take on such a charge. All generations that follow would suffer. Please tell no one of the consequence," she implored.

"How could you ask me to accept such a thing?" Devis countered. "And what of the generations to follow your bloodline?"

"We must all bear our burdens. I, too, wish I did not have to ask you to bear mine."

He nodded. When she left, he stared at the podium. A tear fell from his eyes and then another. Inside the glass vessel pooled the most cherished blood, and he blamed himself.

Kyle stuck the fine instrument in one of his deeper pockets and chuffed at the fallen soldier. "This belongs to me. How did you get it?" A scream alerted him back to the battle in the cafeteria. Four left after this one. Not counting Korac, of course.

John's knee fucking hurt. It's all he could think about as he ducked again. For the fourth time that day he felt the air displacement of something swinging over his head, narrowly and fortunately missing. Four attempts on his life in a matter of six hours. That had to be a world record. And of course it's the first and only accomplishment in his life; he won't have a world to share it with. This whole day was seriously fucked. The worst part was how much the people he was with kept eating it up. They're all, "Oh Rayne says let's do this, so this is what we're gonna do," and, "We don't want anything happening to Rayne." Pfft, if it wasn't for her he wouldn't be in this mess in the first place.

Throughout today's events, he allowed a sparse momentary thought for himself, he reflected on that day two years ago when first approached by her mystery trainer.

"So you followed me all the way home because Rayne Callahan asked you to teach me how to defend myself in an oncoming apocalypse?" he asked. Why the hell was she even mentioning him to strangers? They weren't even close like that. This girl tortured him daily in their late afternoon classes for two years, listing off delicious food while he complained about his empty stomach. Diabolical.

"If you must put it in terms that simple, then yes, that's what I'm here for." The annoyingly good-looking and tall man—and John was tall so anyone taller than him was really tall—agreed almost as if it was a chore to him or an errand she had him run.

John stopped at the end of his driveway. "Look. I don't want you to be here, and you don't seem to want to be here. So let's just tell her whatever we have to to make this go away." He turned to walk away, and X-man guy appeared in front of him several yards away. Did he blink? Or have a seizure? John's mouth gaped. He couldn't help it. Gravel crunched as his bag dropped from his hands. It was like his brain had shut off or something.

God, was that embarrassing. He cringed as he recalled how pitifully bad he handled it all. He was such a sophomore then in every way. But the worst bit came later. After dinner, John followed Xelan two houses down to Sagan's place. Apparently, this was their regularly scheduled night, and superhero guy wanted to "ease you into it with a preview of the training."

Rayne tortured him for two years in class, and this whole time she led a double life and only just now felt he was important enough to get clued into it. Whatever. He didn't need any training wheels. "I know Aikido," John stated, feeling more than a little self-sufficient in defense.

Xelan offered a simple nod without turning back or stopping. "That should prove useful. I studied under Takeda Sokaku and Morihei Usehiba in the early 20TH century. Turning your opponent's momentum against them is a very valuable aspect of the style I teach."

John allowed his mouth to fall open again as he gaped at the back of Xelan's head. "Osensei?"

Xelan threw a glance over his shoulder. "The same." John didn't know what bothered him more: that Xelan claimed to train with a guy who died several decades before John was born, or that he wasn't even bragging about it. His face held nothing like boasting or mocking. He stated a simple fact.

"Hey, I was worried. You were later than usual," Sagan started. She glimpsed John, and after a flash of confusion, smiled. "Hey, John! This is my new boyfriend, Xelan. He goes to college. Did he miss my driveway and park at your house?"

"Well, actually—" John started.

Xelan's groaning stopped John's explanation. John spared Xelan a glare. The tall Aikido master pinched the bridge of his nose. "God, that was pitiful. I never thought I'd have to teach a teenage girl how to tell a decent lie, but it looks like I'll have to add an hour for 'covert operations.'"

At the time, John found all this mildly annoying. He didn't want to get involved with this, but a few moments later he agreed. "I can't believe you can move that fast," he said, staring at Sagan with the light of new appreciation.

"Yet somehow I always end up on my ass," she groused. She swiped a grass stain from her workout pants.

"Your turn," Xelan said.

Reluctant and a little nervous, John assumed a confident, balanced stance. "Before we get too far into this, I want to know how likely all this is to even happen. Like, how much of a chance are we talking here? An invasion sounds ludicrous."

Sagan chimed in, "We've been waiting two years. But I can tell you that in those two years, weird shit happened, and we accept in good faith that Xelan's training is best for us."

"How many of you are there?!" John scoffed.

"You don't need to worry about that. Just get ready to block this punch," Xelan commanded.

John posed his hands for the best defense he summoned and waited with easy breath. Xelan kicked him in the face. "Oh, ow! Fuck!" John shielded his nose and mouth and whined when he tasted blood. Filtered through his cupped hands, he shouted, "What the fuck, man?!"

"Shh!" Sagan hushed him. "Don't wake my parents."

"Jesus Christ!"

"You were watching my hands and not my moves," Xelan explained.

"Yea cause you said you would punch me," John argued.

"Do you think someone intending to kill you will tell you the truth and fight fair?" Xelan asked.

Well, John knew for sure now: Icari did not play fair. Despite the time he spent training with Xelan, he didn't find himself all that good at fighting them, either. But the others? Man, sometimes they actually smiled during these fights. The harder it got, the more likely it was to catch one of them grinning. It bothered him on a spiritual level. He just wanted to get out of there. He wanted an ice pack for his knee. He felt more than saw Andrew tackle the blood sucker behind him to the bloody disgusting table top. He heard the squelch of them both landing there. He gazed longingly at the space under the table beside him. He gave serious thought to crawling under it and waiting until the fight was over, but he knew that wouldn't fly.

He jumped up, ran over to the soldier under Andrew, and forced the thing's arms down. He hoped Andrew got a clear shot for the kill. There! As if Andrew considered the battle already won, he grinned. John shivered in revulsion. What was wrong with these people? The beast below Andrew surprised them both by wrenching his hands from John's grip and grabbing Andrew by the throat.

"Oh. Fuck," Andrew squeezed.

Fang-face threw him to the floor. It whirled on John. "Shit." He turned to run away, felt a loud and disrespectful 'pop' in his knee, and screamed. As he crumpled to the floor, he cursed himself for not hiding under the table earlier. The end was upon him. He squeezed his eyes tight and wished he stood even a slim chance of receiving Last Rites. The bastard breathed on his neck. Oh, hell no, this was not the way he wanted to go! Understandably, he whimpered. At the moment wet teeth touched his neck, the fucker dared to screech into his ear.

"What the hell?!" John needed to look. His eyes popped open, and he spun all the way behind him to see the wannabe vamp flailing around with his arms at his back. He clawed at something there. Just behind him, Andrew faced the Icarus with that perverse smile slapped back on his face.

"Come and get me, alien scum," he shouted. As John watched the "alien scum" pursue Andrew around the room, he realized how much he really didn't like being Rayne's friend.

"I hate what you did to me," Sagan confessed. She swung her fist.

Korac evaded. "Aww, baby. That's mean. You were never mean before. Has Tameka rubbed off on you?" He disappeared.

"Why? Don't you like my best friend?" She anticipated his next materialization and shoved the heel of her palm into his nose.

He took the hit and stumbled back. With one hand over his nose, he said, "Let's just say I don't want her giving a speech at our wedding."

She lunged with the sword. He turned to the side, evading the attack, and hammered an axe pommel on her wrist. Hard. She staggered, dropped her sword, and cursed. Korac's arms encircled her from behind and pulled her tight. One axe dug into her hip, the other on her shoulder, pressing against her face. His presence surrounded her, overwhelmed her, trapped her. No, not like this. She became a victim to a man not known for mercy. Anything but this. She broke out into a sweat, gritted her teeth, and swallowed her pulse.

Korac sighed against her ear. "Seems like you can't stay out of my arms, My Afflicted One." She closed her eyes tight and tried to steel herself against what she knew followed. She faded away. Her disassociation preferred recalling a dream, instead.

Sagan's body flushed to burning up. Sweat streamed down her disrobed skin. And she didn't care. She was so very close, and he would let her this time. He promised. He owed her. From her mind she pushed away thoughts like "What would Rayne think?" or "Am I a traitor?" She couldn't be bothered with that right now, not with his hands on her. He explored her with gentle touches. Every caress took her closer to the edge. The ebb and flow was over. It was finally her turn after four years. Her breath heaved from her lips in a luxurious sigh. Her fingers curled in his hair: a sinful treat. Only a dream could feel this good.

Sated and complete, she kissed the fingers on his hand that reached up to caress her cheek. "And you?" She offered many enticing possibilities with a single question. But he shook his head. His silver gaze appreciated her cooling body, but she detected something was wrong. "Please look at me." He hesitated longer than she liked. She coaxed his chin up with her finger until he met her eyes. The sorrow in his expression struck her. "What's wrong, my love?" she asked him, stroking a lock of his pale hair. She loved the almost silver quality of the silken strands.

His voice filled heavy with remorse she couldn't place. "I have wronged you," he said. She opened her mouth to protest, and he hushed her with a gentle finger to her lips. "I let this go on too long." His voice squeezed as he renewed their physical joining, much to her satisfaction. Her head fell back, and he moaned deep in his chest. "I was fascinated with you. Enraptured, yes." She tried to focus on what he said, but struggled the more he surged under her. "Yes, Elden, yes." He groaned and continued, "I was selfish. You must know that." She wanted to protest his accusation, but the rotation of his hips meant nothing she said at that moment would pass as comprehensible, and the small cry that escaped wouldn't qualify as confirmation or denial either way.

He called out her name so loud his sternum rumbled beneath her hand. She couldn't help herself. She leaned forward and placed soft kisses and teasing nibbles at his throat. She wanted him to taste pleasure, soon, despite the unexpected turn in conversation. He gripped her by the upper-arms, roughly. He maintained the pleasurable assault between them, but his eyes lost the remorse. The mercurial pools went ice and adamantine. "This isn't what I'm like at all. I need to show you." Through lids heavy with bliss, the world shifted down and up as she nodded her consent.

Korac dropped the act. He shoved his hand into her hair in a harsh jerk and gripped tight. He swept the free hand behind her, and held on as he rolled them from the pallet and onto the cold, stone floor. Her heart pounded for reasons which left her conflicted and eager at all at once. The shift stunned her from preventing what happened next. Hands that she found so gentle and smooth a moment ago, tugged at her wrists in coarse, forceful movements.

A wall appeared behind her in the dream, and from it the unmistakable clinging of iron. One wrist against something cold and craggy and the sound of scraping iron followed by the deep finality of a lock in place. Her eyes widened, her pulse surged, and her instincts kicked in. The panic rose and elicited from her a protest. But he did something unthinkable. He twisted his hips deep against hers. She managed a breathy whimper as he locked the free wrist into place. Again, that twist. She sucked her bottom lip into her teeth and shook her head slowly side to side in as tenacious a protest as she managed.

His ministrations were too good to her. She loved him. She trusted him. Even as he rifled through the pile of clothes and withdrew a four-inch, charred blade, she only returned as good as he gave.

She came back to herself in the cafeteria with a braided lock of his hair in her pocket. She said through gritted teeth, "Fuck you."

He chuckled, malice dripping from the sound, as he started drawing the axe down her cheek. She cried out as the skin submitted under the sharp silver, and blood flowed liberally from the wound. The entire time he kept his lips on her ear as he disfigured her.

"Love, why are you doing this?!" she asked. The desperation in her tone caused her to wince.

He breathed against her ear, quiet, meant only for her to hear, "If you come back with me, we can fix it. Just like that. No scarring." The silky tone took on a hard edge. "But if you don't, you'll always have this to remind you of me. And when you tire of seeing it in your reflection, you can come to me anytime."

Nope. She wouldn't have this anymore.

She stomped on his foot at the same time her elbow collided into his ribs. With a grunt, he backed away to catch his breath. Sagan grabbed the axe he held above her and landed a high kick square into his chest. The blow forced him to release the axe to her. He growled in frustration. Nervous about his retaliation, she put a few yards between them and tested the feel of the axe in her palm.

Korac recovered too fast. He straightened to all his height, towering almost a foot above her. His sense of humor remained unphased. "The reality is more enjoyable than the fantasy," he purred.

"With you, this wasn't what I fantasized about," she confessed.

Her honesty struck him. This gave her time to assess him. Why wasn't anything affecting him? No heavy breathing. No sweat. Not even pain. In a voice wrought with yearning, he shared, "I thought about this day for so very long."

Wait, there!

A tiny trickle of blue blood at the corner of his sinful smirk. And something in his silver eyes that seemed transformed. They smoldered like melting pools. His tongue slivered from between his lips to taste his own blood. "The way you look at me..." he said. He chuckled in that heavy bass rumble. "You're the warrior I wanted you to be. How would you tally this fight so far, Lieutenant General?"

Her breathing wrought polluted air that burned her lungs. The smoke began taking its toll. Even her eyes watered. This couldn't go on any longer. But she just couldn't resist a jab. She swallowed a dry lump in her throat, spun the axe once, and said, "You can't seem to stay off the floor."

Korac mirrored her axe spin. "Isn't this familiar? How good do you think you are with that?" He inclined his head at her axe.

She shrugged. "Feels right at home." And it did. And that scared her.

His cold and bitter laugh startled her before he swung his arm high and threw the axe. Sagan dove to the floor and somersaulted toward him. She straightened upright on her knees and plunged the axe with a strong two-handed grip. Her final desperate attempt to rid herself of his power over her.

Korac froze. His eyes went wide, the mercury in them shining. He lowered his gaze to the victim of his relentless, nightly torment and pleasure. Her eyes strained, her teeth clenched and bared, and her breathing labored. But she refused to let go of the axe embedded deep inside his chest. When she heard him grunt, she raised her own violet eyes to meet his.

This wound should be fatal. It should kill him. Xelan taught her so. The bone resisted until his chest gave under the honed blade. The apex of the axe penetrated his brain just enough to affect its functions.

Unsteady, he sank to his knees. His breathing grew more labored than her own. He grunted with every inhale. She gazed into his eyes. What was this feeling? Why ... ? With his blood spattered across her face and clothes, she searched for a feeling of relief. She released the axe, gasped for air, and tried to feel something else through her exhaustion. Korac reached for her with a pale hand. She recoiled, crawling back away from him. At last, his body fell lifeless to the side, his eyes unblinking.

Sagan touched her face to wipe away his blood. What was that? She stared at her hand. Tears. A tug on her heart. Another monster died. That's all. But still she cried for him. When the magnitude of it dawned on her, she fought not to weep. Loss. She grieved for Korac, or maybe just a chapter in her life closed before she was ready.

Kyle shouting at John broke her reverie. With shaking hands, she forced herself off the floor. And took stock of the battle going on around her. Why the hell were these last four still fighting? Their leader was dead. Yet, they continued to attack her friends. They were fighting to the last man. Were they stalling for something? A shriek sounded throughout the building and rang through her ears. Rayne.

"What are you doing?" Rayne asked. She strove to keep the fear out of her voice. It trembled anyway. From where she last landed after he last threw her, she gained a perfect view of Nox's hand stretched over a large mass of flaming rubble beside her. She observed him warily as she recovered from the most recent battering. The heavy, ornate ring shimmered with firelight.

His voice rumbled with gravel as he scolded her, "Patience." An unnerving, vicious smile spread across his lips slicing terror through her. The flames reflected in his obsidian eyes. Her heart raced and her mind reeled with whatever tortures he might devise to deliver upon her next. Just two more minutes, and she could defend herself, again. Come on. In one swift motion, the adorned fist hurled at her face. She recoiled, drew away, and waited for … nothing. Nothing came.

Please, please. What was he up to? Holding her breath, she popped open her eyes in caution and peeked over at him. When their eyes met, he pressed his open palm to her cheek. She shrieked. Her skin blistered under the white heat as the perversion of the Pretiosum Cruor branded into her face.

"That's it, girl. Look in the mirror, and think of me," he crooned.

While she writhed in pain, trapped under his legs, shame washed over her from her tears and her cries. Don't let him have those for free! "FUCK!" Raging against the unbearable, she beat at his arms with her fists with weak, futile efforts to pay him back. Overwhelming hatred replaced the shame, and her eyes blazed with it as sure as the fire creeping ever closer. She knew he could see it. He threw his head back and laughed that full, throaty sound. So pleasant, yet so cruel. So nice to see he was as much of a happy and joyful psychopath in real life. At least he matched his persona in her worst nightmares.

He gripped a fistful of her hair and brought her face to his. This close, death dwelled in his eyes, drowning the reflection of her bruised and soot-covered face. The certainty of her end quelled some of the fire in her. He said, "Destiny is patient."

He tossed her to the other end of the hall. She cried out as she slid across the floor over hot debris and missed a fallen beam by a breath. She groaned. Something ground against her arms and back. She examined the sting of burnt rubble in her skin. She started to sit up. Had to regroup. Needed to get away. Before she even mustered up enough strength to crawl, she froze staring at something beside her. She reached an unsteady hand out to touch it and withdrew with a squeak.

Nikki's body—charred over her hair, face, and one arm—laid spread out amid the rubble. "No," Rayne gasped. How? Did he catch her chasing down that Icarus from the cafeteria? Why? Why couldn't he just let her go? She died a bad death, the corpse frozen in an eternal scream. All the debris set her ablaze - hopefully post mortem. What skin she glimpsed appeared mottled with bruising.

Where was the fatal wound? She groaned when she found it. A deep indentation directly beneath Nikki's ribs. It welled into a cavern, crushing her internal organs beneath her diaphragm. How did that ...? Rayne searched the immediate area and glanced at the ceiling. Almost too late, she spotted the riot gate through the dense smoke. Simultaneously, his shadowy presence appeared beside her. Before Nox hauled it down on her, she rolled out of the way. Well, almost out of the way.

"Shit!" she cried.

The heavy metal of the riot gate crashed into her left arm. A sickening, guttural pop sound erupted from the smashed appendage. Her whole body spasmed in pain. She screamed through clenched teeth, "Oh God, no!"

"Powerless," he said.

The pain subsided replaced with a terrifying numbing sensation. The agony transformed into a tingling of nerves. It wasn't unlike a foot that fell asleep. The numb was probably bad, but she appreciated the momentary break. Gotta get the fuck—

SCREECH! Nox raised the hefty gate. "No!" she gasped. She swallowed three heaving breaths, pinned to the spot, and he slammed it down again. Her body jumped and writhed. She cried out to God and cursed him all at once.

"Hopeless." Amused, he raised the gate again. No, no, no, no …"Accepting." Gazing into her eyes, he rolled the gate down onto her arm again.

She hated the tears, hated the way her limbs flailed outside of her control, but most of all she hated that the pain dissipated in its entirety. That was not good. Her arm lost all responsiveness. Her mind begged her not to look. Not the time or place for denials. Very, very slowly she rolled onto her side and opened her eyes. "Oh, God …" she whimpered.

Her left arm spread out beside her without so much as a finger wiggle. Was this it? Would it never move again? Judging by the limpness of the socket, she guessed he dislocated the shoulder. Blood pooled and poured from the middle of her upper arm. Something peeked out in the blood. Stark. White. Bone. She groaned. He pulverized her arm. All of his intimidating form towered over her with something akin to joy or admiration igniting the features of his face. Like he found a new toy or possession to play with. He stared at the exposed bone in her arm. She needed to get the fuck out and right now. He chuckled. "While I waste my time here, at least I'll have something to amuse myself with."

Thank goodness she couldn't feel her actual arm, because if she didn't get up this was going to suck. Get up. She pushed. Nothing. Get up! Right now. He was about to fuck her up, and her body refused to respond. She tapped out her reserves, and the sweltering brand on her face didn't exactly encourage morale.

Nox fell upon her with a thirst she recognized from her nightmares. "May I have this dance?" he asked. Mock gentility dripped from his words. He bent over beside her, lifted her numb hand gingerly, and placed a soft kiss on the back of it. She locked eyes with the devil and for a moment contemplated falling into them, believing the possibilities that shone there. When his lips curled into a gruesome smile, she held her breath, knowing what came next. He gripped the entire hand hard and pulled her by her broken arm. A striking pain went straight to her heart and out of her throat in a scream.

"I am going to fucking kill you!"

TEN

Rely On Your Confidence Even If It's False

"**WHERE DO YOU THINK IT IS?**" Pablo asked as they approached the end of the Lab hall. He kind of thought all this hero shit was nonsense, but he knew deep down, if he lived through this he wanted to be counted among the heroes. Especially to her.

Lynn peered around the corner opening into North Hall. Right. Then left. Nothing. "When this first started, did you hear someone shouting orders?"

He nodded. He liked the way her braids swayed when down, but he also liked them tied back from her face. They framed her beautiful brown eyes. His fingernails dug deep into his palms. He had to quit thinking like that. Treating injured classmates afforded him some measure of distraction. But now, on their own and facing certain death, he only wanted to focus on her.

She inhaled deep and cleared her throat. The smoke got thick, fast. She said, "I was about to run like everyone else through the hall until I saw him. He dressed different, and he wasn't exactly charging after anyone like the rest of them. In fact, all he did was stand in front of the library."

"And?" Pablo asked. Was he missing the point?

She headed to the left down North Hall. "I think that's where they're coming from."

He followed now. "Oh."

She peered around the corner. When she walked around it, he joined her. Their hands brushed, and he clutched his hands at his sides to keep from taking her hand. She meant all business: searching the library through the glass doors. It appeared dark with no sign of movement. "C'mon …" she muttered.

Why does the sign call it a 'Media Center?' It never made much sense. It wasn't like students could check out videos or anything.

"I wonder why the sign has always said 'Media Center?'" she asked. He decided then and there he planned to marry her regardless of how this apocalypse shit turned out.

"The computers, maybe?" He offered in the way of an answer. He contemplated what his tux might look like.

She scoffed, "Those computers can't run any kind of media."

In one shared moment they looked into each other's eyes and busted out laughing. Surrounded by bodies, the sun went out, and their friends fought for their survival. They hung out in the wide open. And no fucks were given. They needed this laugh, just like, and he was sure of this, they needed to be together when they got out of here.

The humor receded from her face. He frowned when she grew stern again. "We gotta check this out," she said.

With caution, they pulled the doors open and walked through the metal detectors. Ms. Penny called in that morning, but Ms. McGreen came in as usual. Through the darkness, they gazed over the walls lined with musty books. In the center a long table of student-accessible computers. They took a few careful steps forward, trying hard to stay quiet. Both of them gripped their knives firm in hand. They made it past the checkout counter when something caused Lynn to whimper.

"What?" Pablo asked. He rushed over to her and stopped dead. "Oh, God …"

The librarian offices stood off on the right side of the main room. If anyone wanted to speak to them, they just tapped on the large, glass windows. They found Ms. McGreen there. Her arms and legs spread wide, mounted against the window of her office. Her chest cavity splayed wide open like butterflied chicken. The ribs and lungs exposed and intertwined with computer parts wedged in blood where the heart belonged. Blood coated her face from the gouges in her eyes. Someone lodged keys from a keyboard into the empty sockets: "F" in the left eye and "U" in the right eye.

Pablo tried to contain it, but the whole room spun. He crouched to the floor and spilled what little contents his stomach held. He suppressed a sob when Lynn started rubbing his back in soothing circles. "It's okay," she assured. Definitely marrying her. When he finished, she offered him a bottle of water. "Are you all right?"

He swallowed hard and gulped a little air. "You know? I'm really starting to hate that question."

"Are you okay?" Kyle asked Sagan as he offered his hand.

She nodded and let him lift her off the floor. After all the wet, slippery shit she touched that day, she still wiped her hands on her pants leg and grimaced. "Why are you all wet?!"

He gave his signature shrug. "I got my first swirly, and I don't really recommend it."

She decided not to ask for details and instead assessed the situation in the cafeteria. Only four Icari left to fight and Rayne yet to return from Nox. Sagan hated this. Why was Rayne so stubborn? And why was she so often right?

Only three months ago, Rayne gathered them for an emergency meeting in the bookstore. "I know all of our free time is precious," Rayne started. She leaned against the counter of the break room. The group scattered around the space: Andrew at the table, Kyle leaned against the wall, and Tameka and Sagan sat on the couch. "So I won't keep you long. No one's heard from Xelan in a month. That's the longest we've lost contact with him."

To Sagan, Rayne paused not to let the news sink in, but because she found it hard to continue. The stiffness of her shoulders, the strain in her eyes, and sure to follow up with—yup, the hard swallow. Something was up.

Andrew offered, "That doesn't necessarily mean anything."

"Yea, the scrub's around town somewhere up to clandestine shit," Kyle agreed.

"He certainly hasn't abandoned us," Tameka said. She sounded a little defensive. Interesting.

Sagan smiled. They were all lucky to have each other as friends. But Rayne grew more agitated. Was she counting the floor tiles?

After another long minute, she confessed, "He told me once to consider four weeks the limit, and initiate emergency protocols."

All went quiet. Just breathing in the room. A little hum from the heat in the vents. Tameka stared hard at Rayne. Kyle examined his shoes. Andrew looked off in the distance. And Rayne glanced at each of them. Sagan tried to smile for her, but she wore the General hat, now.

"Keep a bag ready if you already don't. You need to have a variety of weapons, but you also want medical supplies. Possibly a change of clothes. Think ahead. Think smart. Anticipate your needs and make one. Keep it in your car if you have one. Or hide it in your parents' trunk. Keep one in your bedroom. We should probably store some at the skating rink. If you think of anywhere else to store a kit, do it," Rayne lectured. "Andrew?"

He snapped out of it. "Yes?"

"Did you get all that?" Rayne asked.

Her voice made Sagan wince. "Rayne," she breathed.

Rayne shoved her fingers in her hair and pulled tight. "I'm sorry, guys. I—"

"We get it," Tameka grumbled and rolled her eyes. "You're in charge—"

"I'm fighting Nox alone."

Now the room went into an uproar.

"Fuck, no!" Kyle shouted.

Tameka asked, "Do you have a fucking death wish?!"

No fucking way was she about to let her best friend just volunteer for suicide like that. And it sounded like no one else was keen on the idea, either. While the others made a chorus of protests, Sagan noticed Andrew remained silent. "The hell you are!" Sagan cried.

"She's right," Andrew said. Kyle, Sagan, and Tameka glared at him.

"The fuck you say?" Tameka's legendary hard frown warded off possessive girlfriends accusing her of stealing their boyfriends, teachers that liked to get handsy, and grown men who threatened her in traffic.

Sagan touched her arm as gently as possible. Tameka snapped to her. "Let's hear him out," she pleaded.

Andrew gestured to Rayne. "Rayne's the most capable out of all of us. She had the most training with Xelan. And most importantly, Nox needs her alive. But not us. If we're there, he can use us against her."

Kyle shook his head and said, "I cannot believe I'm hearing this."

"No, man. I don't want to be a distraction for her and get her killed." Andrew paused to look each of them in the eyes. "And he will kill each and every one of us. He'll get off on it as long as it makes her miserable."

Rayne flinched. Her whole complexion went gray. Her eyes grave. Never again. Sagan hopped off the couch and crossed the room to her. The moment her arms wrapped around Rayne, the trembling torrent of tears started. "You don't know what he can do to you." Sagan squeezed tighter. Rayne let it all out. "He'll butcher you just because I care about you. He'll make me watch. You have to stay away from me."

Rayne started when heavy arms enveloped her. Andrew and Tameka joined the group hug. "We're not going anywhere," Tameka said.

"Promise me?" Rayne squeaked. "Promise me you won't give him any ammunition?"

Kyle joined at last, notably not touching Tameka. "Promise me," Rayne's voice grew firm once again.

It killed Sagan to say it, but "I promise ..."

It took every ounce of self-control not to run and help her. She hoped she did the right thing. As for the rest of the group ... John struggled with his right leg. He favored the obvious weakness as he faced down his Russian soldier. The one for each human civilization thing crept her the fuck out. Andrew stood over the one he fought after shoving a metal shaft through its back. Nikki running off and not returning weighed heavily on her mind. Tameka fought off two Icarean soldiers.

Sagan burst into action. Tameka's curling mass of red hair bounced from the table where one soldier held her arms down on the bloody lunch surface. Another straddled her. His arms raised high and when the weapon glinted in his hands, Tameka screamed bloody murder.

Sagan retrieved the axe Korac threw at her and rushed over to the addition's entrance. She stepped onto one stool attached to the table, ran over the top, and leapt off onto the wall. Pushing her right foot firmly against it, she vaulted in the direction of the fuckhead holding Tameka down. She swung the axe mid-fall. The monster's head landed on the ground before she did. Two more to go.

Before the Icarus straddling Tameka sunk the knife home, Andrew dove into its midsection, and both of them crashed to the floor. Andrew speared the soldier's chest with its own fallen knife. It wailed as cobalt arterial spray drenched Andrew's already messy face. "FUCK!" Andrew shouted. With the wailing cut off in abrupt silence as the beast hopefully died, shouts erupted from the other side of the cafeteria. Sagan's head snapped up, and Andrew bolted upright.

An Icarus dragged John away by his bad leg. Where the Icarus thought he was taking him, no one was sure, but Kyle wasn't having it. He leapt from the nearest table onto the soldier's back hard enough that he rode it down to the floor. "Where the fuck do you think you're going?! John, are you okay? John?" John made achingly slow progress to stand on his good leg. The very pissed off soldier threw Kyle and retrieved him from his landing site only to throw him again.

"Butt biter!" John called.

The Icarus snapped his teeth at John and rushed him. Inches from a pummeling, he gloated "Yea, you know you shouldn't turn your back on an enemy."

Kyle hit the Icarus over the head with a toilet seat he pulled from God knew where. He threw the soldier up against the wall, and John staked it with scrap metal. Sagan surveyed the room. By some miracle, they killed all the invaders. And the unit stayed alive. A twinge struck her as she wondered about Nikki.

"Is that all of them?" Kyle asked.

"Yea, it is ..." Sagan answered with a smile creeping on her face.

Andrew stared at Sagan as she tore the bottom of her tank top, and began wrapping her wounds with her midriff exposed. If she caught him looking, she might think he perved on her. But he meant well. Just checking her for wounds after her fight with Nox's second-in-command. More than wounds, she carried herself as if affected.

John began examining his knee while Kyle checked his potentially broken nose in the mirror.

"Where's Nikki?" Tameka asked. She rubbed her bruised throat.

"She never came back," John answered on a groan.

"What about Rayne?!" Kyle asked.

Sagan and Andrew exchanged a look while everyone watched. "She'll be fine."

"But what if—" Tameka began.

"No, just leave her to it. We promised her." Sagan interjected.

John interrupted, "Well, at least they're gone." He nudged a fallen soldier's corpse with his foot. "What do we do with their bodies? We can't just leave alien bodies lying around."

"The fire will take care of it," Andrew responded. The way it spread, it might take care of them first. Andrew started to move this evacuation along and opened his mouth—

"One hell of a fight, huh?" Kyle smiled when they gave him confused faces.

Why the hell did Kyle have to be so fucking weird? "Dude," Andrew said.

Then they broke into a fit of laughter. Andrew needed that no matter how much it hurt. What a fucking day. Both he and John sagged to the floor, holding their ribs. Tameka knelt to check on him. "Thank you." He appreciated her small smile in return.

Kyle gave his nose a more thorough inspection. When the laughter faded into sighing and deep, mutual relief, Andrew glanced up to see Sagan standing over him.

"How did you know to come here, today?" she asked. Straight to the point.

"What do you mean?" Andrew feigned. He did not want to do this right now.

"You couldn't have known to come today unless you were informed about the attack!" she shouted at him, getting angrier by the second.

It was true. Andrew did not attend the same school, and wouldn't have known to come without forewarning. He stood and faced her. "All right," he began with a reluctant sigh. "He told me not to say anything but ..."

"Who?" Kyle asked, joining the interrogation.

He hesitated. How could he phrase this without breaking his oath? "Xelan."

One word, one name, said all too much. Shit. "Xelan?!" Tameka repeated, more than a little shocked. The news surprised everyone, save for Sagan. She grew further enraged. He couldn't blame her.

"When?! When did you speak to him? No one else has heard from him in four months! How long have you known?!" She backed him against a wall, advancing toward him, gripping the axes with renewed vigor.

Andrew raised his hands in surrender. Time to lie. "This morning, I swear. I had a nightmare of Fair in flames and there he was, all dark and full of warnings." He lowered his arms and relaxed as Sagan loosened a little.

"What did he say?" Tameka asked. She flanked Sagan like she might have to hold the shorter girl back.

He couldn't tell them the truth. No matter what. It's not like they would appreciate that he met with Xelan secretly these last four months. Besides, he was deep in the weeds, and he had more questions than answers, himself. This morning was a prime example.

"Nox is making his move, today."

Andrew stopped fishing his backpack out of his mom's Volkswagen. Just what he needed on this nice spring day. He'd like to say Xelan's appearance startled him, but the handsome Icarus was doing this a lot lately. "Good morning to you, too," he harrumphed, and went back to pulling his bag out. Only five minutes remained until the late bell. He wouldn't make it.

Xelan pulled the bag from Andrew with a sharp tug and chucked it on the ground. "This isn't a drill."

"Look dude, you're making me regret parking in the fucking shade. All I have to do is walk three feet that way, and you'll have to harass someone else. I'm tired of this fucking 'vampire's apprentice' shit you've got going on with me. Everyday last week you told me Nox was coming with all of Cinder to tear apart our planet, and nothing came of it except a lot of marks on my fucking truancy record."

The Icarean giant unceremoniously hauled Andrew up off his feet and slammed him onto his mom's car, leaving a huge dent on the roof. Xelan stood over him. "I can't fucking be there to protect her, and The Brethren picked *you* to do it." He emphasized "you" by painfully jabbing his finger into Andrew's chest. Xelan leaned over him and gripped the teenager's shirt in his fists. He pulled him close, so the message came loud and clear. "If anything happens to her because you weren't there, I will eviscerate you and drag your ass to Nox, myself. If you don't go, she will die. And so will the rest of your stinking race." Just as quickly as he threw Andrew onto the car, Xelan released him, leapt to the ground, and straightened his coat.

As Andrew lay in the crater of the VW's exterior, he felt torn. On the one hand, he really wanted to blow Xelan off and just go about his fucking day. On the other, he never saw that man's eyes filled with such unadulterated terror before. Clearly, this was it. And he wasn't about to fail Rayne. With a groan, he rolled himself off the top of the sedan. Once on the ground, he asked, "Do you know what plan they're going with?"

After Xelan explained, Andrew felt light-headed. He raced up to the tree and lost his breakfast all over the roots. Xelan, for all his animosity, spared Andrew the shit talking for once.

In a soft voice, he said, "I'd offer to hold your hair, but I can't get to you."

Small comfort. But still appreciated. Swallowing hard and gasping for air, Andrew choked out, "Will anyone survive?"

Xelan's initial estimates turned out fairly fucking accurate so far. And now he wasn't around to get this grilling from all their people. The truth, but not all of it. "He said Rayne would die today if I didn't come here. And if that happened, we would all die. Something about the aftermath." Andrew swallowed. "I actually didn't fucking believe him at first, but I was late to school anyway and could afford to drop by. But the Icari are dead, and it's over now." Okay, so he managed it.

As he finished his explanation, the foundation shuddered beneath their feet. His eyes searched the quaking room.

Sagan bolted for the cafeteria's entrance. "No ... it's not over." Everyone formed a line beside her, and a sense of dread filled the air.

ELEVEN

Love And War Are Two Of The Most Unfair Games We Play, So Why Not Play Them At The Same Time?

PABLO AND LYNN ADVANCED AT A CREEP DOWN THE LIBRARY'S SHORT CORRIDOR INTO THE BREAK ROOM. This close to the librarian offices the strong smell of perforated organs curled their nostrils, and both sported a rough grimace. Ms. McGreen was not well liked. She replaced everyone's favorite librarian just this year, but she didn't deserve all this. A wave of nausea overwhelmed Pablo. He began to dry heave with little to no noise. Lynn pulled the door flush closed hoping to staunch the smell.

"You good?" she whispered, eager to move on.

"Yea. Thanks. Let's keep going," he lied. He gestured her forward. He wasn't really ready to press on, but honestly how was he supposed to salvage her opinion of him if he kept cowering and retching. Besides, something gnawed at his morbid curiosity further down the hallway, and despite his fight or flight begging him to give it up, he needed to see it.

The darkness smothered him like a velvety, tangible blockade. He wished for a cell phone for some light. As if summoned, a beam of light pierced the veil of darkness all the way down the hall. She glanced back at him, flashlight in hand. "I'm glad these batteries work," she said.

"You can say that again. The smoke just makes everything so much more . . ." he fought for a word.

"Terrifying? Claustrophobic? Horror movie atmosphere?" she offered. She swung the beam out of one door and into another. Searching.

She was so fearless. God, he was falling in love with her. As much as teenage boy hormones could strum up legitimate love feelings. "Claustrophobic was my favorite. I like when you say four-syllable words. Smart chicks are hot." She snapped back around to him. He really didn't mean to say that aloud, so much so he almost clapped his hands over his reflexively flirtatious mouth. Instead, he gave into the nervous habit, and licked his lips. And she watched him do it.

Seconds ago, he came close to puking his guts up. Now, he wanted to charge the steps between them, sweep her up in his arms, and plant a kiss on her lips. In his little fantasy he wasn't sure if he wanted her aware of his hormonal man-reaction to her, or if he would keep that a secret physically between them. Before he put his plan into action, a dry rasp interrupted the darkness. The mood died as both of them stiffened, alert.

"Did you do that?" she whispered. He shook his head. Any words he wanted to answer with choked in his throat. To his absolute horror, she inched forward. He communicated his disapproval in rigid, frantic gestures. The whisper of his hands moving all manner of ways caught her attention, and she turned back round.

She mouthed, "We. Have. To. Know."

He cocked one eyebrow sky high. "Do. We. Really?!" And hoped all his incredulity seeped into his lip talking.

She just turned around and kept going. Pablo didn't so much as throw his hands in the air with frustration as tried to offer them to a God he wasn't sure existed in exchange for the ability to transfer his logic into the head of the girl he loved. An age-old gesture. Exasperated, he clutched his knife, huffed, and followed.

The corridor ended in a large storeroom. Files and crates of books piled up the walls on all sides. It gave him a new perspective on what librarian work consisted of. Lynn made it to the back of the storeroom, peeking at the corner. Her head vanished into the wall. The darkness was obviously playing tricks on him. He crossed the room after her. At the seams of the wall where they met in the corner, Lynn found a narrow hallway. She glanced into his face. He nodded, and they took the corner.

They gawked at what they found inside. In the floor, beneath a large patch of removed carpet, an access hatch. Glancing at one another again, Pablo held one hand palm up, and the other in a fist on top of it. Realizing what he wanted, she rolled her eyes and mimicked the gesture. Rock. Paper. Scissors. He got rock. She got scissors. Sighing, she passed over the flashlight to him. He was of two minds about winning. On the one hand, he wanted to keep her back here where she was less likely to be hurt; on the other hand, he didn't want to be hurt either. But this was a chance at redemption, and he was not passing it up.

Slowly, painfully slowly, he edged over to the open hole in the secret room of their scary library. He examined the hole itself and found what he predicted might be there: a ladder. Next step, look in the hole. He really didn't want to look in the hole, but he shoved his face to the frayed carpet and peered in with the flashlight. It led down a passageway to a basement he never knew existed. Although the dark obstructed most of his vision, he spotted a connecting tunnel of some kind.

As soon as he found it, the ground shuddered as if it were about to rupture and swallow them whole. Something was coming. Pablo panicked and dropped the flashlight.

"What is it, Pablo?!" she called. The tremor in her voice upset him. He wanted to keep her safe.

He jumped up. "GO!"

She didn't argue. He reached her, and they both started running. Down the narrow hallway. The sound took on form: loud, stampeding boots. They were chased by whatever came out of that hole. "Pass me a Molotov and a light!" he cried as they turned the hidden corner.

"I got you," she said and tossed him the supplies. They rushed down the smelly corridor. He glanced back, and not far behind a pasty, tall motherfucker dressed way different from the others appeared around the hidden corner. He lit the rag and tossed it. They broke into the stacks of seizing books.

"Nice shot!" Lynn shouted.

It connected and burst into flames. At least one caught fire and stopped chasing them. Not bad. Not bad.

They passed the checkout counter, once more through the theft detectors, and all the while dodging equipment sliding out of their shelves, they fled the library. As they ran through the doors, more thunderous boots sounded.

When Lynn and Pablo made it to the mouth of North Hall, they found Sagan and the others standing bloodied in front of the cafeteria. He gave one passing thought that he hoped it wasn't all their blood, before he kicked it into high gear. "Run!" they shouted in unison. The others didn't react fast enough.

"I thought all the Icari were dead?" Kyle asked.

"Those were Colita's soldiers," Sagan stated.

"Yeah?"

"These are Korac's warriors," she said, and stared beyond Pablo.

Just as she finished explaining, sixteen men in chrome armor and silk robes came charging around the corner behind Lynn and Pablo. One sported some nasty burn wounds. His skin damn near melted off his face.

Time slowed down. Everyone turned to retreat just as Pablo and Lynn ran by them. Lynn turned, lit one of the bottles, and threw it on an advancing Icarus. He whooshed up in flames as the alcohol poured over him. Yup, Pablo was definitely marrying her. Asking her the moment they won this battle. And they were winning. He knew she wouldn't let them lose.

The ground shook with the weight of blood suckers like a stampede of elephants quaking the earth. The weapons they held looked strange, serrated like sharp teeth. They just couldn't get out of the way fast enough. Sagan and Kyle led in front. "This way!" Sagan shouted to the rest behind them. She ran past the entrance to the gym, and turned the corner down the narrow corridor. The lights of the back-up generator flashed red across their faces.

"Come on! Just a little further!" she encouraged. Well, she hoped it was encouraging. At this point, she'd settle for desperate. The corridor twisted and turned as they ran in a single file line to the exit. Sagan noticed as she passed the auxiliary gym, the riot gate bore down, blocking it. Why would that gate be down? The only thing in there was … they came to the exit. A large chain with a huge lock looped through the bars on both doors. Fuck. The other exit. They blocked it with the riot gate. Smoke billowed to enter her lungs. And big ass aliens were on their way to butcher them in the school's asshole.

"Sagan, how do we get out of here now?" Tameka asked when she turned the last corner and saw the door. Her words came a little too sharp and fast. Tameka can't panic. If she was panicking, they were all going to die.

John stared at the doors as the rumbling came closer. "We're gonna die here," he whispered.

That was it. Sagan turned to him. "No, we're not." She spun back to the door after she heard a loud crash into it. Kyle rammed into the door with his shoulder. Andrew and John ran into the door with him.

"Shit!" Kyle sank to the floor, the sword wound on his left arm gushing from his efforts. "It's no good. We can't get through here. And the gym is closed off." Andrew and John continued banging into the doors in a desperate attempt to get them the fuck out.

Sagan glanced back to the corridor. Shadows moved in the red and green fading lights. "Oh, fuck! Move! Back away from the door!" she shouted in a firm, authoritative voice. They backed off, and she cleared through them. She raised Korac's axe using both hands and swung down, slicing through the chains with sparks flying. The strike point of the axe blade went red and smoldered, the chains smoked. Only then, she realized she lost the other axe in the cafeteria. She wanted to pout.

"Damn," Pablo said with feeling.

"Come on. We gotta get out of here!" Sagan kicked the doors open.

That's when they realized they weren't safe from the Icari outside at all—the sun disappeared. "Fucking underground school," she cursed loud enough she heard grunts of agreement from her friends.

Andrew said, "Yea no offense guys, but your school is fucking jacked. Before the assault." Plumes of smoke billowing from the old Eagle's nest across the way implied it was beyond jacked now.

Students scattered across the parking lot like a cat jumped into a jigsaw puzzle. When they noticed everyone escaping from the building, they cheered in celebration and relief.

"No!!! RUN!!" Sagan and Tameka screamed. No one moved. They didn't understand. They were still overjoyed to see them alive. "No!!" They ran into the very middle of the gathering crowd. "They're coming. We have to leave," Sagan shouted.

Kyle shook his head. "There are fifteen of them and like a few hundred of us. We can take 'em."

Andrew protested, "We can't just hand weapons to civilians and expect them to survive."

John threw down his bag of weapons and opened it. Sagan rummaged through it. Any swords claimed from Icarean bodies she reserved for her immediate team. She muttered only loud enough for Andrew to hear, "I'm not even expecting them to survive, but I am expecting them to take one or two with them."

Andrew stared at her, open-mouthed, as she addressed the surviving students. "The bastards who attacked our school brought reinforcements. Look at us." She swept her hands around their crew. "We're bloody, bruised, and tired. We killed at least thirty of these things already and one of their leaders. Look at you." Students glanced amongst one another. "There are at least three hundred of you. You, who arranged three jumps at the same time to stretch security so thin the fights went on for thirty minutes. Who rallied behind one student to rid the school of the teacher harassing her and broke his leg in the process. Is this not the most dangerous school in Little Rock?" The crowd cheered. Each student straightened, stood taller. Everyone of them proud of their misguided reputation. Not so misguided right now. "Fifteen. We only have to kill fifteen. Run away, back to the football field if you have to. I won't ask you to fight if you're afraid. But if you think you can do anything to help, grab a stake or a shiv or a shank, and hold the line."

Only three students walked back to the football field. Surprisingly, one of them was Matt. She was sure he wouldn't mind a fight. The crew passed make-shift stakes, and unclaimed swords out to as many people as they could. Kyle walked over to Lucy and asked, "Are you all right?" She gave him a furtive glance and showed little recognition in her eyes. "Take this." He put a sword in her hand and touched her shoulder. Some people grabbed materials for weapons out of the dumpsters and random debris littered across the parking lot. When it seemed like everyone held a weapon, they formed a line, an organized mass of people. A small army.

The fifteen super warriors emerged from the building at a casual pace. A few laughed, mocking the school's pitiful resistance. But several took a fighting stance with serious, cautious expressions. What were they thinking? What's the best chopping method for julienne Fair student?

She stood at the front line. No fear. She fought stronger and killed worse not even thirty minutes ago. Kyle seemed unafraid next to her. Andrew stood amongst the mass of students like a great, unwavering statue. He did not look happy. Their strength helped the others gain confidence, and a wave of defiance surged through the crowd. They would win. Or so they thought. From behind the fifteen super soldiers appeared thirty or more of Colita's varied ethnicity warriors, each of them with a shining sword in hand. The army of students took a collective, hesitant step back. Sagan and the rest stayed put.

Tameka growled, "That bitch! How many did she breed?"

Two Icari pressed forward, and the tension surged in Sagan's gut. Before she made the call to attack, a loud horn blared through the battleground.

"What the fuck?" Kyle called out.

A white Chevy Malibu barreled down the hill from the direction of the football field. The mass of students rushed out of the way, but the Icari stood there. Hadn't they seen a car before?

John muttered, "No fucking way."

Sagan peered into the driver's seat, and she couldn't suppress the delighted smile that spread across her face. Matt smashed his car right into the crowd of bewildered Icarean soldiers. The impact wasn't pretty. Two warriors went under the car, four rolled over the top, and two went flying back into the school. While one of them made a fine hood ornament, the others recovered.

Not fucking around, he threw his car into reverse, backing over the ones under and behind his tires. He shocked Sagan by jumping out of the car and decapitating the six on the ground with a machete. Now was as good a time as any. She shouted, "You fucked with the wrong school!" And charged into the line of Icari. The mass of students surged around her like water parting around a stone. The Icarean forces charged forward, and the two masses collided with Machete Matt in the center.

Nox took a few steps down the hallway dragging Rayne along with him by her broken arm. The debris and glass covering the floor buried inside her back. She twisted against it, her free hand scratching her nails against the floor until her fingertips bled. He raised her from the floor by her arm, forcing her to climb to her feet. She cried out. Dislocated, crushed, and bleeding yet he still felt the need to manipulate her body like a rag doll.

The world stopped spinning once she stood for a minute or two. He snarled into her face, "Is this all your training amounts to?!"

Her whole body feeling like one giant, bleeding bruise, she fell back on her innermost self and hoped she possessed enough energy to pull it off. She summoned all her snark and spat into his face. "Is this all your creative torture lessons amount to?" She wished she carried even half the intimidation his voice did, but what evs.

Blood spattered over his mouth. Much to her dismay, he licked it from his lips. "That's a rude way to address your dance partner." With little effort, he spun her away from him by the worst of her left arm. She landed against the riot gate and lost her sight when her face hit it full-force.

She tried to raise her head and see through the black coffee grounds in her vision. He already appeared behind her, twisting her arm against her back, bending the elbow inward. She suppressed the urge to whimper, but failed to prevent the gasping. Instead, as her sanity deserted her, she muttered, "I never agreed to dance with you."

He pressed his ear to her lips. She ground, "I never. Agreed. To Dance. With you."

He had that signature villain laugh down to an art. He did it so well: a lot of evil and a little sexy. She hated it. He suggested, "Let's make a deal between friends then. I get you to agree to dance with me, and you wear something outstanding."

"Never. Going. To happen," she offered a meager protest.

He bent the elbow again and wrenched her arm the other way. The fire spread, and near that end of the hallway, things started to collapse. Ceiling panels warped and melted, landing all around them. Looking up, the beams above shifted as if they wanted to give. She missed the numb feeling in her arm. This sensation came close to making her faint.

"Had enough yet?" Nox asked against her ear, leaning his full weight on her mangled arm.

She clenched her teeth, sweat and something else dripped down her brow onto her cheek. "Fuck you," she managed in a fierce voice, hoarse from the smoke.

"We could do that or ..." Nox whirled Rayne around to face him. His smile disappeared, setting off alarm bells. This new expression frightened her even more with its emptiness. The horrible sight of her reflected in his eyes. Her reflection drowned in flames. "We could do this," he whispered, brushing his knuckles against her cheek over the open wound of his insignia.

She hissed at him. That same hand clutched strong fingers around her throat, squeezing firm enough to damn near paralyze her, but open enough she drew breath into her dried husks for lungs. He circled her around and bent her until she leaned backwards. The glass and pebble debris dug into her skin more. Agony blanketed every cell in her being. Fire, there was fire.

She turned her neck, craned it as far as she stretched in his firm grasp. He held her over a flaming heap of rubble. The shredded cloth of her shirt gave way to the flames licking across her back, kissing the bloody scrapes.

Rayne drove her nails into the skin of his wrist. Nox clenched his jaw and squeezed his fingers ever so slightly. "Let ... go ..." she squeezed out on a strangled growl. He lifted her by the throat, gradually raising her higher above him. She choked in convulsions against his hand, trying to find air. She raked her nails down his wrists, and little rivers of blood followed.

"Your lessons were woefully incomplete. Tell me, did you ever ask yourself if an Icari would teach you how to take another of his kind down?" Nox queried. Fuck this guy. Xelan wanted him overthrown. But she never really asked why.

Vision blurred. Spots. Couldn't breathe. He threw her, hurled into another section of lockers further up the hall where the fight started. Once she sagged to the floor, her senses came rushing back. Something dripped from her head into her eye. She touched her fingertips to it and winced. Blood from where he slammed her into the riot gate. She let her hand fall to her side and touched something cold. She grasped it, suppressing a smile. The sword. The still bleeding knuckles of her right hand whitened as she tightened her grip, sure of her strength. No more. He abused her body close to the point of immobility, and she was certain the cold at the back of her head was nothing good.

Was she supposed to answer his question? "No. The thought never occurred to me, being only fourteen and all," she croaked.

Rayne lifted her eyes, red with strain from the smoke. Nox stood over her, sword in hand, and that empty expression that unnerved her so. He wanted a challenge. She stood carefully until she planted her feet steadily beneath her despite the exhaustion weighing her down. All the fire in her set ablaze. This ass kicking stopped now. She leveled her gaze with his dark stare and rage filled her, warming the cold, numbing sensations.

Nox didn't miss the transition in her stance. He advanced toward her with a strike for her face. Her sword met his above her head, clanking loudly. He reached for her with his free hand, seizing the meat of her left shoulder and pushed. A sickening sound emitted from her arm, and Rayne cried out. Staggering back, she realized she gained some mobility in her left arm again. It was painful. The bone still broken, possibly in pieces.

"Son of a bitch!" she exclaimed, cradling the arm to her. He lunged for her, and she crouched to the floor. A quick sweep at his legs, and Nox fell on his back. She made a strike for him, but he kicked her in the leg like a little bitch. She landed on her knees. In a sheer defiance of physics, Nox pulled himself upright, feet planted to the floor. He brought one knee to her face, and she grunted as she went down again. Turning her wrists so that her palms pressed flat against the tile, she kicked her feet up and performed a perfect kip-up. She waited in front of him, sword in hand.

"This is much better," that twisted smile returned to Nox's lips. Rayne wasn't sure which expression she hated more.

The battle outside raged on. Out in the rear parking lots of the school, eight of the fifteen elite soldiers laid dead, but thirty-two students also added to the body count. Never mind there were still twenty-four of Colita's brood remaining. The pavement no longer pooled in blood, it bathed in it. A great splashing lake of deep sanguine colors. Once the blue mixed into the red, it all just looked black. Like oil. The abyss swallowed their feet as legs clashed together. The battle was even more intense than Sagan wanted to imagine.

Out in the open air, the Icari found almost no limit to their abilities. They proved capable of carnage unimaginable unless witnessed. Four years of training and preparation and they got so much wrong. Colita's men were the enemies they expected and easy enough to dispense. Their sheer number developed into a grave issue when the good guys' little army comprised untrained students.

Korac's men presented a different challenge. Not long after the fight began, they learned piercing the brain proved ineffective. Only decapitation stopped them. And what might the students decapitate them with? Scrap metal and splintered book shelves didn't exactly make for easy sawing. That left it up to her people and their swords.

"Sagan!" someone called from behind.

She whirled around the massacre. "Matt?" she shouted.

About ten fighting pairs away, Matt shouted at her. He tried to force his way through the throng at the same time. Above the screams and grunts, she made out the words, " …In the woods." What … ? He pushed an Icarus right off of him, and it picked up the fight with another student. This was really important to him. She tried maneuvering through the crowd. She met him halfway. "What is it?"

He stopped to catch his breath for a second. He opened his mouth to say, "There are—"

A high keening sound interrupted him. A sound unlike anything she ever heard. It raised goose bumps all over her arms. A primal instinct screamed at her to get far away. Students around her paused, too. The Icari carried on, unbothered.

"Gargoyles …" Matt finished.

"In the fucking woods?!" Sagan cried.

He nodded and said, "They've kept us trapped on campus." An Icarus bumped into him, and he shoved him off like a mosh pit veteran.

"What's stopping them now?" she thought aloud.

"I think they're only meant to keep us in. We've done a little experimenting. We can go anywhere as long as it's on this campus, and they don't bother us," he explained. "Like really well-trained guard dogs. The biggest ones you'll ever see."

One problem at a time. "Thanks for the info. Are you okay?" she asked. She scanned him over for wounds.

He smiled. A genuine, good looking smile. "Lieutenant General, I think you have bigger problems right now." And he disappeared into the throng.

She really did, too. The extreme underestimation of the Icarean soldiers bothered Sagan. It was all she could do to evade their blows. She only killed one, and several students died during that time. And if they were so hard to kill, then why—

She recognized Andrew's voice shouting through the crowd as one of the excessively serrated blades impaled his midsection on the right side. She made out a fleshy, wet sound as the monster extracted the blade, and blood spurted from the nasty wound.

"Andrew!!" she shrieked. She began pushing her way to him.

He waved her off and knocked the Icarus in the jaw, staggering him. The momentum stumbled Andrew until he fell to the pavement. He laid there unmoving. John, even with his worn knee, fought with all his strength, and severed the head of a monster warrior. He took over Andrew's Icarus.

About eight people beyond them, Tameka fought her own. "Look out, Tameka!" Sagan shouted. She watched as the redhead evade a devastating lunge, blocked the attacking blood sucker with her sword, and landed a well-aimed kick in his face. Tameka thrust the sword into his throat. The force of the blade lodged it into his vertebrae.

Sagan heard Tameka's surprised cry across the battleground. Still alive. A blow like that would kill a lesser Icarus. Tameka turned the sword in his neck and split the spine apart. The beast stayed down this time.

"Well that was easy," she shouted to Sagan. "Aw damn it!" Tameka pulled, and the sword only wiggled. Stuck. Sagan started pushing through the crowd to help. The fights between the students and the Icari washed over her and swallowed any path to Tameka. Tameka couldn't retrieve it from the fallen, Smurf-blooded monster. A body here, a weapon there. Sagan only caught glimpses of Tameka now. She hurried. Through the flashes of bodies, Sagan caught sight of something. Metal. Serrated metal just behind her best friend.

"Tameka!" Sagan screamed. An echo came from nearby.

The strange blade erupted from Tameka's right shoulder. She screamed, and her knees gave.

The blade withdrew, the large teeth tearing even more tissue. A flash of fire, and the beast that impaled her through the back gave an awful shriek. Lynn knelt beside Tameka. Sagan blew the air out of her cheeks in relief as she burst into the clearing.

"Are you all right?" she asked.

Tameka nodded and swallowed before asking, "Is he dead?"

Lynn took a moment to scan the few dozen people that surrounded them. "No. He's just gone."

"Where's Pablo?" Tameka asked.

Lynn pointed, and both girls followed the line of her finger. Pablo and Kyle shared the dubious honor of serving as one of the Icarus' punching bags. Each of them lost their weapons. Their lips bloodied, and their eyes blackened. John knelt on the asphalt beside Andrew. Three bodies laid around them and more followed suit. Swords clashed, people shouted and screamed, flames roared, and bodies fell. Only six super Icari remained, but the good guys gained the upper hand, and proved more than enough to finish them all off.

Tameka allowed Lynn to help her stand and started pulling her sword out of the dead monster's corpse once again. "Give me one of those bottles," she said to Lynn.

Lynn tossed a bottle and a lighter to Tameka. "All right, here you go." She collected the items and pushed into the crowd.

"What are you going to do?!" Sagan asked, worried about the girl's wounded shoulder.

Tameka announced without turning back, "I'll save Pablo! And I guess Kyle, too!"

The Icarus appeared perfectly content with the distracting task of beating the two to death. Tameka set fire to the cloth and wedged it inside the back of the soldier's armor. The flames erupted and clung to his clothes. Sagan heard his screams of agony and panic as the alien fell to the asphalt to battle the fire away.

Pablo said something to Tameka that Sagan didn't catch. He reached out his hand to her. She passed him the sword, still covered in the other Icarus' blood. Pure pissed off rage mottled Pablo's expression. He sliced the sword through the blood sucker's neck and decapitated him. Five super soldiers left.

Sagan enjoyed the swell of pride in her chest. Her people made good on their training. They even acted well together as a unit.

"Ahhh!!!" Sagan shrieked in agony, and the whole crowd turned to her. At the very heart of the throng, she faltered backwards, gazing as her hand came away from her bare stomach covered in blood. Anguish and fear seeped into her eyes. The Icarus behind her tried to take advantage of her hesitation and lunged for her heart with the silver blade. She spun and caught it in the crook of her axe. A test of strength she could not afford to spare. She fell. Just before the blood sucking alien thrust the sword inside her, his head came loose from his body, and Cecily stood where he fell.

"Cecily?" Sagan asked, breathless. She smiled and offered her hand to Sagan. "Thanks."

Cecily said, "I'm—" when her smile broke into a mortifying expression. A serrated sword penetrated through the center of Cecily's body. She clutched Sagan's arm in a death grip, trying to speak, but her voice only gargled. "No, Cecily … it'll be okay. C'mon … don't go." Blood from Cecily's mouth sprayed across Sagan's face, and then she fell.

Sagan glared up at the Icarus with his partially burnt face. His eyes widened at the ferocity of her blood-spattered expression. She gave one strong swing, and the bastard fell on top of Cecily, a headless corpse. Only three left. She spared another glance at her midriff and winced. A nice gaping of tissue diagonal across her stomach, and blood rushed from it. Sagan stumbled and supported herself with Korac's axe propped on the asphalt. She stayed there on one knee, head bowed, wrist perched on the pommel of her axe.

The dream team executed the last three super Icari quickly, but not before the bastards reaped maximum carnage. At great cost, the students dispatched Colita's soldiers. At least seventy-eight out of three hundred or so students laid dead, brutalized. Andrew was still unconscious, Kyle and Pablo swelled like tenderized meat, and Tameka's shoulder wound bled severely. Quite a lot of blood splashed in the back parking lot. It pooled around the feet of the remaining students, and it took on a sickly-sweet smell in the humid, Spring air. This wasn't right.

"Check the bodies. Make sure no one's just unconscious," Kyle shouted and marveled as many complied. Sagan watched a secret, satisfied smile spread over his lips. He finally got to give an order. Pablo and Lynn went to Sagan's side; Tameka and Kyle to John and Andrew's. Bleeding wounds needed packing and tending. All needed rest and well-deserved. No one really thought of a plan for broken bones, yet. So much horror for one day. Surely this was the last. The only thing left was Rayne. And wheels. Sagan called, "Hey, Matt?"

TWELVE

A Partner Might Make You Feel Good For A Night, But Your Wrath Will Keep You Warm For A Lifetime

THE BACK OF SOUTH HALL CRUMBLED IN ON ITSELF. The sounds of collapsing beams a warning to get the hell out. The smoke acted as a black blanket, burning the eyes and searing the lungs. Sweat glistened on Rayne's pale skin, mingling with blood from open wounds. Her left arm, though mobile, lay all but useless. Blood spilled fast all down her arm and fingers. Her scalp wound dripped into her eye, burning with salt and hindering her vision. Her face coalesced into one giant bruise, swelling and pumping blood to places she wished lost all feeling. The sweltering, blistering branding of the Pretiosum Cruor infuriated her with every stinging reminder of its existence. Blood seeped in her mouth. The coppery taste of it meshed between her teeth and oozed out the corner of her lips. Periodic waves of nausea reminded her of the sopping wet, cold matting the back of her head. That concussion definitely warranted a trip to the emergency room. Her back bled and blistered with the raw exposed wounds of second-degree burns. Both hands seared in pain with bits of glass inside, her right knuckles bled from the deliberately sliced wounds, and the sword gash in her palm left her hand slick and gushing. She was a fucking mess.

Despite the condition she was in, she stayed before her attacker with a perfectly balanced stance, poised on the edge of attack. Boiling inside her, she felt only hatred. This gave her strength enough to face him when all of her senses screamed for her to run. She kept her gaze level with his, stretching the sword out from her body. She held it over flaming debris until the sword smoldered. Gonna see how he liked the taste of his own medicine. Nox stared down at her expression, sparing a slight glance at the sword catching fire. In the lines and features of her face, she gave him determination. In her eyes, she wanted him to see pure venom. In return, she saw what he wanted her to see.

"Is that for me?" he asked in a calm voice.

Rayne watched the sword while fire light flashed across her face. "I don't see anyone else around here. Do you?" she responded. She shifted her weight to her side and pulled the sword away from the fire.

They shared a moment in silence. No reason for anymore words. She breathed evenly for the first time since the fight began. The smoke left her throat dry and strangely resistant to the air. Her lungs were probably black from the stuff. She raised her gaze to meet his. Her eyes seethed brighter than the fire as his stare became an icy void. A loud crash from somewhere further in the building signaled the end of their moment.

Nox charged for her, and Rayne blocked the attack with her sword. The sound of metal clashing against metal rang through her ears. The impasse proved only temporary. Nox struck her face with the back of his ring hand. She wavered before recovering her balance and returned his assault with her fist. He faltered and brushed the back of his hand across his mouth. Smiling over the blood from his lips, he gave one long stroke with his tongue. He lapped up his own blood like some kind of feral beast.

Rayne's gaze narrowed at the intimacy in his eyes. "How can you get off on that?" she asked in disgust.

"As soon as you lose this fight, you'll learn how, too," he answered with an air of absolute certainty.

She lunged, and he rose to the challenge. Their swords crossed, and their faces met too close. "Did Xelan try to teach you?"

She answered with her best impression of a growl and leaned harder into her sword.

"Four years and he never once made a move on you? I can tell he's in love with you," he said as if it were a secret between friends. Not as if he just dropped a nuclear bomb on her entire world.

Rayne let her reaction show on her face before she thought to stop it. Wide-eyed, terrified, in shock. What did he say? He took advantage of her momentary hysteria and pushed back against her. She didn't resist. Although her body groaned automatically when he pinned her up against the lockers, her mind was not with them. She didn't want to believe him, but what he said made so much sense. The dream with Celindria. She told him about it four months ago. Right before he disappeared.

"Xelan, I had a dream about Celindria last night," Rayne confessed.

Xelan lowered the throwing knife he was about to launch at her. "Is that unusual?"

"Not entirely, but this one seemed different," she said, feeling defensive.

Ever-patient, he asked, "Why is that?"

Where to start? "I think she was trying to warn me."

Every muscle inside of Xelan's body stiffened. "Warn you."

"She said I couldn't trust anyone. That someone would betray our group. Someone already had in the past." When he kept silent, she pressed, "Do you know what she's talking about?"

Xelan cleared his throat before speaking. Twice. "There are many differences between Celindria and you. Like in this situation, you came to me and you told me about this dream. Celindria wouldn't. She always suspected there was a traitor amongst us, but she never told me who she suspected and I never asked."

Frustrated, she went on, "So you don't know who it could be, either?"

He shoved their training session materials into his duffel. He stopped meeting her eyes. Stopped looking at her altogether. He said, "I don't think you should tell anyone else about this. It was just a dream."

"But she was—"

He did the thing where he moved so fast she barely tracked the air displacement before he appeared in front of her. It always took her breath away. With a gentle grip, he took both her hands and gazed at her with those sincere eyes. "Your unit only works strongest when it's whole. If it's pulled apart, even only a single member, every one of you would be vulnerable." She started to object, and he gave a gentle tug on her hands. "If you weave in even a small thread of doubt, the unit will unravel and fall. No matter what you suspect, no matter what she told you, keep the unit together for now. I will work on discovering any potential threats."

She clicked her tongue. "So don't tell them."

"Absolutely not," he said with a shake of his head.

"What are you going to do when you find them?" she asked.

"End them."

If he was in love with her, and she didn't return those feelings, maybe he's the one. Distantly, she became aware of Nox's fangs pressed hard enough into her throat to draw blood, but she couldn't bother to pay attention. Was this the reason Xelan disappeared after she told him about the dream? No one else heard from him in the last four months. Not even her. Reflexively, she sighed when Nox's tongue pressed to her throat at the open wound and tasted her blood there. What was she going to do?

"ARGH!" Nox punched her hard enough she understood the metaphor about seeing stars. "Am I so little a threat to you now that you can just check out in the middle of a battle?!"

She spat blood on some cindered rubble. "I want to call you a liar," she confessed.

He stepped away from her. Actually, walked away from her. His back was to her and everything.

"You know I tell you the truth. Xelan trained your brood all along to fight an enemy that proved more powerful and more difficult to kill than he ever told you. You should pick your friends more wisely, little girl. Why would an Icarus betray the rest? Unless he never intended to betray us at all." Nox kept dropping bombs.

God damn him. She would show him the extent of her training. She charged to strike him. He stepped aside and retaliated by backhanding her with his ring hand across her eye. She took the blow and thrust her sword at him. Spinning away, she sliced his ribs. He tried to hit her again, only this time she expected it. Tormenting, agonizing, unimaginable, she obstructed the blow with her left wrist. Though the jarring sensation set her teeth on edge, she recovered quickly. Her knee struck the bottom of his hand into the pommel of his sword, sending it upwards into the air. Reaching up, she successfully seized it by the hilt with her bad hand and thrust both blades straight into the center of his chest.

Nox swayed, lowering his onyx eyes to the blades crossed inside his flesh. Rayne held firm as though she wanted to push through him. She swallowed with exertion, and gasped for air. Blood seeped, a dark, rich cobalt. It oozed so slow it almost seemed coagulated. As thick as tree sap or molasses. At first sight, she unclenched her jaw and apprehensively released the hilts of both weapons. Her hands shook. She let her battered arm fall to its side. She over-exerted its abilities for the day. Her good hand tentatively touched her throat, and she winced at the bruises.

Drawing on the surrounding air, needing more, she gazed on as the monster of her nightmares fell shrieking to his knees. The shout carried for miles. It seemed to shake the earth, itself. She forced herself back and covered her ears. Crackling and groaning alerted her once more to the blazing structures surrounding them. Her reflexes acted faster than her body managed, but Rayne leapt away from Nox and dove out of the way. Beams, paneling, and a set of scorched lockers crashed down around her. Panic overcame her when her ankle refused to move. Heart pounding, breathing rapidly, she glanced down the line of her body, and sucked air through her teeth. A flaming beam fell right across her and pinned her ankle to the floor. She barely lifted the heavy thing with her other foot to get free. She pulled her knee to her chest, sparing a moment to examine the burned, sprained ankle.

That large pile of debris crushed Nox beneath it. The entire building fell, and the smoke rose so thick she lost visibility. She tried standing, applying as little pressure on her right leg as possible. Her bad arm laid limp, and her free hand pressed into the wound to stem the bleeding. Slick with sweat and dripping blood from God knows where else, she sought the newly expanded band room. The quickest way out after she realized flames and fallen debris surrounded her.

As soon as she cleared the door, the ceiling fell out behind her. The burning insulation and panel tiles melted away. She rushed through the rows of desks, tried to ignore the body chained to the podium, nearly got entangled by the music stands, and busted onto the stage. That exit door was the most beautiful thing she had ever seen.

Emerging from the burning school, Rayne heaved in great lungfuls of relieving, fresh air. She coughed in an unmerciful fit, grasping the handicap rail to support her. She limped at an agonizingly slow pace. Her eyes watered from the prolonged smoke exposure, but the fresh air was cool and worth enduring the sting of it on her back. All over her body, muscles and joints went numb and cold in some places as the adrenaline drained away. It was unimportant. Was everyone else all right? Had they defeated Korac and survived? These questions kept her from collapsing and moved her further into the back parking lot. Was Sagan alive? Rayne would feel something if she died, wouldn't she? The shroud of smoke cleared. Figures came into focus. She struggled to see them through the film of crap over her corneas.

She expected someone to rush to her side and help her, but no one came. She staggered forward another step before her knees buckled, and her legs fell out from under her. Something jabbed in her the butt. Of all the parts of her body to still have feeling. Cold, hard, and small. She gasped for air and looked down at the small object and instantly recognized it. The mark she carried on her face. And the Earth began to shake.

She clutched the ring in her hand as she put her feet back under her, finding a small miracle in that one action, and shouted to the others, "Run! Get the hell out of here!" Why weren't they moving? Were they too shaken up? She didn't have time for this shit!

She spun and started running back toward the building. Someone followed. *CRASH!* Time slowed down. Debris flew everywhere. Two winged beings erupted from the burning structure. She halted, her sprained ankle gave way, and she slid across the pavement. Nox and Korac glared down at her from the sky with matching sets of beautiful, black wings. The wings fashioned as angels with feathers. Nox recovered his sword and sheathed it at his hip. The two gaping wounds in his chest healed. In their place, absolutely nothing. Perfect, unmarred skin.

"You've got to be shitting me!" she shouted from the ground.

Korac cradled Colita in his arms with her head somehow reattached. Rayne regretted not letting Tameka take her head, after all. Their eyes tight, their brows down, and their teeth bared, the King and the General waited patiently. For what?

Screams and horrific panic scattered the mass of teenagers beyond her toward the wooded hillside behind the school. For all the fear they evoked, the two held a majesty over the impossible. Vampires didn't exist, and only birds could fly. In the distance came a bizarre, keening howl. The likes of which she never heard before. Goosebumps prickled along her skin. The students' screams intensified. Other awful, garbled sounds followed. What the fuck was happening in the treeline? She dared not take her eyes off the two Icari to check.

Between one beat of her heart and the next, Nox dove for her. She watched from where she lay on the ground, unable to move, and remained calm. He wouldn't kill her. He needed her. He stopped within a few inches of her face, his body aligned along the length of hers. His dark, remorseless eyes shifted until the darkness enveloped everything save for the white slits of his pupil. Alien. Terrifying. Above her, the dark angel hovered with fluttering wings. With every beat, gravel blew back and her hair mingled with his swept across her face. Fury at her confidence poured into the solid black orbs of his eyes. She tried to draw back from him as he snarled at her. She was at the mercy of someone who had none to spare.

He reached for her throat and lifted her bodily ten feet from the asphalt. She tried to cry out. No sound came. The span of his wings beat the air around her and soothed some of the ache caused by his rough approach. Maybe he would kill her. Maybe he found another way. He swept an arm beneath her, relieving her throat. She scanned the ground from her periphery. Was Sagan below?

He gave her throat a shake, and she met his gaze. Nox's stare pierced her soul. Scorch marks marred his right cheek. She hoped it was permanent. Evil things should be ugly. She expected him to scream, carry her high, and send her plummeting to a splattering death. Instead, he brought her closer until their eyes leveled.

"Why, Nox?!" she whimpered.

He whispered something to her, and his words layered in varying pitches as he spoke against her lips.

"My brother trained you well."

Nox released his grip on her throat. Rayne fell to the ground, the air rushing around her. She couldn't help herself. She reached out to him to save her from the fall. She landed back on the rough asphalt with a thud, and her breath knocked from her lungs. Sagan ran and knelt at her side, her face horror-stricken. The three Icari soared through the sky to an unknown destination. No relief. No joy. Just pure, icy fear. Fresh tears streamed down her cheeks, and she seemed unable to breathe, and not just from the fall.

"What did he say to you?" Sagan asked.

Several pairs of feet came into Rayne's line of sight.

Andrew shouted, "Xelan!"

Rayne turned her head to see. Her attention shifted to the roof of the auxiliary gym. Five men stood there draped in all black, billowing robes. She recognized only one familiar face. She hadn't seen him for months, but she would never mistake him. Xelan's shoulder-length black hair caught the breeze perfectly over his chiseled features. How had she never made the connection before? They looked so similar. Sure, she never saw Nox's face in her dreams, but ...

"Rayne, what's going on?" Sagan asked, again.

He stood taller than the other four, almost as tall as his brother.

This was The Brethren he never allowed her to meet before today. They—all five—were undoubtedly Icarean, but not entirely evil. Or were they?

White hot anger incensed Rayne's entire being. After everything Nox told her, after disappearing for four fucking months, Xelan was here just in time for his brother to end the world. Confusion and hurt muddled her thoughts. Did they watch the entire time? Would they even bother helping?

She wanted to shout and cry all at once. Her body screamed at her: aching, stinging, burning, bleeding, sweating, and numbing. It was all she could do to keep her breathing even. Cold traveled up her from her fingertips and toes. Her legs became unyielding. Both arms went immobile. Nothing would move. The painful sensation reached her eyes and a blood-curdling, heart-wrenching scream tore from her throat before she fell back on Sagan's thigh, and the world went black.

Epilogue

THE MESSAGE PLAYED OVER AND OVER AGAIN. "We have surrendered. Can you understand us? Have you received the message? The southern United States surrenders. We await further instructions. God save us all."

They hauled supplies and material possessions into the cars on campus. Some people braved the fire to collect keys from bags and purses. They needed to gain access to unclaimed vehicles for the evacuation. The strangers recommended this before disappearing with Rayne and her friends.

"Do you think this is enough?" Lucy carried tons of random snacks she stole from the vending machine outside, using her shirt as a basket.

Matt placed an outward smile on his lips to display his approval. "Yea, this is exactly what we need. Thanks."

"Can you pop the trunk for me?" she asked, her voice straining.

"No," he answered, tersely. "Just put it in the backseat with the rest." When he glimpsed the constraint in her eyes, he tried considering the abuse she suffered over the years by a certain recently deceased, overbearing cock sucker and decided he wanted to try for a more gentle approach. Even if it went against every instinct he had. "We'll want them accessible to us on the drive. No unnecessary stops if we can help it."

This seemed to satisfy her as she visibly relaxed and started storing food rations into the backseat. Well, at least she tried to, anyway. She had every right to ask about the trunk, seeing how the back of the car piled up with makeshift weapons, an abundance of medical supplies, and changes of clothing scavenged from North Hall lockers. The fire engulfed the school at a terrifying pace after South Hall collapsed. All the insulation combusted and withered on contact until it spread onward. There was about a thirty-minute window where they accessed the safer classrooms before the entire school went up in smoke.

"Where are we going?" she asked. She mussed around the backseat between the front bucket seats. He tried hard to ignore her perfectly heart-shaped, jean-clad ass as she rifled through their shit.

He wet his lips and looked straight ahead out the windshield. A few cars pulled away. After the two winged dudes took off, the beasts guarding the perimeter followed. As in, hefted their great bodies into the sky and flew away into the darkness. After that, every single individual looked defeated. "Uhm, do you want to check on your folks?"

She paused in her task. "Wow."

He raised an eyebrow and asked, "What is it?"

"I forgot about them," she confessed.

He knew exactly how she felt. Until he asked her, himself, he hadn't given a second thought to his parents. It was like he survived a battle, and now he was having to contend with a war. "Yea. So, do you want to check on them?"

She said, "Of course."

"Where do you live?" He peered at her through the rearview.

"Oh, uhm." Her cheeks warmed a little, and she started concentrating on packing the food away. Her movements awkward. "I live in Mabelvale."

He nodded in understanding. She was ashamed of her neighborhood, but he learned a long time ago all the students living in Southwest Little Rock, the primary zone for Fair High, lived in lower income areas. "That's the opposite of where I'm headed."

"Where do you live?" she asked on a curious lilt.

"Oh, I live in Otter Creek, but that's not where I'm going. I'm headed to Kavanaugh. Did you know Rayne well or at all?" he posed to her. She shook her head. "Her parents have a bookshop there. I plan to start there in case that's where her crew took her."

She spun around to face him again. "You're going after them?!"

"You got a problem with that?" The thought amused him. As if she could persuade him not to go.

She got closer to his face and said, "Take me with you."

The last thing he expected her to say. "Whoa, this isn't an adventure. People are hurt and dying."

"And if anyone knows what's going on, it's that group of freaks," she charged.

He worked very, very hard to keep his voice very calm and very still. As still as a placid lake, he said, "Nobody is a freak." He examined the effect his voice had on her. She pulled back from his face and turned back to her undertaking.

After a few moments of silence, she made a disgruntled sound. "I understand the food, but can't we put some of this in the—"

"Shh!" Matt interrupted, his tone sharp. He strained to listen, and he noticed her face shift as she realized it, too. Deafening static replaced the message on the radio. For the first time since nine that morning, the message just stopped.

They both jumped in the front seats and leaned forward. His hands gripped the steering wheel until his knuckles went white. With baited breath, they waited for anything to take the message's place. When a man's deep voice invaded the radio waves, Lucy jumped and slapped a hand against her mouth. Matt watched her out of his periphery. She appeared frightened, and he wondered if he should act that way, too.

The insidious voice delivered its address across every station, "Earthlings, humans, homo sapiens, in a presentation of surprisingly sound wisdom the leaders of your planet surrendered all assets, resources, and possessions to me."

Lucy whimpered and shivered. Matt's skin grew chill and his palms went damp. "Henceforth, you shall know King Nox as your Master. You serve me in all things without question. This obedience extends to my people whom you will come to recognize and know very well. You are no longer the dominant species on your planet. The Icari are your Masters, now. There will be no period of adjustment. Effective immediately, we will collect you from your shelters. All of you: men, women, children, and the elderly. Any attempt to resist will result in the total destruction of the surrounding thirty acres. The only hope for your feeble race is to fetch me the woman, Progeny Alpha One Code Name: Celindria. Bring her to me, and we will consider negotiations. Make what peace you will and enjoy the following news reports."

As soon as the voice departed, Matt jumped to turn the volume down. The station flooded with the sound of sirens and explosions. "I don't know how much longer I can go on. I've been reporting since 8:00AM this morning. This is Longview, Texas. I repeat Longview, Texas. Please send any assistance. Wait, something is coming in from the station. Oh, God. No. It seems ... it seems Houston is entirely gone. I repeat, Houston was wiped off the map. As was Austin, Dallas, and San Antonio. Still no word from Western Texas."

Matt pressed the next preset button. The FM radio tuned to a signal, but he wished it hadn't. "The west coast is gone. It sank into the seaboard around 10:00AM. California, Oregon, and Washington state: all gone."

Lucy pressed the next preset. "Please send help," a female voice whispered. "They're outside the building. I know they're coming for me. I just hope—" Silence. Then a shrill scream, the rustling of furniture, and a very unusual whoosh sound. Rubble scrambled in the background.

She pressed the power button off. He met her eyes at the same instant they both looked away, closed the car doors, and he started the engine.

The pearl prodded him. "Put your seatbelt on."

Map

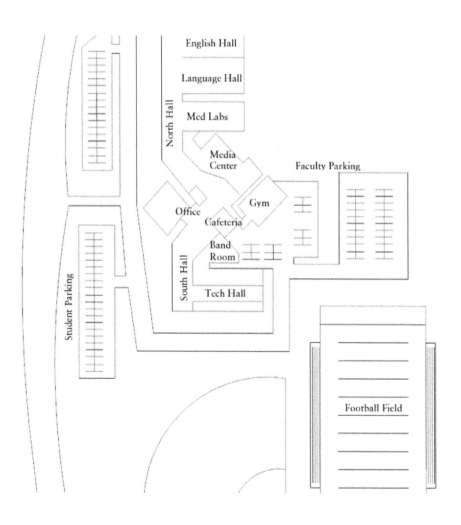

Glossary

Celindria Xelan's first successful Progeny and Rayne's hybrid ancestor. Possessed exceptional abilities beyond that of her kind. Evicted all Icari from Earth near 6,000BCE. Disappeared after. Presumed dead.

T.A.O. Given name for The Afflicted One, Sagan's hybrid ancestor. Moniker assigned due to the madness she suffered. Considered a botched experiment. Left to travel after The Vacating. Whereabouts unknown. Presumed dead.

Merit Tameka's hybrid ancestor. No known abilities. Confirmed dead.

Devis Kyle's hybrid ancestor. Gifted in metalwork and engineering. Forged the Pretiosum Cruor. Missing after the Vacating. Presumed dead.

Andrius Andrew's hybrid ancestor. Counselor. Disappeared a few hundred years after The Vacating. Presumed dead.

The Brethren A council of Icari and humans that govern the Icarean presence on Earth since the Vacating. They work together as a democracy to balance decisions made for the good of both species in regards to the pending invasion.

Cinder   Icarean home planet. Revolves around a sun which went supernova millions of years before Invasion Day. The planet is partially scorched and encompassed by the red giant's expansion.

Conduit   Portals to other worlds appearing as a shift of electricity between seams connecting the planets.

Nacre   A pearl containing the nano computer operating the nanobots which maintain all the functions of the bearer's anatomy.

Pretiosum Cruor   A device forged by Kyle's ancestor, Devis, to hold compatible blood for controlling the conduits, specifically between Earth and Cinder.

Progeny   Xelan's successful interbreeding program between humans and Icari in 8,000–6,000BCE. Made so by introducing nacre into hybrid infants producing amazing and unpredictable abilities.

The Vacating   Designation assigned to the event where Celindria evicted all Icari off Earth back to Cinder in 6,000BCE.

Author's Note

Thanks for joining me for the start of this journey. There's a lot of exciting things going on here with our characters, main and side. How do they reconcile their histories from their presents and their eventual futures? Can Earth and the human race be saved? How far will our characters have to travel to find out? And will Rayne ever figure out what a normal relationship is like?

I wrote this story in high school. I found as I obviously wanted to make it bigger than my small town in Arkansas; I needed to expand the scale and scope of the invasion, the purpose, and the stakes. As you'll see in the next few books of the series, the scale certainly increased. Stories like these create such beautiful brain storms that they practically write themselves. The pieces of this puzzle fell together with beauty and tragedy.

If you ever want to connect with me, please visit my website nicolehayeswriter.com. I'll post deleted scenes there and teasers of books to come. You can join my mailing list and be the first to know when the next book is ready for pre-order. I'd also like to hear feedback on your favorite characters. Whose story are you interested in seeing develop? Do you want Lynn and Pablo to get together? Are you curious about Matt's secret? Who do you think is the traitor in the group? You'll also get news on other authors that I think you'll like and their releases. Also, pick up some tips on how to write and publish your own works. Don't be afraid to try!

I appreciate every single one of you that took the time to read, and I hope that you continue to do so.

CPSIA information can be obtained
at www.ICGtesting.com
Printed in the USA
LVHW091534190620
658546LV00009B/130/J